Aimée Duffy writes steamy, contemporary romance for the 21st century woman who enjoys the 21st century alpha male. She's addicted to reading, shopping and can't go a day without music.

When she's not writing you can find her traipsing up the Ochils (weather permitting of course) or procrastinating on Facebook and Twitter.

@aimeeduffyx
www.facebook.com/aimeeduffyx
www.aimeexdx.blogspot.co.uk

Also by Aimée Duffy

the Office Christmas Party

AIMEÉ DUFFY

A division of HarperCollins*Publishers*
www.harpercollins.co.uk

Duffy

HarperImpulse an imprint of
HarperCollins*Publishers*
The News Building
1 London Bridge Street
London SE1 9GF

www.harpercollins.co.uk

This paperback edition 2017

First published in Great Britain in ebook format by
HarperCollins*Publishers* 2017

A catalogue record for this book
is available from the British Library

ISBN: 9780008197285

This novel is entirely a work of fiction.
The names, characters and incidents portrayed in it are
the work of the author's imagination. Any resemblance to
actual persons, living or dead, events or localities is
entirely coincidental.

Set in Minion by Palimpsest Book Production Ltd, Falkirk,
Stirlingshire
Printed by CPI Group (UK) Ltd, Croydon CR0 4YY

MIX
Paper from
responsible sources
FSC   FSC° C007454

Chapter 1

December was, without a doubt, Natalie Taylor's favourite month. She didn't care much for the cold, or the way the London pavements turned so slick and slippery that wearing heels was just as dangerous as taking a dip in the Thames. She wasn't even a fan of the icy winds or the way the snow stained her favourite boots with hideous white rings she could never cover with leather polish, no matter how many bottles of the stuff she used.

But the evenings were a different story. Tonight, she'd found the perfect way to kick off the month in style.

Trudging up the steps, she pulled a piece of paper from her handbag, then reached for the door of her the flat she shared with her best friend. The smell of cinnamon swirls and baked apples filled her nose and her stomach growled. Just another reason she loved her flatmate. The woman had one of the best bakeries in the city and always let Natalie try her new cakes before she sold them in the shop.

And if the saliva pooling in her mouth was any indication, Rose was switching to her Christmas recipes.

Once inside she tried to ignore the rising growl in her stomach and ditched her keys in the bowl next to Rose's. She headed straight for the kitchen, the piece of paper ready to be shoved into her best friend's face, but froze at the alcove leading to the living room. Rose wasn't alone, and was feeding what looked like a slab of a cinnamon swirl to her boyfriend of almost a year, Tom.

'Hey Nat, there's more in the kitchen if you're hungry,' Rose said, smiling.

Natalie went for a slice of cake and returned with a plate filled with a bit of everything, even the soft apple bakes she'd smelled earlier. She sat down on the coffee table and dropped the sheet of paper she'd been so excited to show Rose. Of course, if Tom was here for the night, that was it for her carefully planned evening.

That man could suck all the fun out of life.

'These are amazing,' Natalie said through a mouthful of the crumbly apple soft bakes.

Tom nodded his agreement as he popped another cinnamon swirl in his mouth. He didn't say much, but when he did it always made her friend's whole face light up. Natalie couldn't really see his appeal. He had thick auburn hair and flawless skin but he wasn't really her type. He was slim in a tall, almost gangly way.

Oh, and ever since he came on the scene, there'd been no more Saturday nights checking out local up-and-coming bands, or Sundays lying in bed with Rose recovering from the night before by eating so many cakes that they spent their Mondays on a sugar crash.

Shaking her head, she smothered the twinge of jealousy. It wasn't nice to be thinking about her friend's boyfriend that way, even if he was as dull as dishwater. She couldn't feel annoyed at him just because he was there when she'd happened to have plans for her and Rose.

But she could stay hopeful that Tom was only staying to taste Rose's new recipes then leaving …

'How was work today?' Rose asked.

'Good, we're booked up well into the new year.' She'd spent all day planning the most exquisite parties her clients had ever seen, but of course the clients didn't know she existed. Her boss, Mick the Dick, was the one who took the credit *and* pocketed all the profits, whether he spent his office hours at the driving range or not.

Natalie glanced at the sheet of paper with a list of some of the best parties to be at this December and sighed.

'What's that?' Rose asked and before Natalie could answer, her friend swiped the sheet off the table.

'Um,' Natalie eyed Tom warily as he leaned over to read the list.

He looked up and turned to frown at her. 'You can't be serious?'

His pissed tone got her back up. Natalie folded her arms across her chest and stared him down. 'Why not?'

'Nat,' Rose interrupted. 'I can't do tonight. Tom's taking me out.'

So he wasn't just there to taste test. Natalie was ready to bet he'd suspected they'd be out on the town again, going from party to party and having *actual fun*. After all, that's how Rose had met him in the first place.

As for what her friend actually saw in him, Natalie didn't know. He put the bore in boring.

Rose sighed. 'Mode was great last year.'

Tom took her hand and rubbed his thumb over the back, then said smoothly with just a tiny hint of pain in his eyes, 'I thought you'd stop this now we're together. Or were you hoping to meet someone else?'

Natalie didn't buy the false slice of hurt in his tone. He was using that to make Rose feel guilty for wanting to enjoy herself. And she'd long since given up trying to tell her friend she was being emotionally manipulated. It only ever ended in an argument, with Rose saying Natalie didn't know how good a guy he was, and how kind and loyal and blah blah blah he was.

3

Rose's chin dropped for a second. 'Of course not, Tom. It's just—'

'Then there's no need to discuss it further.' He took the list from her and handed it back to Natalie, saying, 'I can't believe you use your work connections to find parties to crash. It's ridiculous and completely immature.'

Natalie gritted her teeth before her temper could erupt with a string of insults. See, she could be mature.

'Tom, stop it,' Rose begged.

He just continued to stare at Natalie, as if he expected her to leave. And although she didn't want to give him the satisfaction, she didn't want to see Rose torn between them either. Taking her list, she went to her bedroom without a word.

Well, maybe not *out loud*, anyway. The words boring, rude and twat rolled around her skull all the way there.

If he didn't make Rose happier than Natalie had ever seen her, she'd have told him exactly how much of an arse he really was, and then some.

Instead she dumped her handbag and fell onto her bed. So much for the perfect month of partying. With Tom around, she doubted she'd ever be able to get out with Rose on a normal night. But it had been like that for months, now, hadn't it?

She mentally cursed him, but then let it go with a sigh. Her epic dislike of Tom could also have something to do with how jealous she was that he was monopolizing so much of her best friend's time. Maybe he was genuinely hurt at the idea of Rose going out and flirting with other men.

Or maybe he was a bastard to the core.

Rose came into the room and closed the door behind her. She looked so worried Natalie had to force a smile to reassure her.

'Maybe he's right, Nat. I mean about the crashing thing. It was fun, but things have changed. And if you get caught, you could lose your job.' She sat down on the side of the bed, patting Natalie's hand.

4

So Tom had given Rose another excuse for not wanting her to go. He knew just how to pull at her friend's heartstrings. Of course, Rose was so lovely she wouldn't do anything that would potentially hurt anyone.

He was looking more and more like a bastard all the time.

'I don't just want to do this, Rose, I need to.' Natalie shook the piece of paper at her friend. 'You know why.'

'Maybe this year could be different. We could do Christmas properly, start our own traditions.'

'Christmas party crashing *is* our tradition!' And the thought of celebrating on the 25th made her sick to the point she was sure the apple soft bakes were going to take a return trip. She couldn't, she just … couldn't.

Rose must have noticed, because she back tracked. 'Or maybe I could talk to Tom again. He might feel better about it all if he came with us,' she said, not looking hopeful.

Natalie wasn't either. Tom had a weird emotional hold over her friend and he was clearly not thrilled at the idea of them going out together at all, never mind for a whole month straight. She got the awful feeling that she was losing her only friend, that soon she'd be alone again, as alone as she was when she met Rose three years ago.

And whether it was to Tom or something else, Natalie would have to deal with losing Rose eventually so there was only one thing she could do – get used to it.

Just because she couldn't celebrate Christmas day without guilt choking her, didn't mean she had to stop enjoying the season. And she'd leaned on Rose for so long, she was almost an acting crutch.

Plus, if she wanted to save enough to start her own business then she wasn't going to turn down a chance of free food and drink for a month. Sitting up, she resolved to go solo.

'Are you okay?' Rose asked.

Natalie nodded, realising she really was. 'I'm going to Mode tonight, alone.' At Rose's horrified expression, she added, 'It'll be fine, really. I'll be home before midnight. Promise.'

***

The private club was decked out exactly how Natalie envisioned Christmas as a child. Silky white sheets trimmed in silver sequences dressed tables around the edges, fairy lights elegantly covered the walls and the ceilings, while the arches leading to the dancefloor were twined with holly and had tiny tea lights throughout. She'd done an amazing job, even if she did say so herself.

This was what she loved about December – all the glitz, sparkle and magic – even though she had to face icy wind and freezing rain to get there. But the atmosphere was so warm and full of joy she barely paid attention to her numb feet.

The place was packed already, with women wearing glittering red and gold gowns. The men wore slick suits with festive ties, reminding her of the cartoon reindeer ones her mum always bought her dad when she was little.

The memories were warmer now, not tinged with sadness, maybe because enough time had passed. More than likely it was because, officially, she was there as Nicole Porter the Temp tonight, not Natalie Taylor, the girl who had planned this party right down to the gourmet buffet being set up in the far corner. Separating herself made all the difference. Nicole didn't have guilt or sadness, just a love of all things Christmassy.

Tom was right about one thing though; if Mick the Dick knew about her extracurricular activities his face would be a picture and he would probably sack her on the spot.

She'd turned his company into the first point of contact in the city if you wanted a party, especially during the holiday season. What thanks had she gotten for her hard work that first year? Nothing except a ton of overtime with no extra cash in her wages that month, or any month since. This was her way of getting something for herself out of it. And for Rose. But Rose wasn't with her this time.

She squished down the pang of sadness and accepted a glass of champagne from a passing waiter. Determined to make the most of it, she headed towards the buffet table and grabbed a plate. A few men had already gathered and were stocking up on miniature mince pies, but it wasn't the cakes or pastries she was after – nobody's compared to Rose's. Instead she filled her plate with the cold food that wouldn't spoil easily, leaving the seafood nibbles for her next trip to the table.

When nothing else could fit on her plate without tumbling off, she made her way to an empty table at the back and filled the food bags she'd brought with her, stuffing her stash into her handbag.

When she looked up she caught the dark gaze of a guy across the room. He lifted one eyebrow, nodding to her bag and her cheeks flushed.

Busted.

But the guy just smiled a little mockingly, shook his head in amusement, and picked up a glass of champagne. No doubt Mr Perfect, in his expensively cut navy suit, wouldn't need to stock up on free food to save a penny or two. And going by his broad shoulders and slightly muscled forearms hugged deliciously by the suit, he ate very well.

She waited for him to wave over security, or maybe even a waiter, but all he did was eye her from her silver pumps, all the way to the sequinned neckline of her royal blue dress. He lingered on her chest and she told herself that the increase in her heartrate was down to the stress of almost getting caught plundering, or maybe even indignation caused by the way he was ogling her.

He took another sip of champagne, then winked and she felt her cheeks heat up again. But not from embarrassment.

Now that she was reassured he wasn't going to come barrelling over and chuck her out, she took a moment to really look at him.

His jaw was dusted with dark hair, black or maybe dark brown. He was lightly tanned, either a sunbed lover or he'd just come back from abroad. The answer to that didn't matter though, because she and Rose had rules for successful party crashing and right at the top of the list was Do Not Get Personal With Anyone.

And she'd seen first-hand how important that was after Rose met Tom. Her friend had broken that rule, but kept her alter ego. Rachel the Assistant aka Rose had also gone on to break rule number two – Do Not See Anyone More Than Once.

Nicole the Temp didn't want to see this guy more than once, or find out about his golden glow. She did, however, want to wipe that grin off his face – maybe with some time under the mistletoe or a little indecent grinding on the dancefloor.

And given his unashamed appraisal followed by a wink that suggested he liked what he saw, she guessed he was only interested in much of the same.

Deciding to take the lead, she got up but another man appeared in front of her, blocking the way.

'Hi, I'm Mark, have we met before?' he asked, holding out his hand.

Natalie took the offer and shook back. 'I don't think so. I've just started as a temp. I'm Nicole.'

Mark wasn't so bad. He was a little thinner than the other guy with the mocking grin, clean shaven and had thick, blonde hair, a little darker than hers. No tan either, but he was quite hot.

'Ah, I heard they got temps in to update the new systems,' Mark said, interrupting her evaluation. 'How are your fingers from all that data entry?' He pretended to wince, and she smiled.

Feigning stiffness, she clenched her fingers a few times. 'It's touch and go.'

'Well, maybe this will help.' Mark waived over a waiter and then handed her a fresh glass of champagne.

He pulled out a chair for her, assuming she'd sit with him now and she couldn't help looking over for the guy who saw her plundering, but his attention was on a pretty, petite redhead who seemed to not only be hanging off his arm, but on his every word.

Well, it looked like that ship had sailed.

She took the lead from Mr Perfect and slid into the offered chair with a flirty smile for Mark, trying to steer the conversation away from work or anything personal. He seemed keen to find out more about her, probably to make her feel more comfortable in her new job, so she went with her rehearsed and fabricated backstory.

This was the part Rose always hated, which was why she'd probably told mostly the truth when she'd met Tom.

Natalie held back a sigh. The worry in her friend's eyes when she left just reminded Natalie of her own worry that she was going to lose her best friend. The feeling of impending doom weighed heavily on her so much so she had to concentrate to keep up with the conversation.

Perhaps because of that, or because of the five glasses of champagne she drank on an empty stomach, but she found herself saying to Mark, 'Let's dance.'

Sliding her bag under the sparkly trimmed tablecloth, she took his hand and he led her to the dancefloor. The live band playing Christmas music made it hard to navigate through all the bodies that seemed to have the same idea.

Little bouquets of mistletoe were strung from the ceiling directly above them and she tugged Mark beneath one, looking up, then at him expectantly. A knowing smile pulled at his full lips before he bent down and brushed them against hers.

The kiss was nice, slow and building, but not the sort she read about in books that turned her body into a furnace and buckled her knees. A long time ago, she'd resolved that fiction was not real life, people didn't always get happy-ever-afters and a pair of strong hands holding her up as she clung to muscled biceps with a desperate sort of passion was not in the cards for her, maybe not anyone.

But she tried harder to feel more, feel *something*, throwing everything into the kiss and twisting her fingers through his thick, silky hair. Mark returned her enthusiasm, prying her mouth open with a swipe of his tongue, tangling it with hers. A familiar warmth in the pit of her stomach bloomed and she was about to suggest they find somewhere more private, but it was Mark who broke away first.

'I'm so sorry. I didn't mean to maul you like that,' he said, sounding shocked at himself.

'It's okay, I don't mind being mauled by you.' Which was true. He was a nice guy and she was single. What was the harm in having a little fun? Especially since she was just getting into it.

Someone knocked her forward, into Mark's arms and she bumped against the growing bulge in his pants, a reminder of what she'd been hoping for. A little bit of passion, even if it seemed to mostly be on his part. But she was definitely getting there.

Mark swallowed hard. 'Let's get off this dancefloor and talk.'

What warmth she felt sizzled out. He was really a nice guy – probably wanted to take her out on a date or ten before there would be any more heated kisses. Which would breach her second rule and be her cue to leave.

When they were back at their table with a fresh glass of champagne each, she discreetly pulled her handbag out from under the table.

'Nicole, look. I really like you. How about we do this another time, without everyone we work with gaping at us?'

'Definitely,' she lied, feeling stupid more than anything. Was she so desperate for a connection with someone tonight she just threw herself at him? He was hot, but a one-night stand was something she'd only done a few times. And she'd only done them with men she'd felt at least a little lust for, not just the warm and fuzzies. 'Could you excuse me? I need to go to the ladies' room.'

'Yeah, of course. They're over there,' he said, pointing to the entrance and, luckily for her, the exit too.

She grabbed her bag and made a beeline for the front of the building, feeling annoyed at herself for not realising Mark was one of the few gentlemen left in the city. Holding her chair out for her and asking her questions about herself should have told her everything she needed to know. And he'd only kissed her so intensely because she'd pushed for it.

As soon as she got out into the hall, the redhead she'd seen earlier darted out of the men's bathroom looking flushed with her hair all over the place and her dress ruffled up one side. She smacked straight into Natalie, knocking them both off balance Natalie had to drop her bag to catch herself on the wall. The other woman's face went from flushed to scarlet.

'Oh my god! I'm so sorry. Let me help with this.'

Before Natalie could think or breathe, the woman picked up her bag and handed it over. 'Are you okay? I should have looked where I was going.'

Natalie took the bag and shook her head to clear it. 'I'm fine.'

She was about to ask what the woman was doing coming out of the men's room, when she saw the guy who'd caught her stuffing her bag with canapés coming out of the same door, pressing his lips together as if to keep from laughing at the spectacle before him.

Right, that answered that question. And to think, if Mark hadn't side-tracked her, she might be the one looking like she'd been thoroughly attended to, not the redhead.

'Sorry, I don't mean to be rude,' the redhead said wrinkling her nose, 'but did you know you smell a bit beefy?'

A laugh erupted from the bastard still standing at the door to the men's room, quickly dousing any fantasies Natalie had of having switched places with the redhead. She glared first at the redhead, then *him* and stalked out of Mode with her chin up. Her exit only seemed to make him laugh louder and her face burned so hot she must be puce by now. Her only saving grace was that she'd never have to set eyes on either of them again.

As Natalie hailed a taxi, she vowed her next solo party crash would not be an embarrassing shambles. There was no way tonight could possibly get any worse, at least.

At home, she spread her plunder on the coffee table and was about halfway through when the front door opened. Rose's cheeks were tear stained, like she'd been crying. Natalie stood and whirled on Tom, about to give him hell for hurting her friend when Rose stuck her left hand, palm down, in front of Natalie's face.

The diamond set in a bed of sapphires on her friend's ring finger was Natalie's worst nightmare come to life.

'Nat, I'm engaged! Tom and I are getting married!' Rose said with tears of joy streaming down her face.

Well, that would teach her for stupidly thinking the night couldn't get any worse.

A cold sweat broke out over her skin and what little she'd eaten of her plunder made a bid for freedom. 'I'm going to be sick,' she announced, then clapped her hand over her mouth bolted for the bathroom.

After, she lay with her head on the cold tiles of the floor, gripped with terror that she would soon be alone, really alone for the first time in years.

Chapter 2

Two nights later, Dean Fletcher had just finished up for the weekend when his younger brother came into his office, closing the door behind him.

Well, he'd *hoped* he'd finished up, but Jeffrey had a panicked, jittery look that meant either a deal had gone bad or one of their systems had failed. 'Spit it out, Jeff. I'm running late as it is.'

But his brother didn't speak, he just paced back and forth in front of Dean's desk.

'What's happened?' he asked, pulling his laptop open and switching it on with a sigh.

'It's not work. Christ, I don't know how to say this.' Jeffrey stared at Dean with undisguised pity and his stomach took a nose dive.

There was only one other time his brother had looked at him this way – the day Dean had been jilted at his own wedding. But that was ten years ago, he was only a teenager and was so not about to rehash a past he'd long since buried. If Jeffrey wanted to bring up his personal life, Dean wasn't having any of it – his dates were his business.

Not that he actually dated, it was more a string of flings throughout the year. Nothing serious, just a bit of fun here and there and the women were into it, so why not? It hadn't been a problem until his brother had met Alana a few years ago, then he'd lost his wingman and gained a giant pain in the arse.

'That's not what I was going to say either! I was going to work up to this better but since you're apparently incapable of patience, here goes. I'm going to ask Alana to marry me.'

Dean's chin dropped, he couldn't help it. His brother had seen first-hand how badly a wedding could turn out. In fact, after he was dumped on his *special* day, his family had blamed him. Jeffrey was the only relative who still spoke to him without contempt.

Jeffrey sighed. 'Shit, Dean. Nobody died.'

'Not yet,' Dean said, then ran his hands through his hair. 'What brought this on? I mean, after what happened to me, I thought you'd have learned the same lesson I did.'

That women were never what they seemed. They told you they loved you one minute, then ran away at the thought of spending the rest of their lives with you. Of course, now he could see that he'd dodged a bullet, but it had taken him a long time to realize that. And Jeffrey wasn't made of the same steel he was. His brother had chased Alana around the city for months like a puppy before she'd agreed to date him.

Jeffrey rolled his eyes. 'Love. You might want to hang around long enough to try it some time. You know, Alana's friend is single and—'

'I'm not interested. Now back to this proposal, are you insane? Did Mum drop you on your head as a baby? Have you forgotten everything that happened?' He hated dragging up the past, but a reminder of his own ridicule might knock some sense into his brother.

'Alana isn't *her*. If she doesn't want to marry me, she'll say no.' Jeffrey started pacing again and the wild look was back in his eyes. '*Shit*, what if she says no?'

If Dean had ever worried that he was missing out on something by refusing to commit to a relationship, he didn't now. Over the two years Jeffrey had been dating Alana, his balls had shrunk to pips and now it finally looked like they'd disintegrated.

'Then why bother asking?'

The look Jeffrey threw his way made him feel like an arse, but he wasn't about to apologise. Not when his brother was being an idiot.

'I knew you'd be a knob about this. I don't know why I bothered coming to you first.'

'Because you knew I'd tell you what a complete tool you're being and talk some sense into you,' Dean said, getting tired of this fight already.

'Fuck you, Dean. Seriously.' Jeffrey headed for the door and threw it open. He didn't walk through it, not until he said, 'While you're out tonight with a woman you'll have forgotten the name of next week, I'll be home with someone I love and want to spend the rest of my life with. Whether you're terrified of having that again or just going for the world record title of sluttiest man alive, one day you're going to realize life's passed you by in a blur of anonymous sex. I don't want that for you.'

Jeffrey slammed the door, so he could have the last word, as usual. Dean clenched his teeth. What the hell did his brother know anyway? One serious girlfriend and he was now a relationship guru?

Yeah, right.

Dean closed his laptop, grabbed his keys and headed for the door. He was perfectly happy passing through life on his own terms – it had nothing to do with fear – and tonight he was going to do exactly that.

***

The party tonight had a guest list but he wasn't worried, instead he strolled right up to the bouncer manning the door to the hottest bar in Soho and used the name he'd planted there earlier.

Having their own IT company who supplied the booking software to most of London's hotels, restaurants and bars did more than just make them money. Jeffrey had come up with the idea of using it to get into all these swanky events a few years ago when they were just getting off the ground and what had turned into a few cheap nights out ended as a great way to score those anonymous flings his brother had recently started to frown upon.

But he really wasn't in the mood for thinking about his brother at all, so he headed straight for the bar to take advantage of the flowing champagne. When he wound his way through the tightly packed crowd he changed his mind and ordered a scotch. Bubbly just wasn't going to cut it tonight.

He'd missed the wine and dine portion of the evening thanks to Jeffrey and his stupid arsed ideas. On the plus side, every woman there was already half-inebriated. As he downed the scotch in one go, he welcomed the burn before taking an interested glance round the crowd.

Most of the women looked like they were from the cast of TOWIE, with boobs spilling over low necklines, unnaturally long lashes and wearing more make-up than you'd find at the Mac counter at Selfridges.

And to add insult to his already shitty mood, the same words kept playing on a loop in his head.

Whether you're terrified of having that again or just going for the world record title of sluttiest man alive, one day you're going to realize life's passed you by in a blur of anonymous sex. I don't want that for you.

Fucking Jeffrey. Until tonight, he hadn't thought twice about what he was doing. And until Alana came on the scene, neither had his brother.

In fact, December was their favourite month for crashing parties. The venues were always packed with women looking to have some anonymous festive fun. He usually enjoyed the atmosphere and he was not about to let his brother ruin this for him. So he ordered another scotch and got serious about his surveying.

Until he saw a familiar blonde food thief. She wasn't in that slinky short dress tonight, but a pale gold one that hugged her hips and chest even more. And she was staring at him too, with something close to rage burning in her pretty blue eyes.

He couldn't help the way his lips curved when he remembered what happened the last time they met. It only made her eyes burn hotter and her cheekbones score pink.

But then it hit him. How could she be at two Christmas parties for totally different firms? Unless she had organised the parties. Although he doubted she'd be stealing the food if she had.

So she must be crashing too, just like him. But what his little thief didn't know was that this was his turf, and two independent crashers in a place this small was going to draw attention, then the jig would be up.

Dean knocked back the scotch and headed her way. It was about time for a proper introduction.

***

Just as Natalie thought her week couldn't get any worse, Mr Perfect with that smug smile and another expertly cut, expensive looking suit made his way through the crowd to her. She still hadn't gotten over their last encounter when he'd laughed his head off after his floozy had caught a whiff of her stash.

And with Tom and Rose spending every night together at the flat with that sickly, loved-up couple thing they had going on, she realized that soon they'd either ask her to move out or she'd end up the oldest, rustiest third wheel that ever existed. She couldn't imagine them moving to Tom's rental when Rose's parents had bought her the flat.

But worst of all, Rose had asked her to be the maid of honour, and how could she say no to her best friend because she didn't think Tom was good enough? She wasn't a complete bitch. No way would she have ruined her friend's special night. Natalie was just grateful that, despite the fact she'd planned a dozen or so stellar weddings, Tom was so much of a control freak he'd want to organise it himself.

She really didn't think she'd have been able to deal with it if she'd been assigned the wedding planner role. At least now all she had to worry about was the actual day and she could avoid Tom as much as possible until then.

So, business as usual.

'That doesn't look big enough to hide ten pounds of beef hors d'oeuvres.'

Natalie looked up to catch a glimpse of Mr Perfect's smug grin. 'I've no idea what you're talking about.'

Of course she did, but she had known tonight that meals would be served and she couldn't exactly stuff slices of turkey, stuffing balls and roast potatoes all swimming in gravy into her handbag. Especially not when there were thirty or so other people at the table.

'Oh I think you do. And I know what your game is,' he said, suffocating her personal space with his Lynx effect cologne and his massive-up-close body.

'I don't play games.' *Now run off and annoy someone else.*

He laughed a little, and the sound just wound her up again.

'You're obviously new to this, but I could tell what you are a mile off. Just a head's up, this area is my turf and two strangers at a party this small will get noticed,' he said.

What she was? Like she was some desperate, starving cow who crashed parties without a cover or having done her research? 'You have absolutely no idea what you're talking about and anyway, I didn't see you pee on the walls so what makes you think this bar belongs to you?'

That got the grin off his face. Natalie smiled as sweetly as she could, then stood up and shoved past him. 'If you're so worried about being caught, the door's that way.' She gestured with her thumb over her shoulder. 'I'd say I'd miss you, but …'

With that she slinked away from him, swept up a free glass of champagne, necked it and headed for the dancefloor. She melded into a group of guys and girls effortlessly, the people were too drunk to ask any questions. They were all about the dancing and rounds of shots were brought over, so she helped herself to a few of those too.

The bastard didn't leave, just skulked at the bar with a glass of something brown – not that she was looking out for him. And what was all that rubbish about strangers getting noticed? There were a good thirty people at the party – not to mention the bar was now open to the public after the meal – and the vast majority were smashed. Natalie doubted they'd notice the arrival of the entire Manchester United football team at this point.

As she tried not to get angry at Mr Smug Bastard, the hottie she'd sat next to at dinner joined her on the dancefloor.

Steven twirled her around and around, and her anger melted into giggles. A few shots later and she was ready to show him some of her more indecent dance moves to *Santa Baby*.

This was what she'd been waiting for all year, she thought as she was swung around again, laughing along with Steven. This happy, mirthful, floaty feeling surrounded by sparkly decorations in a room bursting with festive cheer.

***

A loud snore against her ear snapped Natalie into consciousness. She was too warm, her skin had a thin sheen of sweat all over and she realized the problem as her ribs were constricted by a manly forearm, and her bum was pressed against a whole lot of naked groin.

And how did she know it was a groin? Because her underwear was gone along with the rest of her clothes. Crap.

Unfortunately, the hazy drunken memory sharpened with crystal clarity and she remembered agreeing to go home with Steven, breaking rule number three. No Going Home With Anyone. It was a must if you wanted to stick to rules one and two. Not to mention the whole potential serial killer issue.

At least he sounded dead to the world. If she was quiet enough, she might be able to get out before the sun rose and brought questions she didn't want to answer. Not that she could remember him being that interested in who she was last night, but the lack of alcohol and a strange woman in his bed might make Steven a bit more courteous.

Carefully she slid out of his hold, wishing the pounding of her heart wasn't so loud in her ears, but a quick glance over her shoulder told her he was still asleep. Steven was definitely a looker with his light brown hair ruffled from, well, probably her fingers grabbing onto it. And he had a lovely jaw line that was as smooth as a baby's, so thankfully stubble burn wasn't going to be an issue. He didn't look much older than her in sleep, but he probably had a good few years on her.

Still, one-nighters were supposed to be confined to impersonal places. To come back to his house, *alone*, was crazy. Rose would go bananas if she knew. Though, she realized with a twist in her gut, her friend might just be relieved she wasn't at the flat getting in the way of all the romance.

Shaking off the thought, she re-focused on an escape route and climbed out of the bed. A sharp pain cut into her foot and she hissed a chorus of *ows* as she plonked back down. Rubbing the sole, she glared at the belt buckle on the floor then froze as the snoring cut off on a grunt.

Behind her, Steven rolled onto his stomach and reached an arm out, grumbling in his sleep. Dodging out of the way, she was careful not to stand on the buckle again, and tried to remember where her clothes were. She spied silver lace peeking out from beneath a shirt which was abandoned by the door and flushed remembering how those had gotten there.

Natalie swiped up her bra, hooked it on, then snuck out into the hall. Her knickers were by his bedroom door and this time she didn't let herself remember how those ended up there. Instead she just pulled them on and went on the hunt for the rest of her things.

In the living room she spotted her lovely gold dress, just dumped on the coffee table half balled up and so wrinkled she wanted to kick herself. Not only did it cost more than she made in a month, but it was the most festive dress she owned. She examined it carefully but there were no tears she could see, it just badly needed ironing.

She turned on a lamp and the room illuminated. Everything became clear from the empty beer cans in the corner to the half-eaten kebab on the arm of a tatty looking green sofa. A total bachelor pad, sans class. Fabulous, she'd gone home with a slob.

A shuffle sounded behind her. With her heart in her throat she spun around to see a guy who was *not Steven* wearing nothing but his boxers. His frown turned to an astonished blink, then he gave her a good once over. Even with the underwear, she felt utterly naked, so pulled the dress against her front.

As her cheeks burned, she remembered thinking the week from hell could never, ever get any worse. She really needed to stop thinking that because it seemed like fate was really into poking her repeatedly with a sharp, pointy spear of shame.

And she needed to get dressed. Like right now.

'Hey, you here with Steven?' the guy asked.

Who else would she be here with? Then she had a horrible thought that maybe there would be others who lived there. Others who would catch her mortifying floor show.

'Yes. I'm just leaving,' she said, turning around and pulling her dress over her head. 'Have you seen a black clutch anywhere?'

Might as well put his eyes to use and take some of the heat off her.

'Oh, yeah, here.' He picked up something from the sofa, screwing up his nose. 'Sorry, I think it landed in hot sauce.'

Natalie let out a whimper as she took her brand spanking new clutch, pulling a strip of saucy donner meat out of the folds. She had to get out of there, like, now.

'Why not stay 'til morning? I'm sure Steven wouldn't want you walking the streets in the middle of the night.'

She didn't know if this was just a nice guy, or if the distress was showing on her face and he felt sorry for her, but she'd had about as much as she could stand of embarrassment for one evening, so she shook her head. 'I'll get a taxi.'

Without making eye contact or waiting for him to say anything else, Natalie bolted out the door. Maybe Rose was right, maybe she needed to rethink the whole celebrating Christmas properly thing.

She hailed a taxi, but didn't go home. Instead she recited the address of a block of storage units she'd not been to in ages, determined to face the contents and her past so she could finally – hopefully – move on.

Chapter 3

Natalie's head was pounding as she woke to the chorus of Rudolph the Red-Nosed Reindeer echoing through her skull.

She fumbled for her mobile and answered, not bothering to open her eyes. Her head wasn't ready for that yet.

'Hello?' she croaked.

'Where are you? Do you know how worried I've been?'

Rose's voice was like knives in her ears and she had to hold the phone away to listen. As she opened her eyes, she saw why her friend was flipping out. Natalie was lying on a sofa she hadn't seen in years, wrapped in a dust sheet and surrounded by boxes.

Boxes of her mum's stuff.

'I'm fine, Rose.' But that wasn't true. The pain of her headache was smothered by the agony in her chest. Coming here had seemed like a good idea last night, a way to move on with her life, but she hadn't even been able to face looking inside one box.

'Natalie Taylor, I have been up all night terrified something happened to you. I've called you a hundred times along with every hospital in London! I even called the police. Do you know what they said? You're not a missing person until you've been gone longer. What if you had been stabbed and were lying in a ditch somewhere or fell into the river!'

Tears filled her eyes and clogged her throat. What had made her think Rose wouldn't care where she was? 'I'm sorry Rose, I'm so selfish. You didn't need to worry, I was—' Admitting she went home with a stranger was not likely to ease any of her friend's worry, so she decided to skip that bit. 'I'm at the storage unit. I came here to try and … I don't know why. But I wish I hadn't.'

She caught sight of one of the boxes. It was bursting with every colour of tinsel in existence and the tears spilled over. 'I should have come home. I'm sorry.'

'Nat … What's up with you lately? Something's wrong and we're going to make time to talk about it. I might be getting married, but you're still my best friend and I feel like I haven't been there for you this last week. I know how hard this time of year is for you.'

Rose's sudden concern made her feel like a rotten cow. She wanted so much to tell her friend everything, but she had to stop being so dependent on Rose. Besides, the truth would only cause friction with her friend's new fiancé. 'I'll be okay, I promise. I'm coming home now for a hot bath and something to eat.'

'Do you need me to come and get you? I can make it before the lunch rush,' Rose offered.

'No, it's fine. The fresh air will be good for me.' Or the freezing breeze would kill her, but she couldn't face Rose like this. It would be too easy to slip back into leaning on her friend.

'If you're sure. But I'm telling Tom it's girls' night tonight. You and I are going to talk. I'll bring the wine and we can get a takeaway.'

Wine was the last thing she needed, but it would be nice to have some girl time. 'Okay, that sounds good. See you later.'

Natalie hung up and slipped her phone into her bag. The walls felt like they were coming in on her and her heart was going double time. After carefully rearranging the dust sheet over the sofa, she bolted for the door without looking at anything. Outside, she slid down to the ground, panting like she'd just sprinted a mile.

One thing was for sure, she wasn't ready to unpack those boxes, but she didn't want to give up on Christmas either. Which meant she had to find a way to deal with solo Christmas party-crashing that didn't end in total disaster.

***

The girls' night wasn't going exactly as she'd imagined. After apologising to Rose again, they'd had Thai takeout and Natalie had eaten so much curry she thought she might explode, so changed into her Christmas themed pyjamas. She wasn't up for the wine though, and left that to Rose who was uncharacteristically knocking it back.

By the time they'd finished catching up on the television shows they'd recorded, Natalie had come to the conclusion that Rose had something she wanted to talk about too. 'What's going on? Is everything alright with you and Tom?'

See, she could be a good friend. She didn't even call him Tom the Twat.

Rose shook her head. 'It's me, not him. I know you don't like him, Nat, but you should give him a chance. He's an amazing guy.'

Natalie wondered if it was worth lying and saying she did like Tom to avoid a potential argument – or eviction, but that just wasn't her. 'Honestly, I don't know what you see in him. He uses your emotions to get you to do what he wants. That's why I don't like him.'

Rose's mouth popped open. 'You think he emotionally blackmails me?'

'When it comes to you going out with me, yes, I think he does.' She'd said this before, just never as bluntly.

'You're wrong, Nat. Really wrong. Tom had a hard relationship before he met me. His ex used to go out and cheat on him all the time. He gets nervous when I go out too, so I don't anymore. I want him to know he can trust me, but he'd never *stop* me from doing it. It's *my* choice to stay in, not his.'

At least Rose didn't sound offended, more hurt that Natalie would think badly about her fiancé. And how crap did that make her feel? 'You've never told me that before.'

Rose shrugged and poured another glass of wine. She'd still not made much of a dent in her green curry, which wasn't like her. They both *loved* Thai food – in fact most food, really.

'Is there something else going on I don't know about? For someone who's just gotten engaged, you seem ... I don't know, down?' But she hadn't been that way around Tom, which maybe meant Natalie was the problem

'There are other things you don't know,' Rose said, staring down into her glass. 'I'm not a nice person. At least I didn't used to be. I don't want to hurt Tom. I don't want to hurt anyone ever again.'

Natalie shifted closer on the sofa and grabbed Rose's hand, giving it a squeeze. 'What are you talking about? You're the best person I know, and that's just for putting up with my drama alone.'

Rose's eyes were wide and shiny as she looked up. 'I love you, Nat. I don't *put up* with you, I need you.'

'I need you too. Talk to me, tell me what has you believing you're anything other than lovely.'

But Rose hid her eyes and then pulled her hand free. 'I can't, I don't even want to think about what I did ... what I could do again. I'm going to go to bed now.'

'Rose?' she asked, but Rose just shook her head, leaving a pang in Natalie's heart.

Natalie tried to tell herself that Rose's idea of doing something terrible would be standing on a puppy's tail by accident, and not getting it to a vet for a full check-up quickly enough, but the heavy feeling in her gut told her this was worse. All she could do was wait until Rose was ready to talk, and comfort her any way she could.

And to think, that wasn't even the weirdest part of the evening. She was actually beginning to feel sorry for Tom, and even understand why he acted the way he did, in front of Natalie anyway.

It seemed like this was a week for firsts, and she couldn't wait to get it over with.

***

Monday rolled around far too soon, as always, and Mick the Dick was spending a rare day in the office. Unfortunately, that meant he had just taken on a new client, which in turn meant dumping more work on her already packed desk.

After work, her day didn't get much better. Tom had decided he wanted to get married at Christmas *this* year (which would mean he and Rose would be completely occupied with planning for the next few weeks), which would force Natalie to celebrate the day in a way other than staying in bed watching horror movies on DVDs with a bottle of wine and a box of chocolates. Oddly, Rose's spirits seemed at an all-time low, and though she didn't want to leave her friend, she'd never get to talk to her properly with Tom there in full wedding planner mode.

At least he was attentive to Rose's gloominess and seemed to be making an effort to cheer her up, which made Natalie dislike him a little less. Still, she just wanted to get away from them this evening – and luckily for her, she knew a party that needed crashing.

When she arrived at the hotel overlooking Hyde Park, she was glad she came. The party was in one of their lounges with a balcony and the view of the Winter Wonderland bustling through the park was breath-taking. Swiping a glass of mulled wine, she wrapped her poncho round her shoulders and went to get a better look.

She turned her head to the sound of footsteps on the balcony next to her and quickly wished she hadn't. Mr Smug was there, looking none too pleased to see her but there was the edge of something else sparkling in his chocolatey eyes.

'I suppose you've urinated on the boundaries here, too?' she asked, lacing the question with as much sarcasm as she could muster.

'I thought you might try being nice this time, Nicole. Or is that name just a cover?'

Her breath caught, and without thinking she asked, 'How did you find that out?'

The smug smile was back and she wished she'd kept her mouth shut.

'I just checked to see whose name kept popping up and there you were. Or there was Nicole Porter anyway. I doubt that's the name on your birth certificate though.' He folded his arms and waited.

But if he thought she was going to deny it, or give him the pleasure of asking how he managed to get into any of the systems, he was wrong. Instead she shrugged. 'That's none of your business, is it?'

'I disagree. Like I said before, too many unfamiliar faces and people are going to start asking questions. I quite like this set up, so I'm asking you one more time to reconsider.'

She wasn't just hearing this guy though. Mick the Dick's demands to get one pitch after another to his desk had been driving her mad all day. What was it with pushy men thinking women were only there to do what they wanted?

Well this woman wasn't about to bow down, especially not to someone who didn't pay her salary – even a pathetically low one. 'I'm not leaving any time soon so you'd better get used to it.'

She polished off the last of the mulled wine, then turned to leave but he caught her arm and dragged her around to face him again. 'Let. Me. Go.'

He did, but didn't back away. 'Maybe I could let them know all about your little stunt, *Nicole*.'

'You wouldn't! I could just do the same to you.'

'You'd never get the chance. Then again, maybe it doesn't have to end like this with us.' Something flickered in his eyes and her mouth dried up. 'Maybe we could take advantage of this situation and work off the tension between us a different way.'

He pointed above her head to a bunch of mistletoe dangling from the roof of the balcony. Her heart started to hammer and she stopped breathing altogether. He couldn't possibly be suggesting that if she didn't snog him, or go further, then he'd have her chucked out, was he?

Rage burned away the surprise and her heart slowed to a steadier beat. 'Not if you were the last man alive. No scrap that, the last *person* alive. I'd rather change my sexuality than be with a creep like you.'

He didn't look offended, just gave her a hot look that suggested she didn't know what she was missing and even though her stomach clenched, she refused to feel anything other than dislike for this idiot.

'Your choice,' he said, as she turned and stomped back into the party.

Let him try and get her chucked her out. She wouldn't go down without a fight.

***

Dean blew out a huge breath and ran a hand down his face. *What had he been thinking?* He'd never tried to blackmail a woman before – he'd never had to.

After he'd looked into the previous parties, found out the name she used to get in and noticed she'd be here tonight, he'd printed out a list of restaurants and bars having added her name to the guest list of them all. That way, she could go to those instead of risking them both being caught.

It wasn't even about having two unfamiliar faces there. He and his brother used to come to these things together all the time. But they hung out at the bar, separated themselves from most of the guests and only chatted up women who approached them.

His little thief nicked food, mingled and danced in a way that could draw the attention of every man in the room. Even his. Though that didn't give him a pass for what he just did.

But there was something about the way she glared at him, the way she didn't take any of his crap and fought him tooth and nail for what she wanted that triggered an insane need to spar with her. He'd seen her arriving in a cute, red dress and he'd felt the same way he had that first night.

He wanted her. There was no denying it at this point. And so, instead of offering her an alternative to showing up where he was, he delivered her an ultimatum.

Better to move on than risk any more arsehole statements coming out his mouth. A while later, he got talking with Casey, an assistant to the head of HR, which would have normally been risky. Except she never questioned his identity, and who would remember everyone's name in a company with five offices and thousands of employees?

She wasn't anything like his little thief either. Casey was bubbly and fun, suggesting they head to her room after they take advantage of the free food and nibbles. She was exactly his kind of woman – relaxing to be around, easy to talk to, and up for a good time. And he'd long since gotten used to the feeling of repetition. It was a much safer option than the alternative.

Casey excused herself for a bathroom break and he pulled out his phone to check for any messages. Jeffrey hadn't spoken to him since their fight, despite the fact they were supposed to be running a company together, and earlier Dean had decided enough was enough and tried to call him before he came out, but there had been no answer.

There was an email though, but not from his pissed off brother. Worse, it was from his parents. They were inviting him to Jeffrey and Alana's engagement dinner this weekend at a posh restaurant Dean and Jeffrey would be expected to foot the bill for. And he knew the reason for the invite wouldn't be because they wanted him there. Nope, they wouldn't have cared less under normal circumstances. His parents were all about appearances, and the invite could only mean one thing. Jeffrey's future in-laws were coming.

God forbid they had to admit they weren't perfect parents with perfect sons.

He shook his head. He wasn't even fazed by the formal way they addressed him anymore. He'd gotten over all that shit a long time ago.

However, he *was* annoyed at Jeffrey. His brother owed him better than letting him find out from his parents that he was about to get a sister-in-law. Then again, after the way he'd acted when Jeffrey had been about to propose, he could hardly blame his brother.

He caught sight of Casey pushing her way through the mingling crowds, but something had changed. Her lips were tight and her eyes were like daggers as she stormed over to him. When she was a nanosecond away from barrelling into his chest, she lifted her hand and slapped him full force on the face.

'You bastard!' she screamed, then went for another swing.

Dean caught both her hands, wishing he had one free to rub the sting out of his jaw. 'What the fuck was that for?' he whispered, trying not to attract attention. But it was too late for that. The room had silenced and all eyes were on them.

'You know what it's for. Nicole told me. You've slept with half the office and given them all crabs!' she shrieked.

At least there was one plus in what she'd said. Half the party was eyeing each other suspiciously and edging away from what he assumed to be the single females.

Casey tried to head butt him but he dodged it, let her go and took a few steps back.

'I would never sleep with someone as low as you!'

With that she stormed away leaving him gaping at her retreating back. He felt all eyes on him again. At least this story would thaw Jeffrey out – that is, assuming they didn't quarantine him for a good de-lousing.

The cause of his public ridicule was easy enough to spot. She was across the room, right by the exit, almost vibrating with laughter and holding one hand over her mouth to mute the sound. He smiled slowly at her and had the satisfaction of seeing her eyes widen before she cleared off.

It seemed his little thief had just declared war.

Game on.

Chapter 4

By Friday she was desperate to get out of the house. Between spending the days trying to meet Mick the Dick's impossible deadlines and the nights with a quiet, unresponsive Rose, she just wanted to forget about her troubles and let her hair down with a bunch of strangers who didn't expect anything from her.

It also had something to do with the fact that, deep down, she was still reeling from her victory on Monday night. *Finally*, she'd gotten her payback on Mr Perfect and it had been a doozy. She'd also managed to get guest lists and names from the previous events to try to figure out who he was, and the only name that kept recurring was 'Dean'. It was a common enough name, but the surname was always different. So she wasn't exactly sure.

No doubt this guy, whoever he was, had a lot more experience crashing parties than she did. She just couldn't understand why he'd bother. If he could afford all those tailor-made suits surely he could fork out for drinks at a bar if he just wanted to pick up women.

Still, she wasn't going to spend any more energy on him. As far as she was concerned, they were even. If he happened to show up tonight, she'd ignore him and get on with enjoying herself.

All good in theory, but when she did see him, his silk burgundy shirt and black suit combo was hard to ignore. It seemed to work to highlight the colour of his skin and his dark, melting eyes, to the point she was getting annoyed with herself for ogling.

After all, she'd worked all hours planning this party, from the reindeer ice sculptures set in the window archways, to the band. She'd even sourced the gourmet chef and approved the finger hors d'oeuvres being served, and she planned to take full advantage of every last inch of it. She'd started the evening by stuffing her bag with enough grub to see her through the weekend, making sure to take the least odorous items.

Despite the worry that he was going to try something to ruin her night, the guy just mingled with both men and women, striking up the longest conversation with a short, overweight and balding man whose face was so red and sweaty, she worried he had an ulcer churning under his spare tires.

And she really needed to pay attention to what the girl next to her was blabbering on about, not to what Mr Perfect was doing.

'So that's how I got into advertising. What about you?' the girl asked.

Er, what did she just say? Right. Why we're here. 'I love temping, it's a great way to try new things but I don't really want to get into advertising ...' That would just be too hard a conversation to carry, even with a girl who looked no older than an intern.

'But aren't you worried? I mean, people usually pick what they want to do in their twenties, they don't wait until they're old.'

She was in her bloody twenties! There were still two whole years before she hit the big three-oh. 'I still am.'

The intern got all apologetic then, but Natalie didn't want to hear it. She left the table to go mingle with someone else, snatching a flute of champagne from the tray of a passing waiter and downing half the glass in one motion.

She was stopped in her tracks by the short, sweaty man she'd been worried about earlier.

'Let's dance, sweet thing,' he said, snatching away her much needed alcohol and taking one of her hands in his sweaty, chubby palm.

'No thank you,' she said.

'You are a feisty one, aren't you,' he said, ignoring Natalie and hauling her along to where the band was playing a mix of Christmas and chart songs.

She tried to tug free again. 'I said I don't want to dance.'

He just pulled her so close, she could smell a mix of meat and beer on his breath, and feel the perspiration on his shirt soak into her lacy, white dress. That was the last straw. This dress was couture and had cost her more than she paid in rent. Her temper simmered. 'What's wrong with you? I said I didn't want to dance.'

His hands slipped down and cupped her bum, then squeezed hard. 'Dean's right, you've got a tight little arse. If you don't want to dance, follow me to the men's room and I'll take care of you, sweet thing.'

Natalie fisted her hand and was ready to lamp this guy a good one, ulcer or not, but then what he said sank in. 'What *exactly* did Dean say?'

The man's face turned puce. 'Er, well, not much, just that you were good with your tongue and wanted … well … sex so bad you'd do anyone.'

She clenched her teeth together and wrestled out of his hold.

'Sweet thing, I can show you a good time. We could even get a room,' he called, but she'd already spun around and headed for the bar.

Dean – if that was even his name – wasn't even being discreet about his amusement. She heard his bellow over the music, and her temper reached critical level. She didn't look at him, didn't have to. She knew exactly where he was in the room.

'Hi, I'm Rick.'

An older man with skin like leather pushed into the bar next to her. She glared at him, having a horrible feeling what was going to come out of his mouth next. 'I don't have time to chat, Rick.' Turning to the bartender, she said, 'A bottle of merlot, please. And a glass.' Making an exception, she put a bottle of red wine on her credit card – champagne just wasn't going to cut it this time.

While she got served, Rick got handsy, sliding his arm around her hips. 'Come on, love. We can get a room. There's a Travel Lodge not too far from here.'

She snatched his hand before it reached her bum, then spied the gold band on his wedding finger, so held it up to his face. 'I am *not* interested, you scuzzy bastard.'

At least he looked abashed before sliding off the ring and pocketing it. 'How about now? I'll just be a dirty bastard.'

The waiter brought her the much-needed Merlot. Natalie filled a glass, quickly drained it, then poured another. 'Let me guess, Dean told you I'm the office slut.'

'Not in so many words,' Rick said. 'Don't be offended, I can—'

'If you say anything that insinuates you can give me great sex I *will* smash this bottle over your head then stab you in the balls with the shards. Now get lost.'

He took her less than subtle hint, grumbling '*bitch*' as he went. Natalie grabbed her wine and the glass, then made as if to go find an empty table. That's when she spotted Dean, grinning a victorious grin that was going to be short-lived.

He made his second mistake of that evening and approached her, still laughing.

'Don't declare a war if you can't handle one little battle,' he said.

Oh, she could handle the battles, and she was going to win the war too. When he was close enough, she pretended to stumble, guessing his reflex reaction would be to catch her.

She was right.

He was conned.

Her glass 'accidentally' slipped, pouring the contents down

his silk, burgundy shirt. There was no way that's coming out ever.

He let her go, then frowned down at the damage. Sweat on her favourite dress deserved some payback in her book. Not to mention telling all the old, sleazy bastards that she was easy.

'I'm so sorry,' she lied. 'I hope that comes out. You should probably rinse your shirt before it stains.'

His eyes narrowed at her. 'You've just changed the game.'

Natalie glared back. 'I told you, I don't play games. I just get even, and now we are.'

He smirked. 'We're not even close, *Nicole.*'

'Then bring it on, *Dean.*'

With that she left the party with the bottle of wine and her hearty plunder. There was no point hanging round getting hit on by a bunch of horned up ancients who probably had pockets filled with little blue pills.

And even though her night had been cut short, the anticipation of how he'd retaliate together with her second victory of the week left her on a bit of a high.

***

Nobody was up when she got in, so she took off her shoes, pulled out her phone, and started googling all the variations of Dean's name she'd read. After all, it was true what they said. You had to know your enemy if you had a hope of beating them.

But nothing came up that she recognised, not as her Dean anyway.

Rose's bedroom door opened and to her surprise, Tom came out and headed straight towards her. He usually grunted a hello and went to the bathroom or something, but he clearly had other plans tonight.

'Good, I've been waiting for you to get home,' he said, sounding relieved.

Natalie couldn't keep the surprise out of her tone. 'You were? Why?'

He sat on the chair across from her before answering. 'I'm worried about Rose. I know you love her as much as I do, and I just wanted to know if she's said anything about having cold feet to you, or has she changed her mind about me? I know we haven't always gotten on, but something's tearing her apart and if I'm the reason, I promise I'll back off. I'd do anything to keep from hurting her.'

Natalie didn't think she'd heard Tom say more than two sentences before, and she'd certainly never seen him looking so vulnerable. She remembered what Rose said, about Tom having been hurt and that it wasn't him driving the distance in their friendship, but that it was Rose's choice so she wouldn't worry him.

Then later, Rose's revelation about having done something awful and worrying she'd hurt Tom too.

'She hasn't said anything like that to me, but you're always here, so …' Nat shrugged, then as his expression crumpled, she backtracked. 'I don't think it's you, she told me she loves you so much.'

He seemed to relax a little. 'Thank God. I don't know how I could go back to a life without her.'

'I'll try to talk to her, but I'm not sure when. I mean …' She didn't really want to point out the fact that he was there all day, every day, but how did he expect her to get any alone time with Rose when he never left?

'You never get the chance with me here, right? I know, and I'm sorry about that too. I don't know how much Rose told you about me, but I have, well, let's just say I'm not as trusting as I'd like to be.' He sighed and ran a hand through his hair. 'Why don't you take her out tomorrow, either to a bar or one of your parties? I don't want to stop her from living her life, or having friends and enjoying herself. Maybe spending all this time with me is suffocating her.'

Natalie was stunned. She'd thought of Tom as her adversary for a while and figured he was a bit of a controlling bastard too. But now it was obvious he didn't want to be, and she decided to start giving him the benefit of the doubt.

'Okay, we can go for dinner and a few drinks. Nothing too wild,' she said, now she knew he'd worry.

'Thanks, Nat,' he said, getting up. 'I hope we can start getting on better, for Rose's sake if nothing else.'

'Me too', she said and really meant it. Which was not something she'd ever have expected to be saying to Tom. Scrap the week, this was turning out to be a month of firsts.

***

This was going to be nothing if not a shitty way to spend his Saturday night, Dean thought, as he took his place at the table in the restaurant. It's not that the food was bad. In fact, it was one of the best à la carte restaurants in the city. And just happened to be his brother's fiancée's favourite place to eat.

What made it shitty was who he was spending it with. Not that he knew Alana's parents, they seemed nice enough. But directly across from him were *his* parents, and they'd yet to even acknowledge him.

Luckily Jeffrey was so dumbstruck that Alana had agreed to marry him, he'd forgotten about their argument, even if Dean hadn't. But he still forced out the appropriate congratulations, even when he wanted to shake some sense into his brother, and warn Alana that if she broke Jeffrey's heart he'd do everything in his power to make her regret it.

And he might have, if the Wicked Witch hadn't flown in on her broom for the evening, dragging his dad along with her.

The first poison dart came as soon as the starters were served, and it was the first time she acknowledged his presence.

'I see your girlfriend couldn't make it tonight, Dean.' His

mother's disparaging gaze didn't fit with the sweet, doting mother act she was working for the in-laws' benefit.

He was about to tell his mother he'd had two separate women this month, but had gotten bored of their skill in the bedroom already (not that it was true, he just wanted to wipe the smug look off her face and humiliate her for a change), when he caught Jeffrey throwing him a warning glance. Dean couldn't screw up his brother's night and not just because his parent' would never let him hear the end of it. He hadn't exactly been a supportive sibling lately. Even if he thought Jeffrey was making a colossal mistake, he should be there for him no matter what.

'I'm not seeing anyone at the moment,' he said instead.

His mother tutted, and shook her head with a pained expression. Turning to Alana's parents, she explained her disappointing eldest son. 'Ten years ago, he was engaged to be married. I thought by this point we'd be surrounded by grandchildren. But Dean just can't keep a woman. Luckily Jeffrey's loyal. We're so proud of him.'

Dean fisted his hands reflexively, then pulled them under the table. He couldn't believe the witch was making it sound like he'd been unfaithful, when he'd been anything but.

Jeffrey jumped in before Dean could erupt. 'Mum, Dean's so busy with our business he doesn't have time to date. He's creating an updated version of our hospitality program, and we've already lined up thousands of buyers.'

But their mother just shook her head. It was their father who spoke. 'You were forever on that computer as a boy. Now you're a man, son. You need to get out of that office and find yourself a nice wife like your brother. You're not getting any younger.'

Great, now he was an ancient computer nerd. But he wasn't going to argue, he just nodded. Thankfully the conversation turned from his unacceptable (to his parents, anyway) love life to the wedding, and while dates in July and centrepiece ideas were bounced around, he zoned out and unlocked his mobile.

First he hooked up to the booking system to find the next party Nicole Porter was listed to attend, and found it easily enough – a hotel just off Trafalgar Square the following night – then added himself to the guest list.

After all, he wasn't going to let her just get away with ruining his shirt – not that he cared about the clothes. This was a battle of wit and about the only thing keeping him occupied enough so all this wedding stuff wouldn't drag him back to a place in his head he didn't want to be.

And she wasn't just a worthy rival, she was sexy too. With a smart mouth, sexy body and quick wit, she was his ideal fling – exciting, sassy and definitely nothing that would feel repetitive. What made it all the sweeter was that she didn't seem to feel anything for him other than disdain, though he was sure he'd caught an occasional spark of lust in her eyes. There would be no risk of feelings getting involved, and more importantly, hearts being broken.

No matter what she said, they were playing a game. A sparring, lust-fuelled one. And when the time came, they were both coming out of it winners.

***

'I really wish I didn't have that second margarita,' Natalie said, as she bounced up and down on the seat of the taxi. 'I'm bursting for the loo.'

Rose smiled for what seemed like the first time that week. 'You should have gone before we left.'

Hindsight was a funny thing, though not at this moment when she had a bladder full to bursting.

'Finally!' As soon as the taxi stopped, she flung a twenty at the driver and scrambled out. The restaurant was the kind of place where they seated you, but Natalie couldn't wait for that. She was heading straight for the bathroom.

They passed the window and headed for the door, but Rose pulled her back. Natalie crossed her legs, but it didn't help. '*Come on,* Rose. I'm going to wet the pavement.'

Rose's expression was blank. 'I think we should go to that sushi bar around the corner.'

'The one three streets away? Are you kidding? I'm on the verge of peeing myself.'

Calmly, Rose said, 'You told me it was my choice tonight.'

Natalie switched to hopping from one foot and the other. 'You chose *here*, remember?'

Her friend shot a nervous glance at the door, then refocused on Natalie. 'I changed my mind.'

She was so desperate, she could cry. 'Please, Rose. Don't do this to me.'

'Look, just go to the loo in there. They're busy tonight.' Her friend glanced through the window, then quickly stepped away from it. 'They won't even notice you.'

Usually, Natalie wouldn't dare in case the pee police were watching, but she was too far gone to argue.

'Fine,' she mumbled and snuck in.

Thankfully nobody was paying attention to her, but the problem was, she didn't know the restaurant at all and finding the bathroom was not as easy a task as she thought. She tried to look like she knew what she was doing, like she was supposed to be there, but desperation got the best of her and she grabbed a waiter's arm, almost knocking over the three steaks he was expertly holding.

'Bathroom?' she pleaded.

And the second he nodded to the far corner she was off, trying not to knock over tables as she went. But as she neared, a familiar face exited the men's room, blocking her way to the ladies' one. 'No, *please no.*'

Dean chuckled, and she had to resist the urge to hop from leg to leg.

'That's some way to speak to a guy you told everyone was riddled with crabs and then poured a gallon of wine over,' he said with a smirk. 'Are you legitimately here tonight or just in for a freebie?'

Natalie gritted her teeth. She'd have argued with him all night, but … 'I don't have time for this. I'm about three seconds from ruining your shoes too, so if you don't mind, step out of the effing way.'

With a laugh he shifted to let her pass, even though she was fully prepared to shove him out of the way. When she'd regained her composure, she hoped desperately that he'd left, or was on a date. Then he couldn't pester her anymore and she'd be able to sneak out without the lecture that accompanied peeing in a restaurant you've not ordered in.

No such luck.

He was leaning against a wooden archway when she emerged. 'I think the whole restaurant heard you, there. Everyone thought a race horse had snuck into the bathroom.'

'Har, har.' But her cheeks burned as she stalked by him.

'Lighten up, Nicole. This isn't the battlefield. I was teasing.'

'My name is *not* Nicole,' she said, whirling on him. 'And I doubt yours is Dean, either.'

He smiled. 'It is. I don't suppose you'd tell me yours?'

Who knew with his always slightly smug, amused expression? She couldn't tell if he was sincere or if this was another one of those games he kept banging on about. She shook her head. 'I need to go.'

He frowned. 'You're not staying?'

'Why, so you can tell some other sleazy bastards to feel me up because I'm easy? I don't think so.'

Just then, another man approached them and he looked remarkably like Dean. His features were similar, but the other one was younger, and looked worried, not like a smug bastard.

When he spoke, it was sincere. 'I'm really sorry, Miss. Whatever

43

my brother did to you, I can honestly say you can do better. But listen, it's my engagement dinner tonight, and I don't want him to cause a scene in front of the future in-laws.'

His smile was sincere too, especially when he glanced towards a table with a beautiful brunette and two older couples.

Then he elbowed his brother in the ribs. 'For fuck's sake, Dean. Tell her you're sorry.'

Dean just smirked at her in an I-told-you-so way. She turned to the younger, nicer version and said, 'Congratulations to the both of you. And don't worry, there won't be any trouble. I've never slept with your brother, he only wishes. Enjoy your meal!'

She didn't look at Dean, just accepted his brother's gratitude and strolled out of the restaurant with her head held high. She had no idea who won that round, but like Dean said, this was not the battlefield – just an unwelcome coincidence. There would be plenty time to get her own back.

'What took you so long?' Rose asked. She was fully submerged in the shadows.

'Who or what are you hiding from?' Natalie asked. She didn't really want to go into all that stuff with Dean. 'And what's wrong with eating here?'

Not that she wanted to when he was there, never mind with his family, but it was weird for Rose to change her mind at the last minute.

'I was hoping for somewhere quieter so we can talk.'

Natalie wasn't going to argue with that even if she didn't believe it. She wanted to get away from here as fast as Rose seemed to.

***

'There really is a first time for everything,' his brother said as Dean watched his little thief storm out of the restaurant.

Dean was too distracted to ask what his brother was on about – distracted by the way her black, skinny jeans moulded her arse and clung to her surprisingly long legs. But Jeffrey was never deterred by silence.

'The one woman in London who would probably rather poke her left eye out than sleep with you and I got to shake her hand.' His brother laughed.

'It's early days, and I'm fairly sure she'd rather sleep with me than dismember herself.' Though in the mood she was in, he could see why Jeffrey might think otherwise.

Jeffrey shook his head. 'You never knew when to call it quits.'

'I prefer to think of it as rising to face the challenge,' he disagreed, following his brother back to the table. And Nicole, or whoever she was, definitely presented a challenge. But it was much more than that.

'She might beat you down a notch or ten. So I say, go for it.'

'Knob,' Dean said, smiling. As they got closer to the table, he whispered, 'You're just jealous because you can't chase sexy blondes anymore.'

His fiancée was in earshot before his brother could reply and Dean wanted to rub in the fact that he'd gotten the last word for once, but decided to enjoy the win silently. Everyone had already dug into the main course that had just been served and didn't notice the acidic look his mother threw them as they slipped back into their seats.

She struck up a conversation about polo next, and he started on his steak, making sure to stuff his mouth before she asked how he had managed to be such a disappointment at that too. Anyway, he knew his father would answer for him.

It's all that meddling around with the computer, softened the boy up. We should never have bought it for him.

Thankfully not even his mother seemed interested in what he was up to anymore so he concentrated on his dinner instead. Or at least tried to. Jeffrey didn't have the best table manners when it came to spaghetti – why he picked that dish on the night the parents met was beyond Dean – but he was more distracted by

Alana, occasionally wiping the sauce from his brother's chin with a napkin, eyes shining and lips curving in a way that said like nothing but how completely and utterly in love she was with him.

Putting the twinge in his chest down to indigestion, he refocused on his steak.

Dean's mobile vibrated, distracting him from things he'd rather not think about. He pulled it out of his pocket and checked the screen.

Fancy coming over?
xxxxxxx

Mandy. Until a week ago, he'd have taken her up on the offer but his head wasn't in it tonight. Maybe not ever again. She'd started to sign off with more kisses than was necessary and he suspected these infrequent hook ups were starting to mean more for her.

And if he was honest, he'd had more fun sparring with his 'Nicole' for ten minutes than he'd ever had in the hours he'd spent at Mandy's.

He replied, deciding it was time to finish things with her. He never wanted to lead someone on, knowing exactly how crap it felt.

Sorry, Mandy. I think it's time we call it quits.

Her reply took all of three seconds.

Okay, baby. You know where I am if you change your mind.
xoxoxoxoxo

He doubted he would. There was just no thrill anymore when it came to dating the way he had been. Dean blamed Jeffrey and this whole idiotic marriage thing. It was stirring up a lot of shit inside and making him come to realizations he'd been happy enough to ignore before now.

***

The little Japanese sushi bar never failed to disappoint, and when they'd had their fill the place had quietened to the point they almost had privacy as they sipped their complementary sakes.

'So, now we're pretty much alone, spill,' Natalie said.

Rose got so pale even her lips turned white.

'Rose, come on. Whatever you did isn't half as bad as you think it is. You're so kind-hearted. You'd feel awful about the tiniest thing. I mean, it's not like you did something stupid, like went back to a guy's house because you were drunk and—'

'You did *what*?' Rose asked, the colour burning back into her cheeks.

Oops, she forgot she hadn't told Rose about Steven yet. 'I had a one-night stand last week. It's nothing to worry about. He was cool.'

Rose narrowed her eyes. 'Nat, he could have hurt you. In fact, wait. You said last week? Was that the night you didn't come home by any chance?'

Busted.

'Yeah, that's the one. But I really was in the storage unit, you know, after I snuck out.' And after giving another guy a floor show. She still couldn't get the hot sauce smell off her lovely clutch.

'Nat, you're spiralling.' Rose took her hands. 'Why?'

Natalie shook her head. 'Nope, you can take that worried look and flip it on yourself. Tonight's about you, and I want to know what's going on. Is it …'

She took a deep breath, then chickened out of what she wanted to ask, and went with something else. 'Is it Tom? Are you having second thoughts?'

47

Rose studied her face for a minute. 'If I tell you the truth, will you tell me what you were going to ask me?'

Frick, there really was no way to get anything past Rose. 'Deal.'

'Okay.' Rose necked her saki then gestured to the waiter for another. 'I'm not worried about Tom. I think he'll be an amazing husband, a brilliant dad. The thing is, I've been engaged before.'

Natalie blinked, it was all she could do.

'Don't hate me for not telling you. It was ten years ago. And I didn't want you to think I was a heartless cow,' Rose said, looking down at her hands.

'Enough of that, I don't think anything of the sort.' She slid the rest of her sake over the table. It looked like Rose needed it more.

'I don't want to go into the details, but it ended because of me. I left him without an explanation or anything.' A tear broke free from her eye and slid down her cheek. Rose didn't even seem to notice as she picked up the drink and downed it.

And the reason her friend had been so down became clear. 'You don't want to do the same thing to Tom.' When Rose nodded, she went on, 'Then tell me why you left the other guy. I mean, you had to have a good reason.'

Rose's eyes welled to the point Natalie thought she'd break down in the middle of the restaurant. 'I just couldn't see a future with him, not when I looked past the puppy love and took off the rose-tinted glasses. We were opposites in every way. I was ready, even at eighteen, to settle down, start a business and one day have a ton of kids.'

'He didn't want that?' Natalie prompted.

Rose shrugged. 'We never really spoke about it. I was leaving after the summer to go to college here in the city, and he just spent all his time fiddling with his computer. He had all these ideas about designing games and don't get me wrong, he was brilliant at it. In fact, I used to go over to his when I was a kid and play them too. He just lacked the ambition to do anything with it and at the end of the day, I couldn't face supporting him when I wanted to start up a business of my own. So I left.'

Natalie could see it, her friend at eighteen with her future already mapped out. She was so level-headed. Someone who didn't know what to do with their life would have been a poor match.

'But why do you feel you might end up doing that to Tom? He's a banker and does pretty well for himself. In fact, he has a great income, a fancy rental in Chelsea and a 2016 Bentley. I'd say he's pretty ambitious, and it's obvious you really love him, so what's worrying you?'

The waiter approached with another round of drinks, but Rose didn't down this one. 'Even without the money, even without the ambition, I'd still love him more than anything. We just click, you know? And I wonder, did I feel that way back then, or was it just puppy love? If I could walk away from one fiancé, will I walk away from this one?'

Natalie wasn't exactly qualified in relationships, and her experience added up to a handful of one-nighters, two six-month relationships in high school and the occasional fling since she came to London, so she wasn't the person to go to for advice. But Rose's predicament seemed so obvious.

'I think you need to let go of the past and all your guilt so you can move forward with Tom. If you truly believe it is meant to be, then it will work out. You can't hurt him, hon. You care too much.'

Rose sniffled. 'What would I do without you?'

Natalie grinned. 'You'd be lost. So, a Christmas wedding, eh? Do you think Tom would consider moving it to Boxing Day?'

'For my maid of honour? He'd better. Or there won't be a wedding at all.' She chuckled.

Natalie's throat got all thick, and she grabbed at it, like she could stop the emotion from bubbling up and spilling over. She felt like she was somehow closer to Rose knowing her friend wasn't perfect, and also relieved at not having to worry about being a misery at the wedding.

'Are you sure you don't want me to help? I mean, it can't be easy finding somewhere, even for a small party, this close to the day. And I've done loads of last-minute weddings. I could call in a favour somewhere, maybe at the Savoy? I'm friendly with their events manager.' At first she'd dreaded having to help, but now things had cleared up with Tom, she wanted to do whatever she could.

'Nope,' Rose said, shaking her head at the same time. 'All you have to do is go to the dress fitting when it's ready. Tom and I will do the rest. We were just going to have the ceremony at the registry office then have a meal with Tom's friends and family after. I've even invited the girls from the shop and their families, but all in all there won't even be thirty people. Even if you bring a date.'

There was no way she'd take a date. Even spending Christmas day watching the scariest horror films, she could never hide the puffy eyes from all the crying. She'd look a mess on Boxing day. She always did. 'There's more chance of me swimming the channel than that.'

Rose frowned. 'Would you prefer if we moved the wedding to spring, maybe? I don't want you to feel like you have to do this if you don't feel up for it.'

Natalie shook her head. 'I'm not going to be the reason you delay your wedding. Anyway, it's meant to snow this year – how romantic will that be for the photos? I usually put it all away by the 26th anyway.'

If you could call wrestling with her guilt and grief until she felt halfway normal, putting it all away.

'I wish you didn't have to.'

'Me too,' Natalie said, then sighed. 'Anyway, let's talk about less morbid things, okay?'

'Okay then. What were you going to say before?' Rose asked, startling her.

Great. They'd gone from discussing Natalie's unresolved issues with her mother's death and Christmas, to talking about her insecurities. Well, she supposed it was now or never. The sooner she knew the answer, she supposed the sooner she could be proactive about the situation. 'I was worried that the reason you were so down was because you were engaged, wanting to live with your fiancé and were too nice to ask me to move out, even though you wanted me to.'

'Don't be ridiculous, Nat. Of course, I want you to stay!'

Rose looked horrified she'd even suggested otherwise.

'It's going to be different when you're married though. I don't want to be a third wheel and you and Tom have a life to start living. I'm going to have to go at some point.' She just wished she'd had a chance to start up her own business first. Now it looked like her savings were going to go on security deposits and be frittered away paying the surplus in rent. God, and furniture. She'd have to start from scratch since everything in the flat belonged to Rose. Unless she could work up the courage to use her mum's things. But that was too depressing a thought.

As if reading her mind, Rose said, 'You can stay in the flat as long as you like and keep our stuff. I think when we do move in on our own, it'll be to Toms place anyway. And Tom has plenty at his house. I'd just take some of my utensils. I could even find you a roommate if you're worried about paying my parents the rent on your own.'

'Thanks. The idea of moving so soon is scary. And don't worry, I'll deal with the rent.' She was determined to stand on her own two feet, and that meant demanding a wage rise from Mick the Dick. If she could work up the courage for that, then maybe, just maybe, she'd be brave enough to face sorting out her mother's things.

***

Dean slipped away to pay the bill after his mother threw him a pointed look. Tapping the company credit card against the bar, he waited for the bill to be tallied and thought again about the interlude with his little thief.

The way she'd said his name, layered with feigned disgust made him smile. He was going to make it his mission to find out hers.

Jeffrey appeared next to him. 'Listen, I'm sorry about last week. That was a shitty thing for me to say.'

Dean shrugged. 'I wasn't exactly acting like the best brother either.'

His brother laughed. 'Nah, you were acting like an arse.'

With a grin, he replied. 'Always.' He knew by the way his brother clapped him on the back that the fight was over.

'So who *was* the cute little blonde that wouldn't go near you with a ten foot barge pole?' Jeffrey asked.

Where to start with that one? 'Not sure what her name is. We've crashed a few of the same parties and as far as I can tell, she goes by the name Nicole.'

Jeffrey raised an eyebrow. 'It looked like she wanted to rip your throat out with her nails, *after* she kicked you in the balls.'

He chuckled. 'Yeah, she probably did.'

Then his brother got serious, studying him with a look Dean had never seen before. 'You like her.'

'She's sexy and I want her, but that's all there is to it.' Christ, where did all this attentiveness come from? His brother looked like he was examining a specimen in a petri dish – Dean being the object of his scrutiny.

Jeffrey grinned. 'You're a shitty liar, my brother. But I'm not going to say any more about it. Well, maybe one thing.'

Dean rolled his eyes.

'When you were talking to her, or maybe arguing is a better word for it, anyway, my point is, I've never seen you look so alive. Not since … well, you remember.' Jeffrey glazed over the subject after seeing Dean's scowl. 'I don't think you should give up on

Nicole, or whoever she is.'

'You're reading too much into it. She's different, I'll give you that. But I'm not going back to the way I was before so don't get your hopes up that one woman will change me. It's not going to happen.' There was a difference between a strung-out, tension-filled … whatever it was they were heading for, and going back on what he swore he'd never do again.

'Who said you have to be who you were to have something more? You're too black and white. A little colour makes life exciting.' Jeffrey said, then went back to join his fiancée.

As he was handed the chip-and-pin machine, he thought back to the apathy he felt when Mandy's text came in, and compared it to the way his whole self seemed to transform and stand ready to attention when his little thief unleashed her smart mouth on him.

Colour did make life more exciting and sparring with Nicole – or whoever she was – was like viewing life through a kaleido-scope.

Chapter 5

Trafalgar Square was utterly breath-taking at Christmas time. With the fountains lit and the massive Christmas tree in the square draped in silvery lights, Natalie was taken back years to when her parents had brought her to London at Christmas for a weekend to do some shopping and see the sights.

She'd fallen in love with the city so completely that her goal had been to get into a great university here, study business management and hospitality and one day open her own company.

But life had changed. Her father died when she was only ten and her mum's low salary couldn't contribute to the cost of university – and Natalie hadn't wanted a lifetime of debt ahead of her. She'd ended up landing an internship with Mick the Dick, commuting for hours so she could stay at home, clawing her way from making tea and coffee to becoming the best events organiser in the company.

Then she'd lost her mum.

She'd met Rose when she'd turned to sweet treats to try and blot out the pain, and Rose's bakery was her favourite place to binge. One day Rose brought her a coffee and let her try their new recipe for walnut cake and they'd talked for hours about nothing and everything, with Rose being so kind and supportive that Natalie felt for the first time that she wasn't alone anymore, that she had someone who could care about her and she could care for Rose in return. Her life had changed so much after that.

But she wasn't any further forward. She was still on a crappy wage and was now crashing the parties she'd planned for others, just to feel like she was getting something back. It had to stop.

And it would. Tomorrow. She resolved to go to work, demand more money and hope for the best.

It was necessary if she was ever going to save enough to go it alone. And after that, well, maybe she'd work up the courage to finally go through her mother's things and sort it all out – it would save her having to keep up the monthly storage fees at least. As most of the stuff was Christmas decorations – that had been both Natalie's and her mother's favourite day of the year – it wasn't going to be easy.

First though, she was late for a party at The Grand, and couldn't wait to see how all her hard work looked up close.

This was by far the most lavish party she'd planned, and even without all the extras, the hotel was utterly beautiful all by itself. After having her coat taken, she was escorted through the lobby.

The hotel rarely accepted functions, but this international law firm would accept no less so scoring this venue had been a challenge. And the space she'd been worried about worked well. Tables draped in white velvet cloths were strategically set up around the room with a massive centre table, housing hotplates dripping with lamb, veal, venison and all the dressings on one side, with lavish salads, fruits and vegetarian dishes spread out over the other.

The pillars, despite the hotel manager's grumbles, were swirled with twinkling light features but the rest of the décor was minimal. The room was so gorgeous with all its art and antiques there was no need to overdress it.

There was no band tonight either, just gentle violin music whispering in the background, which was a request of the client.

Overall, Natalie was thrilled with how it had all come together and turned to ask Rose what she thought, then remembered her friend wasn't there.

Somehow it made her feel lonelier than she had for a while. Sighing, she took a seat and placed an order for some lamb with baby new potatoes and champagne. There would be no chance of packing up any of this grub. Buffet or not, the staff in The Grand insisted on serving it.

The chair beside her scraped against the marble floor and she looked up, seeing just a tuxedo at first, but the familiar grin caught her eye next. Natalie almost smiled back, not feeling like she was so alone anymore, but she'd never live it down if she looked happy to see Dean.

'I thought you didn't want to get caught. Surely if you've found a way to hack the booking systems, you'd have seen I was coming.' That sounded snippy enough, but her heart wasn't in the sparring tonight.

'Well, this is my turf. In fact, anywhere who uses the 21 Booking System comes under my territory,' he said, taking the seat next to her.

He was too close, his body seeming to suck in all the space around her and she shifted her chair over a touch to give herself room to breathe. It wasn't far enough though that she missed the scent of him, so clean and crisp, but with a spicy undertone that made her feel lightheaded.

She had to pull it together. 'What's so special about that system?'

'I created it. Makes life easier when you can just slip yourself onto the guest list, but because I did design it, I know it's not easy to hack. Which makes me wonder how you manage it?' he asked, leaning closer.

His irises seemed to be more liquid than solid – just like the flowing chocolate in the fountain she'd set up for the deserts. His dark, questioning look scrambled her heartbeat. Frick, when had he started affecting her like this? It must be because she was feeling lonely and down. Any familiar face would have the same affect. At least that was her story and she was sticking to it.

'If I tell you that, you'll just make it impossible for me to do it again,' she said.

'I added your name to other lists for parties I wasn't going to make. When I approached you at Hyde Park, I wanted to give you the list and ask you stick to them,' he said, without any snide or amusement in his tone.

Natalie frowned. How could she believe that, when … 'You tried to blackmail your way into my pants.'

Dean chuckled. 'I was actually after a kiss, and I prefer to see it as an ultimatum. Anyway, I didn't have you thrown out did I? But you made me out to be patient zero in a genital crabs outbreak.'

Thankfully the waiter arrived then with her order. It gave her a second to press her lips together to hold in the laugh. 'I'd never kiss you, not even if you paid me.'

She picked up her cutlery and dug in, trying very hard not to imagine what kissing him would be like.

'You will eventually. We can only win or lose this game together,' he said, sounding very sure of himself.

She welcomed the indignation. 'I told you, I don't want to play any games. And I have no idea where your confidence comes from. You have nothing to base it on. I'm not attracted to you at all.'

As that wasn't exactly true, the attracted bit anyway, she didn't look at him and made like she was concentrating really hard to strip the tender flesh of lamb from the bone.

He tugged her chin round so they were nose-to-nose and she dropped her cutlery, and stopped breathing altogether. Her heart hammered in her chest and fire seemed to sear through her veins. It wasn't rage, and she couldn't convince herself it was.

This was something else, something new, and the anticipation of his next move froze her to the spot.

His breath was hot as it brushed her lips like a caress, making her shiver.

Too soon, he released her. And she was stunned at the realization that she actually wanted to kiss him.

'Now, do you want to try that again? You might be able to talk a good game, but when it comes down to it, your reactions can't lie.'

The smug smile was back and thankfully it wiped away the last of the haze from her mind. Her temper came to the rescue. 'You are a complete bastard. Is this your next play? Try to get me all hot and bothered then cock-block? You'd be wasting your time. I'd never let you near me like that.'

He looked a little shocked at this. 'I was just proving that you want me too. I only pulled away because I wouldn't kiss you until you admit to yourself it's what you actually want. I'm not going to force you into it. Wait! Where are you going?'

She'd already gotten up, so angry she couldn't even listen to him. Another lie? Who knew. His rebuff after getting her hotter than she'd ever been was like subjecting her libido to the ice bucket challenge.

If he was going to play dirty, so was she.

She spied a security guard and almost made it to him when Dean tugged her arm. She didn't want to make a scene, because it would mean drawing too much attention to herself and she'd have to leave.

He stepped in front of her, but she just glared at his bowtie. 'What do you want?'

'You were going to get me kicked out, weren't you?' When she didn't answer, he said, 'Nicole, look at me.'

Well, scowling at him was better than doing exactly what he asked, so she did. 'My name is *not* Nicole.'

'Then why not tell me what it is?' he suggested, but didn't look hopeful.

'Why should I? You're playing some kind of twisted game with me, and I have no idea if what you're telling me is ever the truth. And yes, I was going to get you kicked out. If you want to change the terms of whatever the hell this is, then so can I. It's not like you weren't going to do the same thing to me last week.'

Natalie had to make an effort to calm down. She was getting too worked up over someone she barely even knew or liked and suspected it had more to do with where she was at in her life, than with him. He'd been a fun distraction, but now she felt like she was being played.

'I haven't lied to you and I can prove it. My name's Dean Fletcher. My brother and I co-own Tech Solutions. You can Google us and see for yourself. His name's Jeffrey.'

FML. She knew Tech Solutions, she'd arranged their Christmas parties for the last five years and this year too, at the Savoy. And Jeffrey's name did ring a bell – he was their contact. Of course, it was only Mick the Dick who'd met with him, but she recognised it from the file.

There was no way she could tell him who she was now. It would be like playing with fire. If he found out that the company they'd hired for events was crashing parties – and she'd had every intention of crashing theirs this year for the first time ever – he could do worse than get her all hot and bothered. He could have her sacked, maybe arrested too.

She had to put this back to where they were, before all the talking started. Natalie shrugged. 'I really don't have the time or the inclination to Google you. How about you give me that list of those venues you won't be at and we'll call it a draw.'

Though she had to say the last bit through gritted teeth. She wasn't keen on throwing anything, least of all a war against him.

He shrugged. 'I could email you the list.'

And then find out her name. 'Nice try.'

'Worth a shot. How about I text you?'

Natalie fought back a grin. 'Like I'd give you my number.'

'Well, looks like you'll just have to put up with me a little while longer.' The smug grin was back, but she thought she saw a hint of warmth in those dark eyes.

'Of course, if I quit my party-crashing ways, I'll never have to breathe the same air as you again.' See Dean, she could do smug too.

He lowered his head and stopped just as his lips grazed her earlobe and her heart burst off on a sprint. He slid a hand round her waist and for a second she was glad, because with her nose buried in his neck, his scent just about floored her, and unfortunately not in a bad way.

'If you quit, then it's not just me who'll be missing out, my little thief.' His teeth grazed her lobe and a violent shiver almost knocked her on her bum. 'You feel it too.'

Dean pulled away, giving her room to breathe. Clearing her head wasn't as easy.

He ran a finger down the side of her face, then stroked his thumb over her bottom lip. 'All you have to do is admit what you want, and you can have it.'

At that moment she was ready to ask him to strip her right there in the middle of the dining room, in front of everyone, and take her any way he wanted to have her, but then Rudolph The Red Nose Reindeer started to blare from her bag.

Dean grinned. 'Yours?'

She fumbled for her mobile and looked at the screen. God, thank you Rose. 'I have to take this.'

Natalie darted out into the lobby and answered.

'Hi, is everything alright?' She'd thought Rose and Tom were having another cosy night in by the fireplace.

'No,' Rose said around a sob. 'Nothing's alright. Tom left me!'

Oh no. 'I'll be home in twenty minutes, okay? I'm leaving right now.'

She darted for the exit and started running, as best she could in her silly shoes, in the direction of the tube. It wasn't until she got there and went to get her Oyster card out of her jacket that she realized she'd left without it. Thankfully she had change in her purse.

***

Dean followed Nicole out to the street, but by the time he made it she was gone and he had no idea what way she'd gone. For a few minutes he just stood there outside The Grand, willing the restless tension in his body to dissipate.

Shit, but she smelled amazing. He didn't know if it was her shampoo, perfume or just her. And he couldn't help but remember those plump, glossy pink lips he'd wanted to lick, not just touch. At least he knew now the colour was natural. The residue on his thumb came off clear, so she was obviously a minimalist when it came to make-up. All in all, she was refreshing, and whatever was going on between them was becoming addictive.

Still, how much he wanted her bothered him. For starters, he didn't even know who she was. Most women loved to talk about themselves, but not his little thief. She was an enigma, and he hoped that was why he was so keen to see her again. Otherwise she might be right. Maybe not bumping into each other after this would be for the best.

Lust was one thing, but emotions were another. He was done with the latter.

When it looked like she wasn't coming back, he made to leave but got stopped by a bellman.

'Sir, do you know where Miss Porter went?' he asked.

'She had to leave.' Or at least he assumed she did after the phone call. A boyfriend maybe? He frowned, not liking the idea of that.

'She left this. I couldn't get it to her in time.' He held out a long, black dress coat. 'I don't suppose you would be able to give it to her?'

He was about to tell the man he probably wouldn't see her

again, but stopped himself. 'I'll get it to her on Monday. If she calls, will you let her know Dean has it?'

After all, it looked like an expensive jacket and if she was serious about not crashing anymore, he at least had a reason for her to contact him.

'I will do, Sir.'

The man left and Dean decided a walk home might knacker him enough so he could finally get some sleep. He folded up the coat and felt a card in the pocket, so reached in to investigate. It was a company employee pass, the kind used to get into a building.

'Natalie Taylor, no wonder you wouldn't tell me who you were.'

Now didn't this make things interesting?

Chapter 6

Rose had been inconsolable. Natalie couldn't make out much of what happened over the sound of her friend's sobs, but it sounded like she'd told Tom she'd been engaged before but left the guy. Then Tom had freaked out and left the flat.

It didn't sound like a break-up though. If Tom was really insecure, maybe he just needed some time. Natalie told Rose so, and managed to calm her enough so she could get some sleep.

But now Rose was out like a light, Natalie had her own problems to deal with.

The first, and the biggest pain in her bum, was Dean Fletcher. Or, more truthfully, how he made her feel. She remembered kissing Mark in Mode and wishing to feel something more, to feel real honest to goodness passion.

Seemed like she'd gotten her wish at last. But it was with a guy she could hardly be around without losing her temper. Not to mention a client who could end up getting her sacked.

However, there was an easy solution to her problem. She wasn't going to crash the same parties he was. She now knew how he got on the guest lists, so all she had to do was avoid venues which used his company's system.

The second, and probably more pressing, was she'd left without her jacket. It had her pass for the building inside and it was now well after midnight. The party would be over so she couldn't just nip back for it.

She fished her mobile off the coffee table and called the venue.

'Good evening, you have reached The Grand, how may I help you?'

'Hi, I'm Na … Nicole Porter. I was at the party tonight but had to leave suddenly, and left my coat. I was wondering what time I could collect it in the morning?'

'Please hold a moment and I will find out for you.'

The relaxing composition played by a brass orchestra did nothing to calm her down. If she didn't get that jacket before work, Mick the Dick would be so pissed off he'd give her hell. Not exactly a mood she wanted him in when she asked for more money.

'Thank you for holding, Miss Porter. Your colleague took your jacket home for you and he asked us to assure you he would give it back to you at work tomorrow.'

Crap. 'Which colleague?'

'A gentleman called Dean. Is there anything else I can help you with?' the woman asked.

'N-no, thanks.' She ended the call, staring at nothing and swore out loud.

There was absolutely no chance Dean would respect her privacy and not rake through her pockets, he just didn't seem the type. After all, he didn't respect her personal space or her insistence that he keep his hands and lips to himself.

But after he found out, then what? She chewed on her nail as dread seeped into her stomach. Was he that much of a bastard that he'd get her sacked? She hoped not. And he knew if he did, she was in the perfect position to do the same to him. Though, she couldn't exactly prove that he used his system to crash the parties and she bet he knew that too.

But how was she going to get it back? She opened the browser on her mobile and put his name into the search engine. When all she got was articles in business news, she went to his company's website.

Thankfully they had an 'about us' page and his personal work email address was listed on the site. But if he didn't have that email linked to his mobile phone, he wouldn't get her message until tomorrow. Which would be too late.

Praying for a scrap of luck, she opened an email and decided to keep it light.

To: Dean Fletcher
From: Nat Taylor
Subject: Jacket thief
    Food they're giving away is one thing, but a jacket is another. Are you changing the terms again?
    P.S. You've probably noticed I need that pass to get into work tomorrow and I would appreciate it if you could arrange to let me have it.

It bridled her to ask him for anything, but she didn't want to get into trouble. It would just derail her attempt at getting a salary increase.

After setting her alarm, she changed into her pyjamas, brushed her teeth then climbed into bed.

A few minutes later, her phone dinged.

To: Nat Taylor
From: Dean Fletcher
Subject: Mountains out of Molehills
    I was given your jacket and asked to return it to you Monday, which I promised I would. Say 8am at the coffee shop across the road from your office? I take mine black.
    P.S I'd arrange to let you have it anytime, just say the words.

Natalie scowled at her phone.

> To: Dean Fletcher
> From: Nat Taylor
> Subject: Smart arse
> 8am is fine. I wouldn't hold your breath for that coffee, but
> in case you're feeling guilty for nicking my jacket, I like lattes
> with two sugars.
> P.S. Do I have to put it in writing for you to finally get it?
> Not. Interested.

Maybe that was a bit harsh, considering she was at his mercy and
really needed that pass. Before she could worry about it too much,
her phone pinged again.

> To: Nat Taylor
> From: Dean Fletcher
> Subject: I thought you were sweet enough
> My little thief, that ship has sailed. You want me as much
> as I want you. It's no longer a case of if, but when. That part
> is up to you.
> Sweet dreams
> X
> P.S. If you're feeling at all guilty for any number of things
> you did to me, I can think of better ways for you to ease it
> than with coffee …

Natalie frowned at the email, but decided it would do no good
telling him he was a smug, self-assured bastard who should be
the only one feeling guilty right now, but not when he was holding
so many cards. Instead she put the phone on her nightstand and
waited for sleep to come.

***

She left early the following day. Tom dropped by and it sounded like he and Rose were trying to sort things out, so she gave them some privacy. Still, by the time she wrestled her way through the commuters to get on the tube, she was running late and hoped he hadn't left already with her pass.

But Dean was there, sitting at the window inside the coffee shop with two steaming mugs in front of him. One was black, the other was frothy and had two packets of sugar next to it. She wasn't sure what to think about that as she went in.

He kicked out the chair at the other side of the table. 'Join me for a coffee?'

She recognised the demand delivered as a question but seeing her jacket there and the pass on top was such a relief, she let it slide and sat down. 'Thanks, for this,' she said, picking up the card.

'You didn't think I would bring it?' he asked.

Natalie shrugged. 'I don't know what to think when it comes to you.'

'That's part of the fun, isn't it?' He took a sip of coffee, and she noticed for the first time what he was wearing.

'Is the dress code relaxed at your work?' she asked, wondering why he was in faded jeans and a black tee-shirt sporting some kind of gaming logo. Even the Armani jacket slung over the chair next to him was casual.

He screwed up his nose. 'I hate wearing suits. Especially shirts. And I'm the boss, I can wear what I want. Besides, Jeffrey does all the front-of-house stuff.'

Pity, he looked good in a suit. Not that he didn't now, but he was arrogant enough she wasn't about to tell him that. Instead she ripped open the sugar, poured it into her latte, stirred it with her finger and was about to lick off the foam, but hesitated. 'If I drink this, will I wake up in eight hours not remembering a thing?'

He grinned. 'I prefer my women fully aware and into it. And

anyway, it's not something you'd forget, even if your coffee was spiked.'

She wiped her finger on a napkin.

'You know, big talkers usually overcompensate for shitty bedroom skills. Or small equipment.' She lifted a brow, then pointedly looked at the section of table which hid his package.

Acting all casual, like she hadn't just offended his manhood, he took another sip of coffee. 'There's only one way you can find out.'

'I'm not that curious.'

She nonchalantly took a mouthful of coffee and swallowed.

'We'll see. So, what are the plans this week? I'm assuming you only hit the parties your company organises?'

She dropped her eyes to the latte, hugging the mug with her palms. So there it was, the elephant in the room that couldn't be ignored. The question is, what was he going to do now he knew? 'Something like that.'

'Hey.' He reached out and lifted her chin so she'd meet his eyes. 'Despite what you might think, I'm not a complete bastard. I enjoy our battles. So don't worry, your secret's safe with me.'

She still couldn't tell with him and it made her uneasy. His eyes were open and clear and he'd told her the truth about who he was, but *could* she trust him? It was clear he wanted her and if she was honest, she *was* curious about what would happen if she let herself have him. But then what? This wasn't like crashing, the rules didn't apply here. He knew her name, where she worked and she had the same info on him. And they'd probably see each other again. If not this month, next year.

Then again, he'd been doing it for a while and she hadn't bumped into him before.

She screwed up her eyes, and he reached forward and used his thumb to smooth away the lines.

'You're quite handsy, aren't you?' she said, leaning away from him.

'I like touching you,' he said with a shrug, like he was telling her he liked to read books.

'I'm not like your other floozies. I don't fall for bad lines.' The image of the flushed redhead sneaking out of the men's room at Mode flashed in her mind and her stomach twisted.

Dean sighed. 'I don't want you to fall for anything, especially not me.'

So she was right. A fling, maybe even a one-nighter, was all he wanted. Why did that make her feel sick? 'There's no chance of that. It's a struggle just to like you.'

His smile flashed his white teeth, and a dimple on his left cheek. Her heart stuttered at the sight. Frick, he was reeling her in.

'You don't need to like me to want me.'

Right, this conversation was doing her no favours at all. She was growing more and more confused by the second. Picking up her pass and jacket she said, 'Thanks for the coffee. I need to get to work.'

He threw a tenner on the table – excessive for a couple of coffees, but apparently he did okay for himself – and followed her out. 'Before you go, let me ask you something.'

She didn't turn, just walked to the crossing along from the café. 'You can ask whatever you want. It doesn't mean I'll answer.'

'You know, you think you aren't playing a game here, but your responses tell a different story.'

Natalie sighed, then hit the button. 'Fine, what do you want to know?'

'Does your company throw its staff a Christmas party? I couldn't find a booking anywhere.'

'You want to crash my work's Christmas party? Are you insane?' The green man appeared on the traffic light, and she crossed the road. Unfortunately, Dean didn't leave her side.

'Can you just answer the question seriously?' he prompted.

Natalie stopped outside the building which held Mick's office and turned to Dean. 'Yes, they do but I never go. I'm usually the one who organises it though and they have a tiny budget – then again we only have a handful of staff. Me, one other events organiser, an intern and our boss. Anyway, I doubt you'd want to go into any of the venues it's usually held at.'

He frowned. 'Why don't you go?'

No way, she wasn't even going there with him. 'I don't want to talk about it, and I'm not playing any game, okay? It's personal.'

'Okay, backing off.' He held up both hands, palms out.

Natalie rolled her eyes. 'I really have to get to work.'

'I probably should too. There's a party on Friday at a country estate outside the city, it'll be big – a marquee, a fireworks display, the whole shebang. I know it isn't one of yours, but Nicole's on the guest list if you fancy it? I can email you the details.'

'I prefer to keep it local. It's easier to get home. Goodbye, Dean.'

She left, resolving to put their coffee date – or whatever it was – out of her mind so she could think of the best way to approach Mick the Dick and get the money she deserved.

A little while later, she was back at her desk, fuming inside. Mick had slapped down her request, ridiculing her work and telling her she'd never amount to anything in this company. Which was her cue to move on, one way or another.

Ignoring the unfinished files on her desk, she typed up a CV to get her out the door, then started researching business start-up finance. A little before lunch, her phone pinged with an email. It was Dean, and there were attachments too big to load on her mobile, so she broke company policy and logged into her personal email on her work computer.

If Mick didn't like it, he could go eff himself as far as she was concerned.

To: Nat Taylor
From: Dean Fletcher
Subject: Tempted yet?

Just FYI, the guests are appointed their own rooms in the
main house and guest cottages. Technically we wouldn't be
crashing since I was invited and you're down as my plus one.
Of course when I gave your alter ego's name, I didn't know
yours yet.

Here are some pictures of the place.
So, will I have a car pick you up at 6pm?
Dean
X

Self-assured bastard. But she smiled at his tenacity and opened
the attachments.

The manor was old, maybe built in the 1600s, and completely
stunning. It had at least three levels (or four, depending on
whether they had a basement). Medieval statues were perched
along the ledge below the roof. The grounds looked endless, with
green sprawling lawns, huge trees and a massive marquee which
would probably be where the party was if there were going to be
fireworks.

And, she realized, she really wanted to go. She'd never cele-
brated in December as herself, not since her mum died. Nicole
was how she'd separated herself from the guilt that she still got
to enjoy her favourite season but her mum didn't.

Everyone there would think she was Nicole, and it's not like
she and Dean had any kind of future. He made that crystal clear
today. It would just be a fling of sorts. It might even just be for
the night, and what was wrong with that?

She was beginning to trust him – in the sense she believed
what he'd told her so far – and although she'd never admit it to
him, she did sort of enjoy being around him. Even if he did piss
her off more often than not. And it would give Rose and Tom a

full night all to themselves, which she suspected they needed after last night.

She typed up a reply.

To: Dean Fletcher
From: Nat Taylor
Subject: Sold
    I'll make sure to pack a clean pair of knickers.
    Nat

His reply came through in seconds.

To: Nat Taylor
From: Dean Fletcher
Subject: Lacy knickers?
    I should probably mention it's a black tie event. If there's one thing I hate more than a suit, it's a tux.
    X

Natalie couldn't help remembering how he looked in a tux, or how he smelled when he suffocated her personal space. Her pulse thudded just thinking about it.

To: Dean Fletcher
From: Nat Taylor
Subject: Slinky ball gowns
    I quite liked your tux.
    Here is a preview of my knickers
    Nat

She couldn't help but giggle as she searched the net for a suitably awful pair of panty girdles and attached it to the email before hitting send.

To: Nat Taylor
From: Dean Fletcher
Subject: Holy shit
Well, I do enjoy a challenge and those things don't look like they'll come off easily. I'm nothing if not a trier.
X

She shook her head, then searched the net for pictures of chastity belts, but Mick the Dick stormed into her office with a scowl and she closed the browser. 'Where are the plans for the Holloway party? You should have had them on my desk an hour ago.'

'I gave the file to you on Friday,' she said, with as much politeness as she could muster. 'I've never been late with a deadline, which backs up my earlier point. I deserve better than this.'

His eyes narrowed and she wished she'd kept her mouth shut.

'Careful, Taylor. I could hire a hundred unqualified girls who would work for a tenth of what I'm paying you,' he said, then stormed out of the office.

Her blood boiled and it took every ounce of rationality to stop her from going to his office, telling him where he could shove his job, then clearing out. But she was going to do it the right way, and find something else first. She went back to her CV, determined to have it ready to post by the end of the day.

***

'I know she hates you, but what did *I* do to piss her off,' Jeffrey grumbled, pulling at the cuffs of his tux. 'The sleeves are about five inches too short.'

'At least she didn't order you a shirt with a collar size that would choke a swan,' Dean grumbled, unable to button it to the top.

They'd been sent a package by their mother with strict instructions to try on the contents immediately and email their father photos so she could see for herself what alterations were needed. God forbid she let her sons choose their own tuxes – in case they embarrassed her in front of her posh friends.

Dean flipped his phone open, loaded the camera then snapped a picture of Jeffrey. 'Looks like she thinks you have the build of a gangly teenager.'

Although when he tried to get his jacket on, the seams across his shoulders burst.

Jeffrey snatched the phone and snapped a pic of the tears. 'She'll love this.'

Dean stripped down to the trousers, which were about the only thing the witch got right, and let Jeffrey deal with emailing the pictures. If he did it himself, he'd end up asking if she'd prefer they came as two flying monkeys so they could keep up with her on her broom.

When Jeffrey handed him the phone back, he said, 'Dean, don't take this the wrong way. But this Friday is going to be hell on you, what with the engagement and everything. Why not just ask Alana's friend to be your date, then Mum might give you a break.'

Usually he'd come back with something like, who cares what the witch thinks? But after the poisonous reunion at his brother's engagement dinner, he'd reconsidered. He was sick of being her verbal punching bag, but he'd never give her the satisfaction of not going.

'I already have a date,' he said.

'Excuse me, can you repeat that? I could have sworn I just heard Slutty McFletcher say he had a date.'

Dean balled up the tux jacket and threw it at his brother. 'Knob.'

Jeffrey ducked, the movement caused a tearing sound to come from his own jacket. He sighed. 'Well, that's two fails.' Stripping it off, he looked at Dean and asked, 'Seriously, you're bringing a date? To Mum and Dad's anniversary party?'

'You can pick your chin up off the floor now. It's insulting.' It really wasn't that big a deal. It wasn't like he was taking someone home to introduce them to his mother as his girlfriend. She wouldn't give a toss about anyone he dated anyway.

'Shit,' Jeffrey said, sliding onto the leather sofa. 'Who is she? How long have you been seeing her?'

'You've met her, and I'm not *seeing* her. She's just coming with me to the party.' Dean pulled his tee-shirt back on, then his jeans.

'*You're taking the blonde?*'

'Natalie. And yes.'

Jeffrey frowned. 'Wasn't it Nicole?'

Dean rolled his eyes. It was just like his brother to assume he couldn't remember a girl's name. 'That's the name she uses when she crashes. She's really Natalie Taylor.'

His brother whistled. 'And you even know her surname. This sounds serious.'

'Don't make me throw my laptop at you, because I will.'

Jeffrey held up his hands in surrender. 'Okay, you're just taking a hot girl, who you seem to be really into though she apparently can't stand you, to meet your parents. I hope you've at least prepared her to meet Mum.'

'Don't get your hopes up, we're having fun and that's it.' At least he hoped they would be.

He didn't answer the second part. The truth is, it hadn't been easy getting her to agree to come and he hadn't heard from her after his last email. She was a flight risk as it was. Freaking her out with tales of his venomous mother would only land him there solo. He'd tell her on the way.

'I don't know how you do it. At the restaurant she looked like she wanted to claw your face off, now she's coming to meet your family?' Jeffrey shook his head.

'What can I say? I'm hard to resist.'

'Now who's the knob?' Jeffrey asked.

Dean, for sure. He just hoped when he told Natalie the truth about where they were going she didn't decide to rekindle the war.

Chapter 7

Natalie had been right about Tom and Rose needing some alone time. They'd ended up spending the whole week at his house, but Rose still called her every day. She spent a lot of those phone calls bitching about Mick the Dick and filling Rose in on all the places she'd applied to, but their chats were short and the gaps were filled with wedding talk, so she hadn't managed to tell her friend where she was going tonight.

She'd hoped Rose would be staying at Tom's again, but when they appeared at 5.30pm with Chinese take-out, it was time to spill the beans.

'Nat, we got sweet and sour for you,' Rose called from the living room.

Natalie dragged her overnight case and gown into the hall. She'd managed to get to a salon at lunchtime so they could pin her hair up in a fancy style, and she kept her make-up minimal, not knowing what to expect when she got there, but she had gloss in her purse.

Both Rose and Tom stared at her.

'Your hair's gorgeous. Are you going somewhere?' Rose asked, then eyed the case.

'I was invited to a party tonight. It's at an estate in the country.

I'm spending the night.' She hung the bag containing her fanciest dress over the door and went to join them, picked up a fork and started fishing the chicken and rice out of the containers.

Rose's eyes widened, and Tom asked, 'Who are you going with?'

'Just someone I've been, er, seeing for a couple of weeks.' Though she doubted a few sparring matches at parties and a cup of coffee meant she was *seeing* Dean.

'I can't believe you didn't say anything. Who is he? Is it the guy you went home with?'

Tom pretended to ignore them, focusing on his chicken chow mein while they got into girl talk mode.

'Steven? No, not him. I wasn't hiding it or anything, it's just we've had a lot of other stuff going on.' And Natalie had no clue what was going on with her and Dean.

'Nat—'

'You don't need to worry about me, Rose. I'm not spiralling and things aren't serious with him. It's just some fun and he seems like an okay guy.' Blackmail notwithstanding, but she'd well and truly paid him back for that. It was unlikely he'd try it again, or anything else of the sort. 'Plus it's a fireworks party. I haven't seen a proper display for years.'

Rose smiled. 'Then I hope you have fun. When are you leaving?'

She checked her watch. 'Five minutes, so I better get moving with this.'

After clearing her plate, she hugged Rose goodbye and even got an awkward half-hug from Tom, then she was off. She'd asked Dean to pick her up in a different street. It was bad enough he knew where she worked but if they were going to do the no-strings thing, then she didn't want him to know where she lived too. That would just blur the lines.

She turned the corner and stopped dead. There was a huge, silver limo with blacked out windows parked at the side of the road.

The back door opened and Dean got out with a familiar smile.

He gestured to the inside of the car. 'Your carriage awaits.'

'This is a bit … over the top,' she said, walking up to him. 'Escorting me in a limo isn't going to get you any closer to the panty girdles.'

He laughed. 'Not my idea. It was sent for us.'

'You must know people with more money than sense.'

He didn't reply, just took her bag and dress, and waited for her to slide into the seat. It was all white leather inside and she had to check her fingers to make sure she didn't have any sticky pink residue from the sweet & sour sauce.

'You look like you could use a drink,' he said.

She saw he had a glass of brown liquid in one of the armrests, then he pressed a button and a screen slid down behind him. There was scotch, which must be what he was on, a bottle of champagne, sparkling water and a bottle of the same wine she'd bought to pay him back for getting her dress all sweaty.

'You didn't get that to ruin my dress, did you?' She thought their battling had fizzled out, but wasn't sure. She wasn't sure about anything when it came to him.

'Of course not.' He shrugged. 'I thought you liked it.'

Oh. Well, that was sort of sweet, she supposed. 'I do. Thanks. Could I have a glass?'

He twisted in the corkscrew, but didn't bother with the lever. Instead he just pulled it out. Thankfully he wasn't in his tux yet, that could have ended up a disaster. But he didn't spill any.

He poured some in a glass and handed it to her. She took a sip, then stared out at the city flashing by. Most people had their Christmas decorations up now, so the darkness was bright with multi-coloured stars, angels, reindeer and Santa Clauses in the residential streets they drove through. She remembered her mum always put outside lights through the hedges surrounding their tiny garden, as well as solar-lit figurines. Every window of the house would have a beautiful gold angel stuck to the glass that lit up at night and each would be framed by fairy lights.

The memory was bittersweet and her eyes stung. She shook off the slice of pain and asked, 'So who's throwing the party?'

'Are you trying to deflect me so I don't ask why you look so sad? I thought the point of all the Christmas lights was to bring cheer.'

'It's personal,' she said, downing the wine. 'I don't suppose I could have another?'

'Am I going to have to carry you to the party?' he asked, but took her glass and poured a more generous measure. 'Not that I mind, but I thought you might want to see the fireworks show later. It's really amazing.'

She accepted the glass. 'You won't have to carry me. As long as you don't ask me anything personal again, I won't feel the need to knock back the wine.'

Dean shook his head. 'Most women can't wait to talk about their feelings, even my employees. You're a bit odd.'

'I thought we were done fighting? Or didn't you think insulting me wouldn't count?' She pointedly ignored his comment about most women, because he'd no doubt been with enough to have very accurate statistics.

'We are. I was just making an observation. And odd is good. It's different.'

She frowned. 'I don't get you at all, either. What man who owns a company, can afford to dress in Armani and has limitless tailored suits, would want to crash parties? It can't be for the free booze and food.'

'I mostly drink scotch when I'm there, which isn't free. But why I do it? That's personal.' He smirked.

'Fine, I don't care anyway.' Though that wasn't exactly true. She was curious about him. He just didn't seem to fit his mould. The CEO of a company worth millions – yes, she'd Googled him – and here he was sitting in a stretch limo wearing a ratty looking pair of jeans, Converse and another tee-shirt with a gaming logo. It was bizarre to say the least.

'I'd tell you, but you'd need to tell me why you do it first. I've already given away more about myself than you've offered up,' he said.

Damn her curiosity. She had to know. 'I love everything about Christmas, but I can't celebrate on the actual day, or even bear to decorate my flat. So instead I celebrate with strangers as Nicole Porter. And the free grub helps me save more money. I've wanted to start up my own business for a while. Your turn.'

He frowned. 'Why can't you celebrate on the actual day?'

Natalie grinned to hide the pain. 'That wasn't the deal. I answered your question and I'm not going to expand on it.'

'You're stubborn,' he noted.

'You'd better believe it. Now spill.'

'It's a great way to pick up women,' he said, adding nothing else.

Her dinner swirled in her stomach uneasily. Adding wine to the mix when she felt this nauseated probably wasn't the best idea, but she really, really needed to take the edge off.

'Not what you wanted to hear?' he asked. 'It's why I *still* crash parties, but it's not why I started. That's personal.'

'It doesn't really matter. I saw you come out of the bathroom with that redhead, remember? I already knew you were sleazy.' Which made her wonder why she'd agreed to come with him in the first place. Now she didn't seem so sure.

'I'm not a bastard, Natalie. And I don't mistreat women.'

'No, apparently you're just sewing your seed throughout London.' Another swig emptied her glass, but she just set it down and hugged herself. She didn't want to ask him for anything else.

He blew out a breath, and caught her gaze. The annoyance was clear from the tight line of his jaw. That made two of them.

'You'll probably hear this when we get there anyway. When I was younger, I got jilted by a girl I thought I'd spend the rest of my life with. I swore off relationships then and when Jeffrey and I moved to London to start up the business, we were living off loans and not making much money. We crashed all kinds of parties as a sort of cheap night out, and sometimes we hooked up with women. And don't say it's disgusting. You left the party at Hyde Park with a guy you didn't know.'

'I wasn't going to say anything like that.' She had to swallow back the shock that must have been obvious on her face. 'Someone broke up with you on your wedding day?'

'Technically, no. Her parents told me after. I haven't seen her since the day before.'

'Why?' God, that must have been horrible.

He shifted in the seat, looking uncomfortable. 'I don't know, nobody ever told me. Look, can we drop this? We're almost there.'

'Ok.' She needed time to process it all anyway. At least now she had an idea of why he didn't want another relationship. Still, it wasn't a good feeling to realize she was just another number in his long line of conquests.

'This is it,' he whispered, and the edge in his voice sounded a bit like nerves. 'There's something I was going to tell you on the way, but we got side-tracked.'

Going by his careful expression, Natalie wasn't sure she was ready to hear it.

The driver pulled in front of a giant staircase she recognised from the pictures in the email, then he came around to open the door for her. She got out and took her bag and dress from Dean as he followed. When the limo pulled away, she turned to tell him to lay it on her, but then the mansion doors opened and she looked over her shoulder to see a familiar older couple. It took her a second to place them, but when she did, her temper shot off the charts.

Chapter 8

Dean could tell the second Natalie realized whose party she was at. Those pretty pink lips parted on a gasp and her eyes burned with undiluted rage. He leaned close to whisper, 'Nat, these are my parents, George and Helena. It's their anniversary party.'

'Just so we're clear,' she hissed, 'the war is back on.'

Shit. That was the last thing he needed tonight, but he'd worry about it later. First he had to survive the introductions.

'What time do you call this?' the Wicked Witch asked. 'And what on *earth* are you wearing?'

'Son,' his father greeted. 'And you must be Natalie.'

Her teeth clenched hard at the sound of her name and he remembered what she said about preferring to party as her alter ego. Shit, he was *really* going to pay for this.

His father had the good graces to shake her hand, though she looked so rigid he thought the movement could snap her arm off.

'Pleased to meet you both,' she said, and he could almost believe she wasn't about to explode.

His mother eventually ripped her glare off him and acknowledged Natalie. 'Lovely to meet you, dear.' But she turned back to address him. 'Let's hope you can hold onto this one for longer than five minutes. She's a looker.'

Dean gritted his teeth and waited until he was sure he could sound calm. 'I'm going to show Natalie to her room.'

'There are no rooms,' his mother said, waving a hand in exasperation. 'We've got so many people coming. She'll have to stay with you.'

Natalie's gobsmacked expression might have been funny under different circumstances. Now it felt like he was tiptoeing along a wire, not sure if it was going to trip an explosive, or fall to his death.

'Don't worry, dear. I know your generation don't have the same principles as ours. I've long since given up hope this one will be able to hang on to a woman long enough to actually get her to the wedding, never mind down the aisle. Maybe some practice is what he needs,' she said.

Dean was close to exploding himself, but it was Natalie who addressed his mother. 'That's an *awful* thing to say.'

He was so shocked that she was standing up for him, his mouth could have been hanging open and he wouldn't have noticed.

His mother shrugged. 'When you've lived with the disappointment as long as I have, there's not much else you can say. Now quickly, go get dressed. I need you both in the marquee by eight. And Dean, do something with your hair, won't you?'

He knew how pointless it was arguing with his mother, so took Natalie's hand and dragged her to the stairs. When they got inside, she hissed, 'I'm not sharing a bed with you.'

'Fine. I'll sleep on the floor.' He'd lost all hope of anything going on after her reaction to where they were.

She snatched her hand back. 'You told me Nicole Porter was on the guest list!'

'True, but I had it changed when I found out your real name.'

'So your parents think I'm your latest squeeze, of what, five days? Perfect.'

Dean sighed as he led her up the main staircase. 'My mother

never organises these things. I contacted one of the maids who's working this party. Relax, Natalie.'

She laughed harshly. 'You're unbelievable.'

They walked together down the east wing corridor, right to the end.

'You're overreacting,' he said. Then wished he hadn't because she whirled on him.

'You tricked me!' You should have told me the truth.'

'I know, I should have. It was a shitty thing to do. But as you can see, my mother is a nightmare and it's gotten worse since Jeffrey got engaged. I thought bringing a date to their party would help, and it has.'

The hard lines of her scowl melted. 'That's better?'

He nodded. 'Just ask my brother.'

Opening the door, he stood aside to let her go ahead of him. She looked a bit calmer, but had a small frown on her forehead like she was still pissed off. After a second, she went into his room then froze.

'I think this room alone is bigger than my whole flat!'

'Yup. Over the top,' he said.

She strolled around the four-poster bed, checking out the balcony overlooking the gardens in the estate, his study with an old '90s style computer in the corner, then she ducked into the en-suite bathroom.

'This is … wow,' she said.

He followed her and stopped at the doorway. Dean hated the claw tub bath in the centre of the room – the water always ran too hot and the brass sides had burnt him when he was younger. The shower that could hold four in the far corner was his preference, but Natalie seemed transfixed on the tub.

'There's no time for a bubble bath just now, but you're welcome to later – just make sure you run the cold tap at the same time as the hot one or you'll get burnt off the sides. We need to get ready for the party.'

She turned to him. 'Did you really grow up with all this?' When he nodded, she knitted her eyebrows. 'Then why did you need to get loans to start your own business?'

'Not sure if you noticed, but my mother and I don't get on very well. I'd never ask them for anything. I hate all this stuff. Since I was young, I've been told constantly that we're better than *commoners* because we don't need to work. Jeffrey felt the same as I did.' He didn't want to get into his family drama, but if it took her mind off being angry, he'd try anything.

'Oh,' she said.

He figured as she seemed to be stunned silent, now was as good a time as any to try to apologise properly. 'Look, I'm really sorry for not telling you. I meant to in the car, but before that, I just wanted you to come and knew that if I told you the whole truth, you might not.'

She crossed her arms and was quiet for a minute. 'Did you think showing me all this would make me jump straight into your massive bed with you?'

'No. And if I thought you were the kind of girl who would sleep with me because you thought I came from money, I'd never have asked you to come.' He had some principles, just not the same as his parents.

'Anything else I should know? Tell me now while I'm fairly sane because if I find out when I'm tipsy, I can't guarantee I won't make a scene in front of all your mother's guests.' Her eyes bored into him, and her tone told him she wasn't pissing around.

'Nothing. You officially know more about me than anyone except my brother.' Which had never been the plan. He never talked about himself with women, but Natalie had a way of dragging it all out of him.

Natalie nodded, but she still looked shell-shocked.

Grabbing his tux, he said, 'I'm going to change in my father's study to give you some privacy. There's a lock on the bedroom door. I'll be back in half an hour.'

'Dean, I'm still going to find a way to pay you back for this.'

He threw a grin over his shoulder. 'I wouldn't expect anything less.'

***

The second he left, Natalie grabbed her mobile out her bag, then fell back on the gigantic bed. She was about to call Rose, then decided against it. She didn't want to interrupt something she shouldn't.

Instead she took a minute to look around his room. It was filled with antique furniture and oak wood panels covered the lower half of the walls. The top half were painted a deep blue and there was a gold band at the top, just beneath the artistic rolling coving.

It was incredible, but way too much to take in. And the worst part of it all was the way his mother had ridiculed him in front of a complete stranger. A mother was supposed to love her children and support them through break-ups, or in this case being jilted at the altar.

No wonder Dean didn't want anything serious.

And now, she was even less sure what she wanted from this evening. Knowing as much as she did, she was beginning to sympathise with him. The lines had been blurred and he'd told her so much about himself that it wasn't impersonal anymore.

He'd changed the game again. And that changed everything for her.

Because despite how he tricked her today, and although she wanted him even more than she had, Natalie doubted she could just spend a casual night with him and walk away unscathed the next day.

She looked at the time, and saw she only had about five minutes to fight with her dress that had the most awkward clasp in the world, then freshen up. After wrestling with the gown and failing

86

to twist her arms in a way that should have dislocated them, she gave up and sat at Dean's study, half unzipped, waiting for him to return.

Natalie took the time to type up a quick text to Rose.

Here ok, the estate is beautiful. Off to the party. Speak soon xoxo.

She didn't mention the people, aka his mother, weren't as lovely as the property, but she could wait and give Rose the full run down tomorrow.

A knock at the door was followed by a, 'Can I come in?'

'It's open,' she called to Dean.

'Wow,' he said, taking in her floor length ice pink gown with a slit all the way up to the middle of her right thigh. 'You scrub up well.'

'I've made a pact with myself to try and not fight with you tonight, so I'm going to take that as a compliment.' She stood up. 'I could use a hand with the zip if you don't mind.'

Dean gestured for her to turn around then his warm fingers were on the skin above her spine. She tried to hide the shiver that ran through her, but there was nothing she could do about the goosebumps that rose when he slowly pulled up the zip, unnecessarily stroking her back as he did so.

When he was done, he moved his hands to her shoulders and pressed his cheek against her ear. 'Let me try that again. You always look sexy, and in that dress you're stunning.'

'You're such a charmer.' She was going for sarcasm but ended up with breathless and needy.

He stepped closer, so she could feel every inch of his torso against her. 'I have to try everything I've got since my irresistible little thief won't let me kiss her.'

As her body lit up with a tingling sensation and he snaked his hand around her stomach, Natalie couldn't remember when or why she'd said a daft thing like that.

'Or are you ready to let me now?' Dean asked, turning her round.

He was likely holding her up too, because she was dizzy and could hardly feel her legs. Pulling her closer, he stroked her bottom lip with his thumb. 'What do you say, Natalie?'

She didn't know if it was the fire in his eyes or the flames licking through her veins that did it, but she grabbed a handful of his silky white shirt and demanded, 'Kiss me.'

The surprise widening of his eyes for a second was thrilling, then he bent down and brushed his lips softly over hers, once, twice and a third time. Her impatience flared, she was sure he was teasing her on purpose, so she wrapped her arms around his neck, pulling her chest flush against his.

'I said *kiss me* not drive me insane.'

Dean's breath was coming hard and his heart seemed to thrum along with hers in a perfect, staccato beat. 'You're not the only one going insane. I can't think straight around you.'

'Why do you need to think?' At this point, she couldn't remember her own name.

'Good point.'

He lowered his head and she closed her eyes. As soon as their lips met, the edge turned from desperation to pure passion and it was better than any of the books she'd read could ever describe it. But a knock interrupted, and he pulled back an inch, turning his face in the direction of the door. Natalie took the opportunity to explore his jaw with her mouth and he shivered.

'Fuck. Off,' he said to whoever interrupted them.

'Fat chance.' A muffled voice said, and the door swung open.

Natalie pulled back, but Dean's arms around her waist meant the lower half of their bodies were still melded together.

'Oh, sorry man. But Mum's about to have an aneurysm because you're late and the guests are arriving,' Jeffrey said.

Dean blew out a breath and whispered to Natalie. 'Would you think less of me if I let her have one and stayed here with you?'

She tried not to grin. 'Yes, very much so.'

'Rain check?' he asked hopefully.

'We'd better go.' She pulled at his arms to free herself and he let her, but he was frowning.

'Ready,' she told Jeffrey, who was looking at his brother with worried eyes.

Then he smiled at her, but it was nothing like the smug, mocking grin she was used to from his brother. 'Nice to officially meet you, Natalie.'

'You too, Jeffrey.' She shook his hand, hoping he'd put the flush in her cheeks down to embarrassment at being caught almost necking his brother, and not the raging need for Dean flaring through her.

As she walked down the winding staircase next to the two men, she had a chance to clear the lusty fog from her mind and remember that she'd decided not to go down the one-night stand road with him. But she was more torn now than she'd ever been.

On the one hand, she'd always wanted to experience the kind of passion that melted her bones and burned her up from the inside out, and that's exactly what it felt like just brushing her lips against Dean's.

On the other, the thought of being that out of control with someone who only wanted a night to burn off the sexual tension between them terrified her. That almost-kiss made her forget everything except what she wanted him to do to her. It was hotter than any kiss she'd ever had.

'So, Dean said you've crashed a few parties too? I bet he's been after you from the first,' Jeffrey said, then laughed at Dean's scowl.

'Not quite,' Natalie said, remembering the redhead. Then the way he told her to leave or pretty much snog him. What the hell was she doing here?

'Just ignore him, Nat. He'll soon get bored and go annoy someone else.' Dean said, taking her hand and giving it a squeeze.

Even the innocent contact left her aching in the pit of her stomach. She looked at him, unable to hide the unrestrainable panic rising in her.

'Tell the witch I'll be there soon. I need to talk to Natalie,' he said to Jeffrey, but he was already pulling through a door that turned out to lead to a massive sitting room.

She was too muddled to appreciate the lovely décor or Victorian furniture.

Dean placed his hands on either side of her face and leaned closer. 'What's going on, Natalie? Talk to me.'

Her eyes blurred. Frick. The last thing she needed to do was cry. 'I can't do this. I shouldn't have come.'

'They're not that bad, my folks. Really. And they like you. It's just me they can't stand.'

She knew his tone was soft to reassure her, but that wasn't the problem. Pulling out of his hold, she said, 'I don't mean your parents. I mean this, what's happening between us. I don't want an overnight fling that ends in an awkward car journey home, which, by the way is worse than the walk of shame. And it's not like I can sneak out after and wave down a taxi either, since we're in the middle of bloody nowhere.'

'Who says I want a one-night stand? Natalie, I've brought you to my childhood home. And I didn't just do that because it was easier to deal with my mother if I had a date. Jeffrey's been trying to set me up with one of Alana's friends for ages.'

It irked her to have to ask, 'Then what do you want from me? Why did you bring me tonight?'

'Nothing you don't want to give me. And I asked you here because I like spending time with you.'

'That's a crap answer, at least the first part.' Natalie folded her arms across her chest.

His eyes were guarded when he said, 'I told you I wanted you, and it just seems to get more intense the more time I spend with you. Beyond that …' he shrugged.

'That doesn't exactly fill a girl with confidence.' Sighing, she went on, 'But we'd better go before your mum sends in the firing squad.'

She went for the door, but didn't quite make the handle. Dean spun her round and pressed her against it, using his hips as an anchor against hers. 'Do you know what doesn't fill a guy with confidence? I've told you about my past. I've repeatedly told you how much I want you and other than five minutes ago when you told me to kiss you, you've done nothing but deny feeling any kind of connection between us at all.'

There was nothing she could say to that. He was right. She'd pushed him away and rebuked him at every turn.

Stepping back, he said, 'And you still can't admit to yourself what you want, can you?'

'Yes, I can.' But what she didn't see a point in telling him was that she didn't want to be another conquest.

'And what do you want?' he asked, but didn't approach or crowd her.

Natalie swallowed hard. 'You know I feel the same thing you do. But I'm not sure I can get close to someone for however long this lasts and walk away unscathed when you've had enough.'

Dean didn't speak for what felt like an age and she was considering bolting. But his eyes held hers steadily, even if his brow was lower than normal.

'That's why I did what I did,' he said, then didn't elaborate.

'What do you mean?'

'You're really going to have to catch up with me on the sharing at some point. It's too unequal.' She waited as he ran a hand through his hair. 'I don't want to feel like I did when I was eighteen again. I have flings because I know how shitty it feels to be left behind. So I know exactly where you're coming from.'

A pang of sorrow hit her. Since she met him she'd assumed he just liked scoring women, but now she knew the real reason, it was harder than ever to dislike him for that, or even to feel like one of his conquests. He seemed as affected by her as she was by him and she wasn't sure when it happened, but it wasn't just sympathy that softened her; she'd started to really enjoy just being with him, without the sparring or the plotting.

And still, he'd told her he didn't want her to fall for him which meant there would be a time limit, however long that was. At least she wouldn't be his usual fling or one-night stand, she supposed. And there was always the possibility that it would be her who got bored of him and ended it, though after the kiss that seemed unlikely.

Just remembering the kiss had heat flooding in her lower stomach. Natalie couldn't ignore it, and she wasn't sure she wanted to. The way she felt around him might only be a once-in-a-lifetime thing. Was she really going to deny herself because she was scared to be hurt or left alone?

Not a chance. She'd lived through so much, she should be tough as nails by now. If she could survive the loss of her parents and her dreams, she could deal with his rejection whenever it came.

'What do we do now?' she asked.

He reached for the door handle and opened it, stepping aside to let her past. 'I think we either have to learn to trust each other, or walk away.'

Chapter 9

Dean led Natalie through the grounds towards the marquee and was glad she seemed to be deep in thought, because he needed time to pull his shit together.

What had started as a potential fling, felt like it was getting more serious by the second. He'd had to get them out of the second lounge fast, because he didn't want to hear what she chose, or give her the chance to ask him.

It was becoming clear that he couldn't keep from spilling anything she wanted him to, which meant he was edging into dangerous territory. The problem was, the safeguards he'd put in place to avoid situations like this had never triggered with her.

He wasn't even sure if he wanted them to.

'Wow,' she said, gaping at the inside of the marquee. 'Is this real?'

He wanted to roll his eyes at the sight before them. His mother and father probably spent an easy hundred thousand decking the oversized tent out. It looked like a banquet hall from a Disney movie with all the twinkling lights. Dean would put money on the red carpet covering the ground being velvet, and that each table cloth was made from the finest white silk.

'My parents are ostentatious, and it's a big anniversary' he said, smiling down at her. 'You ready for this?' Dean held his hand out.

'No,' Natalie said, then took his offering.

He gave her hand a squeeze. 'Just try not to believe anything you see.'

The mini-orchestra setting up at the far end were tonight's entertainment, and his mother was fluffing around checking centrepieces. Her guests must be in the conservatory being served pre-dinner drinks and hors d'oeuvres while the rest arrived. She left soon after, seemingly satisfied that her décor was perfect.

He eyed Jeffrey and Alana at one of the head tables and urged Natalie to follow him.

'My brother, believe it or not, and his fiancée are the two most normal people that will be here tonight.'

'Can we sit with them?' she asked, but when they reached the table he saw at the same time she did that the seating cards didn't have his name or hers.

'She got me in the basement?' he asked Jeffrey.

'Nah, at her table. I think she wants to torture poor Natalie.'

Dean grabbed the cards. 'I'll be back in a sec.'

After switching them with his own, he came back and urged Natalie to sit next to Alana. She did, and he took the seat next to hers, placing the stolen cards in front of them both.

Jeffrey laughed. 'She'll make you pay for that later.'

'Then take one for the team,' Dean suggested.

'You kidding? I'm the favourite.'

'Are they always like this?' He heard Natalie ask.

Alana smiled indulgently. 'Unfortunately. It seems I've agreed to marry a ten-year-old boy.'

Natalie laughed, and to Dean's relief, seemed to relax into the banter. He learned she had a flatmate who was also her best friend and the girl was getting married Boxing Day. But that was it for the info because his mother got hold of him and Jeffrey so they could do the meet and greet – after he was told to go to the bathroom and comb his hair again, of course.

By the time he found his way back to the table, Natalie and Alana seemed to be hitting it off. Nat even acknowledged him by reaching out and squeezing his hand, which had Jeffrey's eyebrows shooting up his forehead.

He ignored his brother and just tried to just enjoy the moment. After all, he was not at this second being yelled at by his mother and was surrounded by his brother, future sister-in-law and the girl he, well, liked spending time with.

A pretentious six-course dinner was served, champagne flowed freely and his mother didn't even annoy him once. Afterwards, the music changed to a waltz and a curtain slid open revealing another part of the tent which was lit up with a shiny chandelier.

People were already getting up and pairing off.

Natalie's eyes widened. 'Is that a dancefloor?'

'Yup. This tent even has a dancefloor.' He shook his head.

Jeffrey rose and held out a hand to Alana. 'Care to dance, love of my life?'

Ordinarily, he'd have rolled his eyes at his brother's idiocy. But he wasn't feeling the old familiar worry for his brother at the moment. Not when he saw the way Alana's eyes lit up and her cheeks scored pink.

'Always, with you.' She turned to Dean. 'And if you don't give Natalie her whirl on the dancefloor I'm going to tell your mother that you want to dance with her.'

'You wouldn't,' he said, pretending to scowl.

'Oh, I would. Don't underestimate girl power.' She winked at Natalie, then let Jeffrey lead her away.

'I can't dance like that, anyway.' She eyed the others whirling round the floor.

'I could teach you,' he offered. Not that he liked dancing, ever. But with Natalie it might not be so bad.

She leaned closer. 'It's probably better to wait until everyone's drunk so they won't remember when I stand on all their feet.'

'You're forgetting I've seen you dance. You don't have two left feet. In fact, we can stick Santa Baby on and you can show them all how to *really* dance.' He grinned at her flush.

'Seriously, though. I don't want to make a fool of you. Or myself.'

He stood and offered her his hand. 'You won't. Come on.'

'Please, Dean,' she whispered, looking around in case anyone saw their exchange. 'I can't dance in there with them. I'll end up slipping and toppling them all like dominos.'

'Who says anything about dancing with them?' He took her hand and urged her out of her seat. 'I have a better idea.'

Natalie followed him through the grounds, paying less attention to the barren trees laced with twinkling lights and more on staying upright in heels. He stopped when they reached what looked like an old fashioned, concrete music stage. There were twisting pillars lit up with fairy lights all around it which joined at the top in a huge arch, still giving a great view of the sky above. It was stunning. And made her feel like she was dreaming.

'How about here?' he asked.

She couldn't speak, she was too gobsmacked at the sight. She nodded.

Dean led her up the stairs then stepped in front of her. She no longer saw the beautiful place he'd brought her. All she could see was his smile, which was much more open than she'd seen on him before, and she wondered if what she'd mistaken as smug, was actually just caution.

'I should warn you, I was never good at choreographed dancing. You might lose a toe.'

'I'll take my chances.' He took her hands and placed one on his shoulder, but kept a hold of the other. His free arm circled her waist, pulling her much closer than the other couples had been.

When they were pressed together she couldn't seem to work her lungs right, but she had no time to recover.

'Just relax. Follow my lead.'

They started to move. His steps were so smooth and graceful, and she was anything but. She kept looking at her feet, terrified she was going to chop off his toe with her stiletto and instead ended up head butting him in the chest.

He laughed. 'Is that how you're going to pay me back, with violence?'

'Of course not.' She'd actually forgotten about how he'd tricked her, and didn't care so much since she'd been having such a fabulous time. 'I'm sorry. I knew something like this would happen.' She'd never be able to master this dancing thing.

'Don't worry about it. How's the head?' he asked, stroking his thumb across the skin above her brow.

'It's felt better. You've got boobs of steel.'

Laughing, he pulled her over to the low railing edging the music stage and sat her next to him. 'Boobs of steel? I don't think anyone's ever accused me of having those before.'

'Clearly nobody's head butted you before.' She looked up at the sky through the arches, surprised to see stars at this time of year. But she was just stalling again. They were finally alone and she had to talk to him. 'Dean, when you said we need to either start trusting each other, or walk away from this, which did you want to choose?'

His expression shut down again, except for the smile she was convinced now meant he was being careful. And she realized why. He was right. He'd opened up to her, told her stuff that must have been difficult and she'd given him glazed-over snippets of the truth.

He went to answer her, but Natalie got in first.

'Wait. You were right earlier. I've not exactly been forthcoming with you.' She looked at the stars again, trying to draw courage from them, but that had to come from her. 'My mum loved

Christmas. It was her favourite day of the year. Mine too. We didn't have anything like this, but she always went over the top. Every inch of the house was always covered in glittery, sparkling decorations, even after my dad died. She'd changed, probably because a part of her was missing, but she always made the effort at Christmas. It became our day.'

He listened patiently and even let her grip his hand harder for support and she drew some strength from it. 'My mum died three years ago. Breast cancer that was diagnosed too late. She fought it, but it got the better of her in the end. Ever since, I've not been able to do anything at Christmas. I can't even face any decorations so my flatmate has to do without. And I'm useless on the 25th, I just feel so guilty knowing I still have that day, our day, and she's gone, you know?

'So that's why I crash Christmas parties. I don't feel as guilty celebrating with people I don't know and I'm pretending to be someone else. It's my way of enjoying the season again without disrespecting my mum by being selfish and doing all the things we used to do together.'

She closed her eyes, willing the tears not to spill over, and felt his warm arms encircle her. Dean pulled her on to his thigh and held her close. *Please don't let her bawl all over his lovely tuxedo.*

He kissed her hair. 'You're not being selfish by wanting to live your life, and I don't think your mum would want you to give up something you love.'

She nodded against his shoulder. 'I just can't get over the guilt. I've tried. I have boxes of her stuff stored away and after the night at Hyde Park, I went there. But I couldn't bring myself to look at them, never mind open them.'

'Healing takes time. You'll get there. Just don't stress yourself out about it.'

Funny, that's exactly what Rose said every year when December loomed close, and Natalie felt guilt-ridden about not wanting decorations up in her home. 'Thank you. For listening. And not making fun of me.'

She pulled herself together and sat up.

Dean was frowning again. 'I'd never make fun of your feelings, Natalie. I'm not a complete knob, despite what my brother says.'

'I didn't mean that, it's just. I don't know. You're the only person other than my best friend I've told. I don't know what people who don't know me that well would think.' Even she was torn between feeling pathetic and like a coward. She wrapped her arms around herself.

'Are you cold?' he asked, taking his jacket off before she could stop him, then draping it over her shoulders. 'Just say the word and we'll go back to the oversized tent.'

She smiled and shook her head. 'Can we stay here for a while?'

'Whatever you want.' Dean took her hand, and they sat there just looking at the stars.

A pop and whir sounded out and a burst of light came from the direction of the tent.

'Looks like the fireworks have started already,' he said, then led her over to the edge of the stage to get a better view.

As three more rockets shot into the air and burst into bright, whirring sparks, he shifted to stand behind her and wrapped his arms around her waist. She relaxed against him, watching the spectacular display that reminded her of fireworks she'd only seen at New Year on the television.

As the last explosion in the sky fizzled into the darkness, Dean said, 'You asked me earlier what I would pick. I can't imagine walking away and never seeing you again.'

She turned in his arms, watching the way the fairy lights danced off his shirt collar. 'Me neither.'

He met her gaze, and she saw something a bit like fear in his eyes. 'So we start trusting each other, and telling each other the truth?'

'You know, I've only ever lied to you about not wanting you, and to be honest, at the time I was lying to myself too.'

His lips curved without the edge and it made him seem more real, honest even. 'I knew that all along.'

'Cocky bastard,' she said, then laughed when he did.

*****

When they arrived back at the marquee, guests were already filtering out and Natalie couldn't say she was sorry. These people were not of her world. They were dripping in expensive jewels, luxurious handmade gowns and tuxedos. But despite that, she'd had fun during dinner with Dean, his brother and Alana.

And even her awful attempt at a waltz hadn't put a dampener on the evening. The stunning display in the sky had made it kind of magical.

Then she spied Jeffrey coming towards them with an exasperated edge to his stride. 'Where have you two been? Mum's giving me hell because you switched tables, then disappeared before she could get a chance to introduce Natalie to her guests. Come on.'

That sounded like her idea of a nightmare. She looked up at Dean, pleading with her eyes.

He smiled. 'Tell her to get over it. We've had a long day and are going to bed.'

Jeffrey's jaw dropped. 'You're throwing me to the sharks.'

'Well, that's two I owe you,' he replied. 'Goodnight, brother.'

Jeffrey rolled his eyes and lightly punched Dean on the shoulder, before turning to Natalie. 'Goodnight Natalie. It was good to meet you properly.'

She tried not to laugh. 'You too, Jeffrey.'

'Dean, will you give her Alana's number? She wanted to see if Natalie fancied a shopping trip sometime. In case, er … well. Just in case we don't see her for a while.'

'You'll see her again.' He turned to Natalie. 'How about crashing our Christmas party at the Savoy next week? Alana's coming to check it out as a wedding venue.'

She really shouldn't feel so ridiculously happy that he wanted her around for more than the night, and tried to keep her beam to a minimum. 'Sounds fun.'

Jeffrey's mouth dropped open for a second before he recovered, then he looked at Dean and seemed genuinely happy for some reason. 'Cool. I'll see you then. Goodnight, guys.'

As Dean escorted her through the mansion and up the stairs, she said, 'He's surprised you're seeing me again, isn't he?'

'When I told him about you after we saw you in that restaurant he said he'd never seen me look as alive as I did when I was arguing with you. But I didn't know if you'd ever come around, so I brushed it off. You're so stubborn.'

He dodged her light jab. 'And you can be so annoying, but you never hear me going on about it.'

Dean led her into his bedroom, then stopped just inside the doorway. 'Regardless of what my mum says, there's bound to be an empty bed in here somewhere. I don't have to stay in this room.'

'Do you want to sleep somewhere else?' she asked, wondering if she'd laid too much on him today and he was backing off.

He cocked a brow and his eyes melted. 'What do you think?'

'I think you should lock the door. We don't need to be inter-rupted.'

The sound of the lock clicking into place set the fire in her veins burning. There was no going back now, not that she'd want to.

'If Jeffrey even thinks about knocking this door tonight ...' Dean said, coming closer.

Her heart raced faster, and he hadn't even touched her yet. He was close enough to.

'What do you want, Nat?' he said softly, brushing her jawline with his knuckles. 'I don't want to push you into anything you're not ready for, or don't want to do.'

'I know you don't. What I want is for you to kiss me deeply, thoroughly, and make me so hot I can't stand it. Then we can see about getting me out of this dress.'

His smile was slow and sexy. 'I've always enjoyed a challenge.'

Chapter 10

Dean didn't kiss her straight away like she'd hoped. Instead he took her face in his hands, slid them down the sides of her neck slowly and then onto her shoulders, knocking her borrowed jacket to the floor.

'Can I undo your hair?' he asked.

Natalie nodded, trying to control her breathing so she didn't pass out from the exertion. Not that she'd exerted herself at all yet, but the feel of his skin against hers had her heart racing in a way no jog on a treadmill could.

Torturously slowly, he carefully removed the pins from her hair and bit by bit, loose strands fell in waves around her shoulders. He placed the pins on his desk, then stepped closer so their bodies were pressed together and wrapped his arms around her waist.

Leaning down, his nose brushed against hers and then finally, their lips met.

She grabbed his forearms, bunching his silk shirt beneath her fingers as her lips parted. Dean pressed his mouth to hers harder, pulling back only to nip gently at her lower lip with his teeth until the room swirled and the fire at her core raged.

Her hands found their way into his hair and she tugged him

close, filling with an uncontrollable need she could never have imagined. His tongue was hot and smooth in her mouth, tangling with hers in the sexiest dance ever and she didn't notice much else until cool air hit her overheated skin as her dress slipped off her body and onto the floor.

The intensity didn't dim, but he pulled back slowly, kissing her softly a few times before he took his lips away completely. When she looked up at him, she saw the heat in his eyes as his gaze slid down her body.

She'd thought he might make a crack about her lack of panty girdles, but instead he whispered, 'Beautiful.'

Natalie was on the verge of tearing up, her emotions were all mixed up in the passion and his unexpected sweetness was almost her undoing. But she got to work on his shirt, pulling it out of his waistband and unbuttoning it from the bottom while Dean took care of the bowtie first, then his belt. While she dealt with the zipper, he slid off the shirt just as she let his trousers fall to the floor.

Swallowing, she found him difficult to take in. There was nothing she thought sexier than Dean in a tux, but now he stood before her in boxers she had to reconsider.

He wasn't just beautiful, he was ripped with hard edges. Not only were his pecs steel-like, but his abs and biceps could give them a run for their money, they were so well-defined. He was clearly religious about working out. There was no way a programmer who spent most of his days in the office could ever look this fit otherwise.

And all she could think about now was finding out how he felt, flesh against flesh with her.

Tilting her chin up, he asked, 'Are you okay?'

The concerned tone didn't fit with his rigid jaw, like he was holding himself back from getting his hands all over her too. 'I've never been better.'

Or so overwhelmed by something so basic as stripping a guy.

Picking her up, he carried her to the bed and deposited her on top of the covers. She was glad he left the lights on. This she had to see. Though, *needed* might be a better word for it.

Dean blew out a shuddering breath as he looked at her, then peeled his boxers off and dropped them on the floor. There was no way he was lacking anything and the sight had her burning between her thighs.

He got up on the bed and kneeled between her legs. Bending, his mouth captured hers, eating up her cries. As the pulsing dimmed, his kiss grew hotter, his lips moving with a desperate edge and the craving for him rose. She wrapped her legs around his waist and dug her heels into his rear.

Dean held her gaze and she saw the same sheen of pleasure in his eyes that must be shining from hers.

Then he started to *really* move. She rolled her hips in time with his thrusts and before long her head was spinning – she felt unable to convert air to oxygen. Or maybe it was the way staring into his eyes made her feel like she was falling and being tugged forward at the same time. Their slick skin slid together effortlessly as more pressure built at her core.

Gripping his shoulders, she kissed him, making pleading noises at the back of her throat. He understood and shifted his hips, moving quicker, grinding into her and the pressure exploded until she was throbbing around him, pulsating with little bursts of ecstasy.

Dean thrust deep one last time and gasped into her throat. The muscles on his back tightened beneath her palms and his hips jerked into her as he found his own release. Careful not to crush her, he withdrew and rolled them both so they were facing each other.

Unable to stop herself, she ran the pads of her fingers over the smooth skin on his chest while they caught their breath together.

'I suppose I'd better give in with good grace. I'll definitely never forget that,' she said.

Tangling his fingers into her hair, he said, 'Me either. You, my little thief, were more than worth the wait.'

***

When they'd both freshened up and Natalie had slipped into a pair of Christmas themed pyjamas, he pulled the covers back and they climbed into bed. She came straight into his arms and warmth flooded beneath his rib cage, but there was nothing sexual about it at this moment – after the long day he was just about spent.

Unease slithered into his consciousness and it roared louder than the after buzz he'd been floating in. He might have made the decision that he didn't just want Natalie for a bit of fun but stepping into a relationship after all this time though made him more nervous than he'd care to admit, even to himself.

Maybe Jeffrey was right. It could be his fear that had held him back from taking the next step with any of the women he'd met in the past. Still, that didn't mean he was ready to give himself up to someone else completely. He never wanted to put himself in the position of being jilted again.

The chunk it had taken out of his pride and the discord it had caused with his parents had been the worst part of it all.

Natalie lifted her head from his chest. Her sleepy eyes seemed wary. 'Why so tense? Is this the part where you tell me you don't want more than a one-night stand?'

Instead of being pissed that she still clearly didn't believe a word he said, all he could feel was relief that he wasn't the only one unsure about what was happening between them. 'I want you more than ever. I can prove it now to you if you'd like?'

Just kissing her wiped everything else from his mind. The sex had heightened each of his senses – sight, touch, sound, smell and taste, all completely focused on Natalie.

Her lips curved and her eyes cleared to sparkling blue. 'As

much as I want you to, I don't think I'll be able to stay awake for the best bits.'

'Is that why you put on your Christmas pudding PJs, to turn me off so you could get some sleep? Because it's not working.'

She laid her head against his chest again, relaxing into him. 'Nope, I just like them. They're warm and comfy.'

'Sexy too.'

Her hand slapped his chest lightly. 'Stop teasing, I know I look like a weirdo.'

Holding her tighter, he disagreed. 'You might *be* a weirdo, but your jammies are cute.'

'I'm too tired to come up with a witty retaliation tonight. Remind me of your insult in the morning.'

He laughed. Christ, he was doing that a lot since he'd met her.

'When are we going back tomorrow?' she asked, then yawned.

'Whenever you want to. Mum will probably have her guests for breakfast around six, but if you don't want to meet them, they should be gone by ten.'

'Six? That's insane. Tomorrow's a Saturday,' she mumbled.

'True. Nat, tell me something.'

Slowly, she lifted her head to look at him. 'O-kay …'

'You said you wanted to start your own business? Would you be organising parties too?'

Nodding, she added, 'But I'm not just a party planner. I do weddings, charity events including a few televised ones, and baby showers since they've started coming into fashion, along with anything else a client wants. My boss's company does everything you could imagine, but they only have me and Gary managing client files. Gary tends to do the sports-related events. I do everything else.'

'So you organised all the parties we were at by yourself?' he asked, impressed.

Natalie yawned again. 'Just me. Mick the Dick aka my boss usually spends his days at the driving range. I'm sending my CV out to other companies. I finally worked up the courage to ask for a pay rise and he told me he could find a hundred unqualified girls to do my job for a tenth of the salary.'

She scowled at the memory.

'Bastard,' Dean said, wondering if he should go to the next meeting with Mick and play the awkward, pissed off client. Then again, that could get her into trouble. 'Why not just go it alone now? There's no time like the present.'

Her anger drained from her face and she slumped back onto his chest. 'He won't let me have client contact so they don't know what I can do. If I leave, I have to start completely from scratch and I haven't saved enough yet to keep me going until I get on my feet.'

'I'd help. I know how hard it is those first few years while your company gets off the ground.' Though as she stiffened, he added, 'I mean I could loan you the money, if you wanted. You could even pay some interest if it made you feel better.'

'Please don't take this the wrong way.' She lifted her head to look at him. 'This is something I want to do for myself. I want to accomplish it on my own, or fail knowing it's all on me without the worry of having someone to pay back lots of money to. Especially someone I'm ... well ... sleeping with.'

'I can respect that. But if you need anything, even just advice, Jeffrey and I are here to talk to.'

The wide, wary look in her eyes was easy to understand. She didn't know how long he was offering, and to be honest neither did he. But this wasn't going to be a fling with a time limit. Not for him anyway, and he needed to start believing in her too. At this point he wasn't sure if he could even go without seeing her till his work party on Wednesday.

***

The next morning Dean woke at 5 o'clock out of habit. For as long as he could remember, their parents had woken them up around now, insisting they were bathed and dressed before breakfast was served at six. God forbid either of them left their rooms without the proper attire.

And he knew someone else who would be up now too. Pulling on a robe, he ducked out of his room and strolled down the corridor, stopping in front of a door he'd just barged into for years. Not this time though, he didn't want to get an eyeful of something he shouldn't.

Instead he knocked lightly, waited a bit, then rapped against the wood to show his impatience.

Jeffrey opened the door, rubbing his eyes with his knuckles. 'What the fuck, Dean?'

'Come out and shut the door,' he said, pulling a face when he saw Jeffrey's man-sized Spider-Man pyjama bottoms. 'Alana seriously agreed to marry you?'

'She thinks they're cute,' his brother said, scowling. 'What do you want?'

Now they were alone in the corridor, there probably wasn't a point in whispering but just in case they woke Alana, he did. 'Have you two hired a wedding planner yet?'

Jeffrey eyed Dean suspiciously 'Who are you and what have you done with my brother?'

'Just answer the question.'

He shook his head. 'You're acting like a psychiatric patient lately, you know that? And no, we haven't yet.'

'Good. I want you to talk to Alana about something for me.' What he was about to ask would probably give his brother more ribbing fodder.

'What?' Jeffrey asked seriously, his focus sharpening with curiosity.

'Natalie has single-handedly organised our Christmas parties for the last few years and probably the summer balls too. She does weddings, and is going out on her own soon.' She'd also probably kill him if she knew he was trying to help with this,

109

but she seemed too smart – and definitely talented – to go through life letting someone else take credit for her hard work.

'Well, that was the last thing I expected to come out of your mouth. Dean, look, I know you really like this girl but Alana is probably going to need more to go on than your word.'

'I agree. But she's coming Saturday, so you'll both see what Nat can do. You don't have to decide now.'

'It's not just that. I mean, I've been to the parties, and if you're right, she is really great at what she does ...'

His brother got that cautious look again, like he was trying to find a solution to world hunger or something. But Dean knew it meant he was trying to find a tactful way to say something that would piss Dean off.

He sighed. 'Just spit it out, will you?'

'Fine. It's too early in the morning for diplomacy anyway.'

Dean snorted. 'Like you've ever had any.'

Jeffrey scowled. 'Do you want to hear what I have to say or not?' At Dean's nod, he continued. 'What happens if she falls for you? Because after last night, even I can see this is more than 'just a bit of fun'. Alana thought so too.'

He frowned, not having an answer for that. When he'd told Jeffrey that's all they were going to be, it was before he'd got to know her, and let her get to know him. The real him, not the closed off version of himself he'd presented to women for most of the last ten years.

'Think about it Dean. What happened to Mandy anyway?' Jeffrey asked.

'I broke things off with her last week, but that was different.'

'Why though?' Jeffrey pressed, and when he couldn't answer, his brother said, 'Because your default is to push someone away when you think they're getting in too deep. I'll bet you haven't seen Mandy for a while because you thought she was too into you. And you wouldn't let yourself feel anything meaningful for her.'

Dean was shaking his head before Jeffrey even finished. 'You're right about one thing. I did think she was getting too attached. But I didn't stop whatever it was we had going because of just that. From the first conversation I had with Natalie, I realized that meaningless and anonymous sex isn't as fun as it used to be. I don't know what I'd do if Natalie started to really feel something for me, but if I didn't feel the same? I'd walk away. I wouldn't drag it on – I don't want to hurt her.'

'And if you did start to feel something for her? Would you walk away then, too?' Jeffrey asked.

Dean played with the idea of brushing the questions off with a shrug and a 'who knows?', but he really wanted Jeffrey to get on board and try to convince Alana that Natalie would do an amazing job of their wedding, so he went for the truth. 'I already *have* feelings for her and I'm still here aren't I?'

Jeffrey's chin dropped, then he shook his head. 'What happened to going for the title of world's sluttiest Fletcher?'

'Keep your knickers on. It's not like I'd ever put myself through anything more than dating again, but as long as she's happy with what I can give her, we can stay together.'

But this meant he really needed to explain how far he'd be able to go with her and let her make up her mind about where they went from there.

Jeffrey whistled. 'You really do have it bad. I told you letting go and opening up to someone was amazing, didn't I?'

Have it bad? Well, he couldn't get her off his mind, and hadn't been able to for weeks, but he still had limits. Limits he had to explain to Natalie.

'You're a complete bell-end, bro.' He turned to hide his smile and headed back to his room. Over his shoulder, he called a little louder, 'But I suppose this time there's a slight possibility you could be right, about the second part anyway.'

***

Natalie knew it was too early – like middle of the night early – when Dean's bedroom door opened and he walked into the room, spot lit from behind by the blinding light in the hall. She was half sprawled over his side of the bed and it was still warm, so he couldn't have been away for long.

'Did you decide to have breakfast with your parents?' she croaked.

'Like I'd miss quality time in bed with you for that. Sorry, I didn't mean to wake you,' he said, quickly closing the door and bringing back the darkness.

She scooted over in the bed to make room for him. There was a muffled thud as something light hit the ground, then the mattress below her dipped as he climbed in beside her.

'My mum would combust on the spot if I turned up for breakfast in my robe,' he chuckled.

'Your parents are strange. Who gets dressed at … what time is it?'

'Quarter past five.'

So it *was* the middle of the night.

'Strange is too mild a word for it.' She yawned.

He lay down and opened his arms. Natalie snuggled into her favourite spot at the nook of his arm, half resting her head on both his chest and shoulder. 'What woke you up?

'Hard to sleep with all the snoring, you know?' he teased.

She was already half-asleep and moving her hands to swat him on the chest seemed too much like hard work. Instead, she feebly nudged him with her chin. 'I don't snore.'

'It's a sexy snore. Not your average tractor ploughing the field kind.'

That snapped her fully awake. It seemed he lived to tease her, and she couldn't not defend herself. Lifting her head, she stressed her point, 'I. Don't. Snore.'

'Relax, Nat. I was kidding. I got up because I always wake up at 5 o'clock. Old habits and all that.'

She wished she could see his face. His tone sounded too light. After getting to know him a little, she got the feeling he didn't really like growing up here. 'I can get up now if you want to get back to London?'

He ran his hand over her hair and down her back before settling on her bum. Even through her Christmas pud pyjamas, she could feel the warmth in his palm and her blood simmered, like it was waiting for his skin to be on hers without the barrier before starting to boil.

'My body clock is just set for now. Go back to sleep, we can leave any time. And didn't you want a bubble bath?'

Yes, she really wanted to try out that tub. It was gorgeous – huge too. She'd never been in a bath that sat in the centre of the room before. In fact, as soon as she'd laid eyes on it, despite the fact she was still reeling at where Dean had brought her, all she could see was them both in it together, surrounded by bubbles and the marble floor tiles covered with candles.

'Only if you join me?' she asked.

'If you want me to,' he said, unenthusiastically Must be a guy thing. Rose said Tom didn't take baths either.

'I want to get all naked and wet with you,' she said, running her hands up the bunched muscles on his abdomen. 'But you could probably fit a quartet in your shower, so that would do.'

'Hold that thought a sec. Are you really awake?' he asked, sounding as serious as she imagined a serial killer would be before confessing his sins.

Natalie sat up on the bed, though she still couldn't see him. A second later the room flashed with bright light, blinding her briefly. When she refocused her eyes, he was lying where she'd left him except he had a line between his brows and his expression wasn't as open as it had been.

'If I hadn't been awake then, I am now. What's going on?'

Chapter 11

Dean shifted back so he was leaning against his iron clad headboard, then reached for her hand. She took it, despite the fact she had a feeling he was going to tell her something that would trigger her temper. Or maybe even crush her.

'I feel shitty about bringing you here without telling you where we were actually going, and I'm really sorry.'

His wide eyes were completely sincere, she couldn't doubt now that he'd dropped whatever shield he'd worn around her. But a chill creeped into her bones, and it had nothing to do with the temperature of the room. There was something else coming, something else he had omitted and she wasn't sure she wanted to know.

'I know, and I've forgiven you. Mostly,' she added lightly, not feeling very light at all.

His lips curved, flashing his dimple and for a second she felt silly for thinking there was more to his sudden apology, but his smile disappeared leaving a tight, wary expression in its wake. Dean closed his eyes for a second, taking in a deep breath, then opened them again and stared at her. She thought she saw a flicker of fear.

'I'm not saying I don't want us to be together here. I just want

114

to be upfront with you and let you know I still have limits.'

'Time limits?' she blurted, wondering if she had one more night, or a few more hours. Maybe not even that. Frick, she shouldn't have ignored her doubts yesterday. She should have—

'No, no time limits. It's just … what's happening with my brother and Alana, your best friend and her fiancé? I can't give you that. Not now, not five years from now if we're still together. And before you start I know you're not plotting a way to get a ring on your finger—' He'd clearly noticed her scowl '—I just want to let you know that if we are together for weeks, months, years, whatever, I don't think I'll ever be at that place where I can plan to marry someone again.'

Natalie folded her arms across her chest. 'I'm not an expert when it comes to fledgling relationships, but I'm pretty sure you're not supposed to talk about marriage till you're at least six months into one.'

'Maybe. But by then you might have realized you've spent all that time with someone who can't give you the future you want. Isn't it better to get that conversation out of the way now?' he asked, his brows pulling together in the middle. 'Or would you rather wait 'til you're in too deep to hear it?'

Her first reaction was to joke it off, ask what he thought made him believe he was so irresistible that she'd fall for him. But she didn't.

Dean had been so worried about leading her on, he'd brought up the M word before they'd had a proper date. The more she got to know him, the more her emotions became tangled up and she couldn't honestly say she'd never fall for him.

He was giving her a chance now to decide whether she wanted to move forward with whatever they had while laying his cards on the table and she had to respect him for that.

Natalie squeezed his hand. 'I was never the kind of girl who dreamt of having a big white wedding. I've never even dreamt of falling hopelessly in love with someone and, well, after losing my parents the idea of going the truly, madly, deeply route appealed even less.'

He rubbed his thumb along the back of her hand. 'Losing one person you love is hard enough but the two people you love more than anything in the world? I'm awed by how strong you are. I might not get on with my parents well, but I doubt I'd be able to keep myself as tight as you have when they're gone.'

He thought she was strong? All Natalie ever saw herself as was an emotional wreck who'd needed someone to lean on for so long, she'd forgotten what it was like those first few months before Rose. 'I'm not as strong as you think. I use Rose as an emotional crutch and have for so long that by rights she could have me institutionalised. I was a mess when I met her.'

He frowned for a second, like something she'd said triggered a horrible memory, but he shook his head once, and then all she could see was concern. For her. Natalie wondered if all this depressing talk was making her see things.

'The girl I know is brave, strong and quick-witted. And I don't know the Natalie you are with your friends, just the girl who declared war on me – and might have even won too, if I hadn't managed to get you to kiss me.' He grinned, and she couldn't help smiling back.

'Of course I'd have won. I'm amazing.'

'You really are,' he said, then pulled her in and kissed her in a way that made all her worries drift away.

***

Dean stood over the brass torture device, his jaw clenched with determination. There was no way this thing was going to get a chance at it again. He was an adult. Thirty years old. This was not going to beat him.

The hot water tap groaned a protest when he turned it on and the cold one did the same. He dropped in a cupcake thing that one of the maids had assured him was better than a bubble bath and cursed to himself when he saw it dissolve, turning the water pale pink and glittery.

He had to do something manly after this – like go out hunting or wrestle a bear. He couldn't think of anything more emasculating than a glittery bubble bath.

'The noise of that plumbing could wake the dead.'

He turned to see Natalie in the doorway to the bathroom. Her hair was sexy and rumpled from sleep and her pyjamas were so cute and baggy, he had no idea how she still managed to turn him on as much as she did fully naked.

Maybe it was because he could still imagine her naked. Or maybe it was because he now had a new appreciation of what sexy actually meant.

It wasn't just about a gorgeous face and rockin' body, or clothes – Natalie could be standing in a bin bag and he'd still want her more than anything.

Being sexy was the full package. And to him, it was her wit, her smile, the sparkle in her eyes, the way she ribbed him. The rest of it – her looks, the way she dressed, her silky blonde hair were all just dressings that made her even hotter.

'It's old,' he said, answering her.

'Looks like it's just about ready.' Natalie pulled her top over her head, then tossed it to the vanity at the side of the room. 'Are you going to join me?'

Slowly, she shimmied out of the bottoms, revealing the smooth, silky skin at her thighs he'd wanted a better look at last night. And the sexiest thing of all about Natalie was the confident way she met his eyes and stepped out of the trousers, kicking them away.

His blood arrowed south to the point that not even his robe could hide what was going on beneath.

'Because if you are, you might want to stop the water now. Or we'll make a mess of these lovely marble tiles.'

Right, he had to stop staring at her and deal with the bath. He turned and switched the water off.

Natalie pressed herself against his back, sliding her hands round to untie his robe. 'Let's get this off. I like looking at you too.'

She undressed him, then scored her nails down his sides, right over her ribs then licked up his spine until he was tingling all over.

Standing back, he watched her lift one leg over the huge edge, spinning all kinds of fantasies about holding her curvy hips as he bent her over the tub. She lifted the other leg, going wide and he had an illicit view that made him want to haul her back to the bedroom and take her like a wild animal, but when she lay down and the bubbles filled in the space around her, Natalie closed her eyes and sighed blissfully.

Maybe later.

'Are you coming?' she asked, not opening her eyes.

Almost. But knowing that wasn't what she really meant, he followed suit and climbed in with her. She pulled her knees to her chest to make room for him, but she didn't need to. They'd probably get another person of Natalie's size in there. Not that he'd want anyone else here when he had her.

Moving over, she turned to lie between his legs with her back to his chest. He had to hold back a groan, but couldn't stop from tensing all over.

'I'm not hurting you, am I?' she asked, jerking forward and turning at the waist, the movement splashing water against the sides of the bath.

'Not in the way you think. It's more of a pain caused by lack of, er, attention.'

She looked down. 'Well, we can't have you in pain.'

Before his mind could catch up with what she'd said, Natalie got up on her knees, the water lowered and more of him was revealed. Placing her hands on each of his thighs, she leaned down.

Holy shit.

***

He groaned and maybe even gasped her name a few times, he didn't know. The orgasm seemed to last an age, pulsing down his spine, straight through him and into her. She didn't pull away, only slowed down, eased off on the pressure, nursing him through until it was over.

He was panting, utterly spent, but somehow found enough energy to open his arms for her. Natalie settled back against his chest, submerging both their bodies in watery bubbles.

'As soon as we get out of here, I'm going to pay you back for that,' he promised.

Her twinkling laugh vibrated through him. 'You make it sound like I committed some injustice against you.'

Sliding his arms around her, he held her close. 'Worse. You've taken whatever self-control I had and made me feel like a complete teenager again. And going by the glitter and all this pink,' he swished the water in front of them, 'you've turned me into a teenage girl.'

She tilted her head to look up at him. 'There's nothing adolescent or girly about you, trust me.'

But Dean was still going to prove himself after this, and wasn't leaving this estate until he'd repaid her thoroughly.

***

'*Now* we're about even,' Dean said, then nuzzled her neck from behind.

It took Natalie a minute to process her thoughts. She was half sprawled in his lap with her shoes resting on the white leather seats in the limo and could barely find the energy to worry about getting it dirty. He'd reduced her into a melted mess of nerve endings after their bath, and had just finished doing wonders with those fingers of his.

When she caught her breath, she said 'Sexually, I think I owe you a couple. But as far as the battles are concerned, I still have to pay you back for taking me to your parents' house under false pretences.'

Dean laughed against her neck. 'What do you have in mind?'

'Something game-changing,' she said, but really didn't have a clue. She hadn't thought much about being tricked after he kissed her properly for the first time, having been too blissfully distracted.

'I'll keep my guard up. So, are you still going crashing tonight?'

'I think so. It's low-key, not much security and the design company is big enough that even two unknowns could slip in undetected. There's no food though.' Natalie wrinkled her nose.

He smiled. 'Perish the thought. I'll just have to take you out for dinner first.'

'Well, I'm easily pleased. A pizza or a hoagie will do. I had my fix of fine dining for the weekend.'

And she wasn't kidding. Who knew brunch could have courses? And last night they were brought plate after plate of food, albeit small fancy portions, until she lost count of what course they were on. Mussels, salmon, chicken, cakes, tarts, antipasti, bread, sorbet – she'd never eaten such a wide variety of food at one sitting before.

Dean readjusted her until she was sitting sideways in his lap. 'I'd like to take you on a proper date, and not to a fast food restaurant.'

'Wait a minute. Don't guys usually do that *before* taking a girl to their parents' country manor and defiling them in their four poster bed?'

His eyes widened and she smirked.

'Defiling? If anyone was defiling anyone it was you with all that dirty talk.'

'And here I thought I was just giving you good advice.'

Shaking his head, he laughed a little. 'So I need advice too? Would you like to kick me in the balls next?'

'Tempting, but if I did you wouldn't be ready for this ...' Natalie twisted and straddled him.

Dean kissed her hard, moving them until her back was against the mini-bar. She was so hot and ready for this next first – sex in a limo. And it was perfect since the back area was totally blocked off from the driver's view.

But just then, the driver's voice came through the speaker. 'Sir, we're almost there. Will we be dropping Miss Taylor off at the same place?'

Dammit.

Dean pulled back and pushed a button on one of the armrests. 'Natalie, it's up to you?'

'Er, no. Round the corner is fine.' There was no point in hiding where she lived now. In fact, she was tempted to bring Dean back. She gave them her address.

Dean released the button and the driver said, 'Very well, Miss.'

'So,' he said, then went to work righting her dress. 'Dinner, tonight?'

'You could come in and I'll whip us up something edible. Or close enough.'

He laughed. 'As much as I'd love to, I have some work I need to finish. I'll pick you up at six and we can get something before the party.'

'Fine, but if I spontaneously combust you'll only have yourself to blame.'

Dean kissed her again, but it was softer than before. 'We have all night for that.'

Her mind ran wild with all possibilities at the venue. But one was a no, no. 'Not the bathrooms.'

Shaking his head, he said, 'I meant after the party back at mine. I'm not going to drag you to the loo and *defile* you at a party you organised. I like having you in my bed.'

She quite liked him having her in his bed too – and, she was curious to see where he stayed and wondered if it would be as grand as his bedroom at his family manor. She didn't think so. When he was out of the suits and tuxes he was more urban geek – in a really hot way – than posh and stuffy.

The car pulled to a stop and she saw her building through the glass. Dean opened the door and took out her case. 'Can I take this in for you?'

'Thanks, but I can get it.' Natalie took the case from him, and got all tongue tied for a second. What did she do now? Kiss him goodbye? Were they there yet? Given the things they'd both done to each other with their mouths, it shouldn't be so hard to work out.

Dean answered that question for her, sliding his hand onto her cheek and leaning down to kiss her in the middle of her street. Not expecting more than a peck, she got all fired up as he laid a little French kissing on her and she dropped her bag on the pavement so she could wrap her arms around his neck.

She lost feeling in her legs after a minute but that was okay, since he now had a firm grip on her waist and it seemed to be the only thing holding her off the ground, before he broke the kiss and asked, 'Six?'

That was *hours* away.

Natalie pouted and he laughed.

'I'll make it up to you tonight,' he promised.

With anticipation curling her stomach into knots, Natalie picked up her case and headed for the steps to her flat, being careful to make sure she had her footing. At the top she fished her keys out of her handbag and unlocked the door.

'Nat?'

She turned to see he'd rolled down the window of the limo.

'Bring a clean pair of knickers. I'm making you breakfast in the morning.' Dean winked.

She had to bite her lip to hold the laugh in. 'You're awfully confident for a guy who hasn't even taken a girl on a proper date yet.'

'Tonight I'll date the knickers right off you. Don't worry about that.'

The window zipped up before she could think of a witty retort, but it didn't matter. She'd get him back later. When the limo pulled away and was out of sight, she let her full smile loose and went into the flat, grinning like an idiot.

***

The flat had been empty again so she had a chance to do more research into business start-up loans and also some job hunting, since the first option was more like a pipedream with her current bank balance.

A few new vacancies caught her eye, and she'd just finished sending off her CV for the third time, when her mobile rang.

Natalie answered. 'Hi, Rose.'

'Nat! Are you back? I need you at the bridal shop tomorrow at eleven. It's the only time we can get a fitting this close to the big day and I'm sorry, but I can't be there. I'm trying a different recipe for the cake because Tom's mum has a wheat allergy and the first attempt was a total disaster. I'm also knee-deep in flowers that were supposed to come as bouquets for you and me but instead they're unarranged! Can you believe it? And apparently no florist in this city can have two lined up for Sunday – that's a whole week away!'

'Rose, you need to relax. Take a deep breath. Come on, let me hear you.'

She did as Natalie asked, once, then again.

Natalie heard the same edge of hysteria in Rose's voice that she'd heard before in brides-to-be. Going a hundred miles a minute just made things a lot more stressful.

'Feel better?' she asked after Rose had taken about five.

'Yes. I'm sorry, I don't know what came over me there.'

'It's stress, just try to relax. It will be perfect with or without flowers. You have each other and that's what really counts.'

Rose chuckled. 'You're right. I'm being a Bridezilla, aren't I?'

Natalie lay back against the sofa, smiling at the ceiling. 'Nah. More like the Incredible Bride but with less green and more pitiful smashing skills. Seriously though, how are you doing? If I can help with anything … Maybe one of my contacts can get the flowers done for Thursday?'

Rose sighed. 'No, I don't want you working this. You're a guest, and my maid of honour. I forgot how much goes into planning a wedding, even a small one. Anyway, I meant to ask, how did last night go?'

'It was … amazing.'

'Hmm, sounds like you took the next step? So, spill. Who is he and when do I get to meet him?' Rose asked.

The next step? Natalie frowned, remembering what Dean said. This was pretty much as far as they went. But then she hadn't been looking for a boyfriend, let alone a husband, just three weeks ago. If she could even call Dean her boyfriend.

'I'm not sure what to say to your first question, except I think I'm spending the night at his house. I guess you could meet on Wednesday. He co-owns Tech Solutions and I've been invited to his Christmas party. You could be my plus one?'

Well, technically she was Dean's but since she organised it, she'd have no trouble slipping Rose onto the guest list. She grinned at the thought of getting her best friend to crash his party.

'You know, any other time I'd have said no but this wedding lark is driving me off my head. Count me in.'

Natalie sat up so fast her head swam. 'Really? I can't believe you're coming! It's at The Savoy and I can't wait to see it how it looks. They had a massive budget with hardly any input. I really went to town on this.'

'So he's Mick's client? Are you sure that's okay?' Rose asked.

She snorted. 'Who cares, Mick's a dick. And it's not like Tech Solutions is my client. I can date who I like.'

'True. I can't wait Nat. I'll be home tomorrow night, you can tell me all about it then and I promise to dial down my inner Bridezilla.'

'Okay. See you tomorrow.'

They hung up and she opened her email app, then typed out a message. She really needed to make a point of getting Dean's number tonight, but he said he'd be working …

To: Dean Fletcher
From: Nat Taylor
Subject: Wednesday
    Can I bring a plus one, or was the invite just for me?
    X

It was probably mean to be so vague, but she did owe him a few paybacks so … His reply was instant.

To: Nat Taylor
From: Dean Fletcher
Subject: Bored already?
    Not unless you want him to be able to walk at the end of the night …
    X

Smiling, she typed a reply.

To: Dean Fletcher
From: Nat Taylor
Subject: Keep your knickers on
    She will need her legs for her wedding this weekend, so I'd appreciate some restraint.
    You know, I could always just add Rachel Greenfield, the assistant, to the guest list myself. I'm sure you've noticed Nicole

Porter is already on it.

X

P.S. How's work?

She noticed it was after four and ran what would be her second bath of the day. After settling in, she checked her emails again.

To: Nat Taylor

From: Dean Fletcher

Subject: Where's the fun in that?

I did indeed, my little thief. But you're now officially attending as my date. Your friend is welcome to come, with her husband-to-be if she'd like.

Work was productive until your email about gave me an aneurysm. Of course, then I remembered you had me so there was no need to be concerned.

I'll see you soon. Don't miss me too much.

Dean (all the man you need) Fletcher

X

Natalie chuckled at his closing line.

To: Dean Fletcher

From: Nat Taylor

Subject: Productivity

Dear All the Man I Need,

I'm not sure if I miss you but I'm definitely feeling deprived. Any ideas how I might resolve the matter?

Natalie (squirming in her knickers) Taylor

X

While she waited on a reply, she got out the bath, dried herself off and slipped on a dressing gown. After she'd started on drying her hair, the phone buzzed.

To: Nat Taylor
From: Dean Fletcher
Subject: Delayed gratification
    Dear Squirming in Your Knickers,
    Be patient my little thief. Tonight will be all the better if
you do.
    X

Shaking her head, she smiled remembering how he'd said she'd been worth the wait. She couldn't deny that he had been either.

***

Dean vaulted her steps at ten to six, telling himself he was not going to push his way in for a quickie before dinner. Natalie might have been kidding about doing things backwards, but now they were trying the whole couple thing, he wanted to do that right. She wasn't like his other flings and he wasn't about to treat her like it.

When she opened the door he had to shove his hands in his pockets to keep from grabbing her. Her deep pink dress covered everything from her cleavage to her knees, but it was the most indecent thing he'd seen her wear yet. It was like a second skin and he knew at a glance that she hadn't bothered with a bra. He swallowed hard, trying not to think of what else she'd gone without.

'Would you like to come in for a drink?' she asked, smirking a little and batting her eyelashes.

It wasn't a drink she was after, and neither would he be. 'The taxi's waiting.'

She looked around him at the car idling by the curb. 'You could always send it away and we'll order another. Later, maybe …'

Natalie pressed her hands against his abs and curled her fingers. Even through the thin cotton of his shirt, the way her nails scored him lightly was almost as good as when she did that against his bare skin.

She looked up at him, her blue eyes full of promise and expectation and he almost forgot about his intentions. He took her wrists, rubbing his thumbs over her erratic pulse and lifted her hands off him. But this close he could feel the buzz between them and was almost knocked stupid by her floral scent and the silkiness of her skin. It was like that all over. And this morning's antics in his bathtub, then again on the bed, flashed through his mind.

He had no idea if his need for her was showing on his face, but her triumphant smile gave him an idea. Shaking his head, he said, 'Nice try. But I'm taking you out.'

Releasing her, he moved back. The view he had now wasn't just of her face, but every inch of her from her silver stilettos to the loose blonde curls around her shoulders.

Natalie pouted. 'Delayed gratification sucks.'

'Just trying to take my girl on a date. Come on.'

She grabbed her bag and keys, then turned to close the door.

He couldn't help it, his attention slid down her back, to her curved hips and he had to grit his teeth. There wasn't a VPL in sight. *Was she really naked under there?*

After she locked up, he took her hand and dragged her to the taxi before he decided to find out for himself. When they were in and he'd given the driver the address, Natalie's eyes widened. 'I said I'd be happy with a takeaway.'

'Our first date isn't going to be at some greasy spoon.' He lifted her hand to his lips and kissed it. 'I might not act it all the time, but I was raised to be a gentleman.'

'A gentleman would have helped me out this afternoon, or just now.'

He grinned. 'Still squirming in your knickers?'

She leaned close, whispering in his ear. 'I'm squirming, but there's no room for knickers under this dress.'

His heartbeat roared in his ears. Now she wasn't the only one close to squirming.

'You've changed the game,' he managed after a minute.

'I don't mind playing these kinds of games. And it seems like I'm winning.' Natalie ran her hand up his knee, along the inside seam of his trousers, but stopped short before she got to what was going on beneath. 'How are you feeling about delayed gratification now?'

Like he wished he'd never mentioned it. Ever.

It was very hard not to drag her onto his lap but he doubted the taxi driver would be thrilled with the show they'd give him. Thankfully they were at the restaurant already, so he focused on getting a note out his wallet and paying, then they were both out on the street.

Natalie hugged her arms against the chilly bite in the air. He put his arm round her shoulder and led her to the restaurant. 'Didn't you bring a jacket?'

'Nope. It would have ruined the effect of my dress.' She winked at him.

'That's dedication,' he murmured, impressed. Then gave his name to the woman at the front podium.

They were led through the restaurant to a private table at the back. All the way, Natalie was smiling full on, taking in everything from the real Christmas trees decorated in silver and purples, to the glittering light features shining through the windows. He didn't understand why she couldn't do this in her own home, not when the decorations seemed to make her this happy.

The private booth he'd booked was almost like Santa's grotto, with fake snow covering the furniture, a twigged tree with sparkly lights and a table that looked more festive than his parents' house on Christmas day.

She froze, staring at the space around her and he noticed she wasn't smiling anymore. Shit.

'What's wrong? Is it too much?'

Natalie hugged her arms again but she couldn't be cold. There was a log fire burning away across from the table. 'No. It's just … This place brings back memories.'

He wondered why the difference, but then this area was more authentic, less modern and glitzy than the rest of the restaurant. Pulling her into his arms, he tilted her chin up so he could see her properly. The guilt in her eyes slayed him. 'You're doing nothing wrong.'

'Then why does it feel like I am?' she whispered.

'We can go somewhere else, or ask for another table?' he suggested. He really should have thought this through better.

Natalie shook her head. 'No, you went to all this trouble. I'm sorry.'

'You have nothing to apologise for.'

Dean kissed her. It was supposed to be reassuring and light. Natalie fisted her hands in his hair, clinging to him, kissing him with a desperate kind of need that probably should have terrified him. Instead pain sliced his chest in two. He felt her grief almost like it was his own, and he wanted to make it go away for her. He kissed her back, showing her he was there and he would be for …

How long? As long as she needed him? As long as he needed her?

Someone cleared their throat and Natalie broke the kiss. She turned away from him, sliding into her chair and wiping her eyes with the backs of her hands. His heart constricted.

A waiter apologised, then asked what they wanted to drink. 'A scotch please. Neat. Natalie?'

'Scotch sounds good.'

The waiter disappeared to get their drinks and he moved the other chair so he could sit beside her. 'Onto the hard stuff already. Is dating me that bad?'

He was teasing, trying to lighten her mood but also his. Something had changed between them with that last kiss, but he couldn't put his finger on it. All he had was this feeling like he was falling in slow motion, knowing he was going to hit something hard. Maybe even break every bone in his body. And there was nothing he could find to grab onto to stop it.

Her eyes were shining still and there was a flush across her cheekbones. 'You must think I'm a mess.'

'I think you're stunning actually. Especially in that dress.' He hoped that would earn him a smile, but he was disappointed.

'I'm not sure I'm ready for this.' She waved a hand round their private slice of the restaurant. 'It reminds me of my mum's dining room at home. She even had a log fire like that one.'

'I'm sorry. I didn't know.'

Natalie took his hand and her lips curved, but her eyes remained haunted. 'I know that and I don't blame you. I need to get past feeling like this. My mum wouldn't want me to.'

He kissed her head. 'I saw how your eyes lit up when you came into the restaurant. You were so happy. Nat, you get to enjoy Christmas. I know you miss them, but it doesn't mean you have to give up something you really love just because your mum loved it too.'

She snuggled into his shoulder and he wrapped his arm around her. 'Easier said than done, but I'm going to try.'

The waiter returned with their drinks and said he'd be back shortly for their orders. Natalie picked up her scotch, took a sip and screwed up her face. 'It burns.'

'The first sip always goes down the worst.'

She tried again, swallowed, then coughed.

'Second's not much better,' she croaked. 'I think I'll stick to wine.'

Dean took the offered glass, watching her pick up the menu. She seemed determined to get through this, but her gaze didn't stray far from the table, like ignoring the decorations would make them go away. He felt like such a dick, bringing her here and dragging up all this pain.

There was one way he could distract her but this wasn't the time or the place. He'd have to try something else. 'I didn't just bring you here to wine and dine you. I was hoping to butter you up so I could ask you something.'

She put the menu down on the table. 'Ask me what?'

'How would you feel about being our events coordinator?'

When she walked into the private area Dean had booked for them, the wind had been knocked out of her so forcefully, she was sure a car had smashed into her full speed. But this left her gobsmacked. 'You want me to work for you?'

He shrugged. 'Not exclusively. But we have enough things coming up that would keep you busy and give you a steady income.'

Her heart started pounding, and she could feel every beat rattle around her skull. 'That's a really sweet thing to offer, but I don't think it's a good idea.'

'I don't see why not, and I didn't ask to help you out. If you go it alone, or go to another company, Jeffrey and I would book you anyway. Everything you've done for us has been amazing. This way you get all to keep all the profit.' He shrugged.

It sounded reasonable enough and she really wanted to say yes. It would give her a steady income so starting on her own would no longer be a pipe dream. Then she remembered their last kiss and knew she couldn't accept his offer. She'd never felt like she'd needed anyone more than she did when his lips met hers, and she'd poured all of that need right into the kiss. If she wasn't careful, she was just going to switch out one emotional crutch for another. And there were no guarantees right now that either would stick around.

'Dean, it's an amazing offer. But we've only been together for less than twenty-four hours. We don't know what will happen in a week, never mind a year.' She could hardly believe the words she was saying. It felt like she'd known him for months.

His reply was interrupted by a waiter taking their order. She went with the first thing she glanced on the menu – a steak – and he had the same.

Even after they were alone, he remained quiet and his forehead creased a little like he was deep in thought. Natalie wished she could hear what he was thinking – or that she had a crystal ball and knew where they'd end up. If it was together, she could let herself go with him. As it was, she was surprised that after her emotional and needy outburst he wasn't already running for the hills.

Instead he just looked like he had when she'd first met him, with a guarded expression that turned into a cool smirk.

'You're right,' he said, then necked her scotch.

She hated the tight smile he offered her, but didn't know how to bring back the warm Dean she'd gotten to know and like. They ate dinner in almost silence, with Natalie trying to flirt a little to get him back. Thankfully the heat in his eyes was real, but he was still cautious and didn't touch her again. Not until they left, and he put his arm around her as they crossed the pavement to get into the taxi.

He was almost aloof on the way to the party, to the point she thought she'd lost him for good. And she knew why. He'd been walked out on before when it mattered the most. Someone he'd thought loved him enough that they wanted to spend the rest of their life with him had run away without so much as an explanation.

Despite everything he'd been through, he had opened up to her. He told her all about himself and even agreed to try more than a fling. What had she done in return? Shut him down from doing just that, for planning any kind of future. And it wasn't only because she was scared to need him. She was terrified of falling in love with him, because despite what he thought, she wasn't strong – losing someone else would destroy her.

When they arrived at the party and gave their false names to get in, he headed straight for the bar. She followed behind, ignoring the packed hall filled with hundreds of guests and stopping only to swipe a glass of champagne from a passing tray.

She watched him order a drink, then froze when a gorgeous blonde sidled up to him. Panic constricted her throat as the blonde reached for his arm, and rage boiled when he turned to smile at something the woman said.

Her temper unlocked her joints and she stormed over, ready to chuck the contents of her glass his face. Nothing could save them now.

Until she heard him say, 'Sorry, I have a girlfriend.'

Her anger evaporated under a swarm of emotions she couldn't name.

The floozy didn't give up though, just stepped closer and pushed back her shoulders so her fake boobs strained against her gaping neckline. 'That's okay. I'm not looking for anything permanent.'

Natalie would have been pissed again, except Dean didn't ogle the woman at all. He just said, 'I am. With my girlfriend.'

Again she was stopped in her tracks, not more than three feet away. He wanted permanent? What happened to his *I can't give you what your friend or my brother has* speech?

'You're no fun,' the blonde complained, then walked away.

Dean turned back to the bar and picked up his drink. She joined him there, placing her glass down. 'I'm your girlfriend?'

His shoulders tensed and he looked at her warily. 'You heard that?'

'Yes. I was on my way over to give you a champagne bath and play footie with your balls. You're lucky. I'm a good shot.'

He smiled, but it was still cautious, not open and warm like he'd been with her earlier. 'I'm assuming you heard the rest.'

'Did you mean that, or were you just trying to get rid of her?' she asked, but he looked away quickly. 'I know that expression.

You don't have to hide from me.'

Dean necked the rest of his scotch. 'I don't hide.'

He was being too distant, too closed off. She wanted the guy back who made her laugh, made her so hot she couldn't think straight, and cared enough to kiss her until she forgot about her guilt. But she'd either hurt or offended him in the restaurant. Maybe a little honesty would make this right.

'I want to trust this, I really do. But at the same time I don't want to start to need you, Dean. I have to learn to stand on my own two feet, emotionally and financially, and I don't know how long you'll be around.'

His expression softened as he turned to her. 'I'm not planning on going anywhere.'

That was the funny thing about plans. They could change. She remembered the last plans her mum had made didn't come to pass. Fate sometimes dealt you a shitty hand.

'Natalie, really. I'm in this as much as I can be and I'm not even considering us ending.' He cupped her face with his hand and met her eyes. 'I need to know if you are too.'

The rush of emotion was almost overwhelming. She didn't think she'd ever felt this much this quickly about anyone. In fact she was sure of it. But terrifying as it felt, there was no going back. New and unsure as the relationship was, she wanted him. 'I'm in too.'

His answering smile made her heart pound. Taking his face in her hands, she pulled him down for a kiss, telling him everything she didn't have words for.

Her heart constricted. He really was sexy, and sweet and he was right, they needed to start trusting each other because she didn't want this to end. Not ever.

'Were you serious about Tech Solutions hiring me to do all the events?' she asked.

He lifted his brows and nodded.

'Then … yes. I'll do it. But you'll be my client.'

His lips curved so much that his dimple winked. He pulled her close and wrapped his arms around her. 'This is going to be great, Nat. You'll see.'

And she believed him. There was still so much to work out and she'd have to keep her job for a while until she built up a fuller client base, but she could do it.

He slid his hands over her backside and squeezed. 'You'll finally be able to leave that shitty office you work at.'

She frowned a little. 'That will take time. I'll still need to keep my job until I get on my feet. Maybe even find something part-time ...'

'You can use a room at Tech Solutions whenever you need to. That'll keep your overheads down. I only have one request.' His smile was wickedly sexy.

'Which is?' she asked.

'You leave your knickers at home.'

Pressing her lips together to hold back a grin, she ran a finger up his forearm and poked his shoulder. 'That sounds like a sexual harassment claim waiting to happen.'

'But technically, you won't be my employee ...' he suggested, raising an eyebrow.

'Worse, you'll be my client. In fact, my only client. Doesn't that breach ethical laws?' she asked, enjoying this game.

'You're not my doctor, so I doubt it. And if it makes you feel better, look at Jeffrey as the client. You're not having sex with my brother.' He said this deadly serious and she chuckled.

'Oh, I don't know. Jeffrey is kind of hot ...'

Dean pressed her against the wall with his body, claiming her mouth with a groan. Her reaction was instant; her breath came in gasps and the taste of the scotch on his tongue was so good she wondered why she couldn't stand it at the restaurant.

He released her, too soon for her liking, and stepped back. 'I don't think Jeffrey could get you hot and ready like that, do you?'

'No, and I was only teasing. How did I end up the one thoroughly teased?' She shook her head to try and clear it.

Dean took her hand. 'I'll make it up to you later, we have all night. Dance?'

'Are you sure you want to risk it again?' she asked, still wobbly from the kiss.

'I'll put in a request for Santa Baby.'

Natalie laughed. 'I better not grind too low or I'll end up flashing everyone at the party.'

'I wouldn't mind the view,' he said, then led her in the direction of the dancefloor.

She didn't feel nervous now. This wasn't choreographed dancing, and the night was going so well she didn't think it could get any better. Well, it could have, if he'd followed through after the kiss. But instead of feeling frustrated, she couldn't wipe the grin off her face. He'd been so possessive and delicious. She couldn't wait until they got back to his place.

Unfortunately, her luck had run out.

'*Natalie? What the fuck are you doing here?*'

Dread danced down her spine, sending a chill through her.

Dean turned to see who it was, but she didn't need to. She'd know that voice anywhere. She'd heard the acidic edge more than she'd like to remember.

'Who the hell are you?' Dean asked.

Feeling like her stomach was at her feet, she took a deep breath and turned around to face the music – or raging bull might be more apt a description. Mick's face was so dark it was almost purple and he had a glare that would have stopped the grim reaper in his tracks.

Frick, this time she really was busted.

Chapter 12

'Come with me right fucking now.'

Mick stormed through the crowd and she went to follow, but Dean caught her arm. 'Nat, who is that prick?'

She was sure all the blood had drained from her face and she was ghostly white when she looked up at him 'My boss.'

'Shit.' Dean ran a hand through his hair. 'We'd better deal with it.'

As much as she wanted him as a buffer against Mick's rage, she could tell from the hard line of Dean's jaw he was pissed off. 'Please, I have to do this myself. I don't want it turning into a fight. He's my boss.'

'He's a dick,' he growled.

'Yes, Mick the Dick. That's what we call him, but I need my job until I get on my feet. I need to try and smooth this over.' Though she didn't know how.

He sighed, then nodded. 'I'll be at the bar if you need me. Do you want a glass of red?'

'I think I'll give scotch another go. I'm going to need it after this.'

He gave her a quick peck on the lips then she was off, pushing her way through the crowd spilling over from the dancefloor. She found him pacing outside at the smoker's balcony, but luckily nobody else was there.

Natalie tried to decide the best way to deal with the situation. Be defensive and apologetic, or use offense as the best defence? Mick caught sight of her. The rage in his eyes could melt the ice in Antarctica.

Taking a deep breath to steady herself, she pushed through the patio doors. 'Hi Mick, what are you doing here?'

'What am I doing here?' His voice was so low, it sounded even more menacing. 'Do you know how much time it took to convince Stephen & Bell we were the right events company to go to? They were worried we'd fuck it up, that something would go wrong, so I came to make sure that didn't happen. And what do I find? You. Crashing their party and doing who knows what else with their employees!'

'I came to make sure it all went smoothly too,' she lied, but when his eyes glowered, she knew that wasn't the right answer.

'Let's get something straight right now. You're nothing but a PA to me. You're an oily rag, I'm the organ grinder. I can't trust you with the clients, they don't even know you exist. Do you know how many clients we'd lose if they found out an unqualified child was working on their files?'

An oily rag? A child? She was used to his comments about her lack of qualifications but she had experience now. And he'd just pushed her too far. 'Is that *really* why you won't let me deal with the clients, Mick? Or are you just worried that if I did work closely with them and left your shitty, underpaying company they'd follow me?'

'You have some fucking nerve talking to me like that after breaking company policy like this. Consider yourself free of my shitty company as of now. Pack your desk up Monday morning and get out. You'll have until ten.'

Her anger evaporated as the reality of what she'd done sank in. 'But—'

'No buts.' He walked close, so he was towering over her. 'Know this; you'll never work in this business again. I'll make sure of it. I hope you like stocking shelves at the local supermarket because nobody else will have you. Now get out of here before I have security call the police.'

'Mick, please. This is an overreaction.'

'GET OUT. NOW.'

Natalie's heart skipped a beat, but her feet got moving. She went through the patio doors, and was about to head over to Dean, but Mick grabbed her arm and squeezed. 'Ow. Let go of me.'

'The exit's this way.' He frog-marched her to the door and when they passed security, he told them to make sure she didn't come back in.

Mortified, humiliated and on the verge of tears, she walked away from the venue and pulled her phone out her bag. Crap, she'd still not exchanged numbers with Dean. She tried to email him, but the 4G connection was slow and her vision was too blurry to see much on the screen.

The icy wind nipped at her bare arms and legs and she started to shake, whether from the cold or the fact her career was now over. Before she froze to death, she managed to pull up a new email.

She hailed a taxi and somehow kept it together until she stumbled into her empty flat, before the tears really started. Shit, Tom had been right. What had she done?

***

Dean couldn't see much past the crowd but after five minutes the tension in him couldn't be confined to one spot. He'd wanted to punch her clown of a boss for the way he'd spoken to her, and wasn't thrilled that she wanted to face him alone. But Natalie was right, he was far too pissed off and a confrontation wouldn't have gone down well.

But where was she?

When he saw Mick stroll back into the party with a glass of champagne and a charming smile, Dean scanned the crowd for her. She was nowhere to be seen. Had the fucker upset her? Gritting his teeth, he abandoned the drinks and went to find out. After a loop round the conservatory and the rest of the club, he couldn't see her anywhere.

Time to face her dick of a boss.

Reigning in his temper, he approached the guy and interrupted his conversation with a group of suits. 'A word. Now.'

They all turned to him expectant, but Dean glared at Mick with narrowed eyes until he excused himself.

He led them over to the entrance hall before turning on him. 'Where is she?'

'Who?' Mick asked, his expression closed and giving nothing away.

'Natalie Taylor. The woman you dragged off five minutes ago who never came back,' he said, his voice laced with menacing sarcasm.

The only reaction Mick showed was a slight thinning of his lips.

'Look, old man. You don't want to piss me off more than you already have. Tell me where she is.' He stifled the urge to take Mick by the throat and shake him.

'Whatever she told you is a lie. She doesn't work for me. I can assure you no employee of mine would dare crash one of our most respected clients' parties. I have no idea how she managed to sneak in,' Mick said, calmly with a hint of authority.

If it wasn't for the fact Dean didn't trust the man as far as he could throw him, he might have bought the lie. It was clear Mick thought he was an employee of this company and was trying to smooth things over. He didn't care about any of that. He just wanted to find Natalie.

'Where. Is. She?' He said the words slowly, carefully, so this idiot would understand him and might actually answer the question.

Mick's calm facade slipped and his eyes burned. 'She's gone, and she won't be back.'

'You threw her out?' he asked incredulously. It was freezing outside and she didn't have a jacket.

Not waiting for an answer, Dean jogged to the exit and flew past security. He ran down the street a little either way but she was nowhere to be seen. He approached one of the bouncers on the door.

'Have you seen a girl in a pink dress, she has blonde hair?' he asked.

Short and bald answered. 'Left 'bout ten minutes ago mate, caught a taxi.'

Shit.

Dean pulled his mobile from his pocket, cursing when he remembered he didn't have her number yet. His email app blinked with new messages, but there was only one he cared about reading now.

To: Dean Fletcher
From: Nat Taylor
Subject: rain check
   Got sacked and kicked out of the party. It's freezing out so I'm going to get a taxi and head home. Sorry, not really in the mood for tonight. I'll be in touch.
   Nat
   X

She'd been sacked? He had to take a deep breath, then another, to cool down enough so he could convince himself smashing Mick's face in was not a reasonable thing to do. Then he replied.

After adding his number he hit send. He stood for a minute, trying to get his head around everything that happened tonight. He'd gone from being excited to see her, to so hollow at the thought that she wouldn't even commit to working with him because she was unsure of their future together.

Then there was that kiss. The one so full of her need it had freaked him out. Beneath the panic though, it had almost been reassuring. After all, if she needed him there was less chance of her walking away from him. He realized now Jeffrey was right and that was what held him back from dating properly – he didn't want to face being stood up like that again.

While he waited for her to call, he walked aimlessly down the street, away from the party and tried to remember how shitty he'd felt when Rosaline didn't turn up to the church that day. It was hazy, a memory he rarely revisited, but he remembered waiting at the pew as time ticked on, listening to all those hushed whispers from friends, family and whoever else his parents had invited. Some had looked at him with pity, others with a gleam in their eyes knowing this was the best gossip they'd had all year. It had made him wish for a hole to open beneath his feet and swallow him up.

The kicker was, deep down, part of him had known she wouldn't show. She'd been distant for weeks and honestly, if it hadn't been for his mother giving him his nan's engagement ring and convincing him of what great idea it would be to marry his best friend, he wouldn't have thought to ever ask her. That's all they'd been growing up, even into their teens and sure, they'd snogged and experimented with each other, and had even been referred to as a couple at school.

But it wasn't his heart that had felt the pain that day she left him. It had been his pride.

He had been devastated, but now he looked back, he could see that it spawned from being betrayed by his best friend rather than heartbreak.

Of course, he still remembered the humiliation of being jilted and probably would forever. But if Natalie was happy just being with him, he wanted her to stay. He frowned when he realized that if she left, he'd be right back where he was ten years ago, except this time it wouldn't be his pride that took the hit.

It was mind-boggling that a girl he met a mere two weeks ago had the potential to hurt him more than Rosaline had.

But he couldn't think about that now. Nat was at home, maybe alone and who knows what that bastard had said to her. Dean checked his phone again, but there was nothing. He hailed down a taxi, having made up his mind to go see her, but his phone buzzed before he got her address out.

To: Dean Fletcher
From: Nat Taylor
Subject: Re: rain check
  I'll call you tomorrow. I need to be alone tonight.
  X

Dean frowned at the phone for a second, then gave the driver his own address. He felt worse than useless at the moment, but then he realized something. A plan began to form as he scrolled down to Jeffrey's number and hit call.

'What's wrong?' Jeffrey asked, his tone wary.

Dean sighed. Like the only reason he'd call his brother on a Saturday would be because something bad had happened. Though he supposed it had.

'Nothing, I just need a favour.'

144

Jeffrey laughed. '*Another* one? You owe me for so many last night, you'll be paying me back all of next year.'

Dean rolled his eyes. 'Put it on my tab. Listen,' He explained what he needed from Jeffrey and for once his brother stayed quiet, even when he'd stopped talking. 'So, will you help me?'

Finally, Jeffrey said, 'This is more serious than I thought. Dean, you barely know her. Why are you going to all this trouble?'

Frowning, he realized his brother might be right again – about the serious part anyway. But he did know Natalie. He knew she was smart and witty and strong. And as for the reason ... he cared about her a lot more than he'd let himself care about any other woman, and he had to try to help her now.

Choosing to ignore what his brother said, he asked, 'Jeffrey, will you help or not?'

A sigh sounded in his ear. 'Yeah, of course.'

'Thanks.' He ended the call before Jeffrey could grill him. He wasn't keen on examining the reason he was doing this right not. And he had other things to worry about. Natalie might go ballistic when she found out what they were up to.

***

Natalie waited for Dean at the bridal shop, picking at a cream cheese bagel and sipping coffee. She was surrounded by white lace, silk and chiffon so understood why the shop attendant was glaring at her from behind the till.

Maybe coffee was a bad idea with all the wedding dresses in various shades of white stacked around the shop. It wasn't like she could afford to pay if she ruined them. The thought made her mood plummet again.

She'd spent the night crunching numbers. She couldn't afford to live off what she'd make from Tech Solutions – she'd typed enough of their invoices to know exactly what they paid Mick. Not without taking on new business too. And if her ex-boss meant what he said about blackening her name, then she'd never get any new clients.

It was too risky, and she'd been up half the night wondering what her next move would be. Maybe Mick was right, maybe stacking shelves was all she could do. After all, you didn't need qualifications for that …

She shook off that train of thought, not about to let his callous insults affect her. Qualifications were not as important as instinct when it came to planning events, and Mick didn't have much of that. He was an overqualified scumbag with a business degree that had nothing to do with what his company did.

Just then, she spied Dean through the shop's glass door, and her worries seemed to fade to the background. She didn't think he'd offer to come with her when she'd called this morning, after all she figured he'd had enough of weddings to last him a lifetime. But here he was with his sexy casual attire making her mouth water and her pulse quicken.

His dimples winked as he smiled at her, but the shop attendant was on him as soon as he got through the door. 'Hi, I'm Louise. Can I help you with anything?'

With her gaga eyes and suggestive tone, it sounded like Louise's offer would cover more than her job description. Just like last night, her temper simmered. Couldn't pretty women just leave him be? Didn't they realize he was taken?

'I'm here with Natalie.'

She repressed a smug grin when he strolled by the woman and bent down so he could kiss her.

'Are you okay?' he asked.

It was probably petty of her to twine her fingers through his hair and pull him back for a kiss that was a little too hot for a bridal shop on a Sunday morning, but the irritation from the shop assistant's blatant drooling made it hard to resist.

When she released him, she whispered, 'I am now.'

She stood, taking his hand in hers and smiled sweetly at Louise.

'I'm ready for the fitting when you are.'

Dean lifted an eyebrow as he looked down at her, squeezing her hand in question. She just shrugged, feeling a bit pathetic at her possessive reaction to yet *another* woman flirting with him.

Louise grabbed a garment bag and led them to fitting rooms at the back of the store. Dean leaned close, and whispered 'Ever done it in a fitting room?'

Her face flushed, and she felt a warmth spread all the way through her lower stomach. But nothing would be happening here. Louise was with them and would stay to see if adjustments were needed. After her little jealousy-fuelled stunt, she just hoped the woman didn't take in the dress so much that she couldn't breathe in it.

'Behave,' she whispered back, and he chuckled.

Louise opened one of the red velvet curtains and hung the garment bag on one of the hooks.

'Is this the kind of dress you have to wear commando?' he asked.

The husk in his voice made her bones feel gooey. 'I can always make an exception.'

His eyes darkened and she bit her lip. Lust crashed into her like a wrecking ball. 'Did you only come here to drive me wild? Because it's working.'

Louise cleared her throat, snapping Natalie's attention away from him. 'We close at noon today, so if you don't mind?'

Yup, she'd pissed off Louise. 'Sorry.'

Natalie went into the cubicle, then tugged the curtain. Before it closed she saw Dean's wink. It was a little erotic stripping down to her undies, knowing he was on the other side of the fabric.

That was, of course, until Louise started to speak.

'Is that logo on your tee-shirt the new Tech Systems game? My little brother has been dying to get his hands on it.'

Natalie unzipped the bag, gritting her teeth against the purr in Louise's tone.

'Yeah, Zone Craft. I designed it. We launch next month.'

She frowned, unhooking the dress from the hanger. She had no idea he designed computer games too. What else didn't she know about him?

'That's amazing,' Louise gushed. Natalie could imagine the her twirling her dark curls around her perfectly manicured fingers and fluttering her long eyelashes. 'I can't wait to give it a go. I'm pretty good at … most games.'

The way she hesitated suggestively made Natalie's blood boil. She unzipped the dress, then pulled it over her head. It stuck at her underarms, and frustration did not help when she tried to wriggle free.

'Really? You don't seem the type,' he said.

Was he flirting with her? Natalie struggled to tug the bust over her chest, gritting her teeth and emptying her lungs, hoping that would help.

'Yeah. In fact, it's my brother's birthday in January and you've just given me a fab idea. Would you mind giving us a go before it releases? It would make me the best big sister ever.'

Natalie froze, half twisted at the waist to reach the zipper. The nerve! She was right here! Dean was clearly taken and now the cow was asking him for a date?

'Um, I think we could arrange that,' he said, and the urge to strike him in the crotch flared again.

'Here's my card. Call me.'

Natalie yanked up the zip and then opened the curtains. The ice pink chiffon dress skimmed along the floor as she stormed out. Dean was just pocketing the card and she scowled at him. Some boyfriend.

He only looked confused as he took in her expression, like he was surprised that arranging a date with another woman in front of her was something worthy of such a reaction.

'That looks almost perfect. The bride has a good eye,' Louise said, circling her with a cheery expression.

Natalie fisted her hands until the urge to tug Louise's curls out by the roots subsided.

'Maybe just a little tight across the chest and hips. We can take it out a few millimetres. These gowns usually have a few spare inches in case anyone puts on weight before the big day.'

Her face burned, but from mortification this time. She wished she'd never let Dean come. But then at least now she knew what he was capable of. Natalie welcomed her temper, because she couldn't face hurt right now.

'It looks perfect to me,' Dean said, his gaze raking over her.

Her hand twitched with the desire to slap him. How dare he look at her like he wanted to devour her when he had Miss Home Wrecker's phone number in his pocket.

He stepped towards her but she shot him a *don't you dare* look and turned back to the dressing room. To Louise, she said, 'It'll be fine. I'll just try not to gain any more weight before the big day.'

The bitch smirked.

Getting out of the dress wasn't easier than getting into it and she made a vow to cut back on the cheese and steak and deserts and champagne and the million different things she'd eaten at Dean's country manor. No wonder the dress was tight. She'd done nothing but gorge all weekend.

And not to forget the bucket of ice cream she'd made a dent in last night after she'd been sacked and chucked out of the party.

She dressed in record time, refusing to give the Miss Game anymore time to flirt, but when she opened the curtain it was just Dean there. Louise was distracted with another customer.

'Fancy some lunch? I'm starved,' he said.

Natalie just gritted her teeth.

His brow puckered. 'What's with the death stare?'

'I know you've been out of the game for a while but FYI, you don't arrange dates with other women when you're out with your girlfriend. In fact, make that ex-girlfriend.'

Ignoring his shocked expression, she stormed past him, picked her bag off the table and despite her best intentions, lifted the remainder of her bagel. She didn't even acknowledge Louise on the way out the shop, or ask if there was anything else she needed to do. Rose would deal with that.

'Wait, Nat.'

She ignored him and upped the pace until the next corner, then rounded it. The icy breeze nipped her eyes until they watered. It had nothing to do with what had happened at the shop. Weaving her way through the Sunday shoppers milling through the streets didn't distract her from the fact that, now her temper had ebbed a little, the pain was creeping up on her.

'Will you just stop? Please.'

He was close behind her and she picked up her pace. But strong hands gripped her shoulders and spun her round so fast she had to grab onto his arms to keep her balance.

'I wasn't arranging a date.' His eyes narrowed. 'I agreed to do her a favour for her brother's birthday, that's all. How could you think I would do something like that?'

'For someone so smart, you can be a complete idiot.' She didn't mean to lash out, but being angry was much better than showing him how hurt she really was.

His eyebrows lifted and he laughed, spurring on her anger. 'Are you jealous?'

'Of course not!' His *oh really* look irked her. 'As far as I'm concerned you can sleep with whoever you want.'

She tried to turn away again, but he grabbed her round the waist, pulling her flush against his body. She almost melted at the proximity, at the clean and somehow spicy smell on his neck, the heat of him seeping through her clothes and melting her bones.

His eyes flared with anger.

'Do you really mean that?' he asked, his voice hard.

NO! But she couldn't get past the way he'd been so chatty with a woman who'd been all over him. It wasn't as severe as last night, but at least then he'd told the floozy he wasn't interested, that he was taken. He hadn't said a word to *Louise* and a lump swelled in her throat when she realized it was maybe because he'd been attracted to her.

Still, pride wouldn't let her admit any of that. She shrugged.

With his eyes blazing, he released her. Clenching his jaw he pulled both his phone and her card out of his pocket. 'If that's how it is.'

He read the numbers from the card and pressed them into his phone one at a time. Natalie's breath cut off halfway to her lungs and her eyes filled with moisture as she stared at him in horror.

His thumb hovered over the call button and he looked at her. 'You really don't care?'

Chapter 13

Natalie closed her eyes, trying to free herself from his intense gaze but it was the wrong thing to do. The moisture spilled onto her cheeks and poured down her face. She was in his arms again, being pulled to his chest and as she took a breath to try to calm herself it hitched in her lungs.

'Don't cry. Shit, I'm sorry. I was just calling your bluff.'

She struggled, trying to push away from him but he held her securely. 'Leave me alone, Dean.'

He released her at once. 'You're blowing this out of proportion. I wasn't flirting with her. It's you I want to be with.'

Her cheeks flushed, but from embarrassment this time. Maybe she was overreacting. The jealousy, the petty way she'd gotten possessive was not like her at all. Wiping her eyes on the sleeve of her coat, she wondered if the whole being sacked thing was the reason she was acting like a lunatic.

'You're right, I was jealous. I'm sorry.'

He didn't look at her like she was some kind of deranged bunny boiler – and after the way she'd acted, he was well within his rights. He was looking at her like he was ... pleased. That just confused her all the more.

Dean handed her the card. 'Here. I won't need this.' He then made a show of deleting the digits from his mobile.

She breathed a sigh of relief. 'I don't know what came over me.'

Still, she put the card in her pocket.

Dean shrugged. 'I'd feel the same if it was you getting chatted up. Except I probably would have punched the guy.'

Natalie smiled a little. 'My hand was twitching.'

He laughed. 'Come on. Let's get some lunch. Your bagel is bound to be freezing.'

He held out his hand and she took it.

***

To overshadow her mortification for acting like a crazy girlfriend, Natalie made a point of getting to know Dean better over lunch. He told her he'd been creating computer games most of his life, but when he and his brother started Tech Solutions, they'd played it safe by sticking with systems and software. Now they were established and had enough capital behind them, that if it all went tits up with the gaming side (his words, not hers) they wouldn't struggle to make a living. She understood the need for having back-up cash, which only made her worries creep to the forefront of her mind.

He noticed her picking at the salad and sighed. 'There was nothing wrong with the dress. You looked stunning, really.'

She forced a smile. 'I'm not worried about that.'

Well she hadn't been, until he brought it up.

'Your job?' She nodded. 'I'll take you tomorrow to clear your desk. You can even move your stuff to Tech Solutions. We were thinking about having a launch party for the game. Do you think you could pull something together in a month?'

Natalie frowned. 'You don't need to fabricate an event to make me feel better.'

He put down his cutlery, after having munched his way through an enormous plate of pasta. She envied him. It looked and smelled mouth-watering. 'I'm not orchestrating an event to keep you in work. This is important to me. Programming games is my dream. I want the launch to be perfect and, seeing what you can do, I know you're right for the job.'

Natalie wasn't used to being complimented on her work and his praise made her feel giddy. Wanted even. But also ashamed at the way she'd behaved earlier. To make up for it, she'd go all out for this function. She'd give him the best launch party ever. And since she had no other job or commitment, she could give it a hundred percent.

'A month is plenty of time. I'm going to need to speak to you both, go over budgets, venues and guest lists.' It was easy to fall into the planning, except now she could cut out Mick who did no more than convey the information to her. She had even given him a list of questions to take to prospective clients. 'Then I can flesh out a few ideas, see what you prefer. And provisionally book a venue. Is there anywhere you would prefer?'

His smile was indulgent and his eyes glowed. It was like he was just happy to see her happy and she was lost for a minute in the swell of emotions pulsing through her.

'We can have a sit down with Jeffrey this week but I'm happy for you to take the lead on this.' He reached across the table for her hand. 'I trust you.'

The fact he was placing this in her hands was a little intimidating, but she couldn't help but feel flattered. 'It'll be the best launch anyone's ever had.'

'Do you want to come back to mine? There's something I'd like to show you.'

Natalie could guess, but his tone wasn't hinting at anything sexual. His eyes did though, and they made her heart pound. She was about to say yes, then remembered Rose was bringing the flowers back to the flat so they could arrange the bouquets and then taking over the kitchen to practice her wedding cake. Natalie had volunteered to be the taste tester. Now, after the fitting, she wished she hadn't.

'I'd love to, but I have to help with wedding stuff.' She chuckled. 'I'm glad she's spending most of her time at her fiancé's because I haven't been a very involved bridesmaid so far.'

Dean grinned. 'Can't say I envy you. Do you want a lift home?'

'If you don't mind. Thanks.'

Despite her protests, he paid the bill. It irked her that he had to, that she couldn't really afford to pay half now she was jobless. But she took solace in the fact that by the end of January, she'd have her first invoice paid. And since Dean was letting her borrow an office, the only overheads she'd have would be her rent and bills at the flat. Rent and bills which were going to double after the wedding but she wasn't about to tell him that. He didn't need all her worries dumped on him, and she suspected he'd find a way to help her pay if she told him. But she was determined to do it herself.

Hand in hand, he led her back to his car and asked a little about the wedding. She didn't want to get into it too much, knowing it must dredge up awful memories for him. He didn't seem fazed or even upset, and she had to wonder if getting jilted was something you could get over, even after all those years. Natalie couldn't imagine she would if he left her at the altar. Not that it would ever happen. Dean had made himself very clear that marriage wasn't on the cards.

He stopped them next to a sleek, charcoal McLaren Spider, and she only knew what it was because Tom was forever showing them pictures and saying when he'd made his first million, he'd buy one.

Dean held the door open, but she couldn't bring herself to climb in. She'd known he did well for himself, even knew his family had money, but somehow this made it all too real.

'I don't drive like a maniac, Nat. Don't worry.'

She just stared at him. They both lived such different lives. He had expensive toys and a company that made stupid amounts of money. He was also kind, generous and sexy as hell. Not to mention the fact he was going out of his way to look after her.

And what did she bring to the table? Petty jealousy at every woman who drooled over him. Guilt issues with Christmas. A temper to rival a bratty two-year-old.

His expression changed, the humour morphed to worry. 'Are you okay?'

'I don't know why you're with me. You could have anyone you wanted.' She hadn't meant to blurt out her insecurities, but she couldn't take it back now. She hung her head, feeling very inferior.

Dean took her face in both his hands and his warmth seeped through her skin, barely touching on the icy despair. He tilted her face up so he could see her eyes.

'I thought we'd established you're who I want?' He didn't sound annoyed though, his tone was reassuring.

And she hated that she was so insecure around him. Why was that? It seemed the more time she spent with him, the worse it got. 'I don't understand why. I'm a jobless bum with enough issues to sink a cruise ship.'

Well, it was out. In about four seconds he'd run for the hills. And how could she blame him? She was far too wrapped up in him. It wasn't healthy, or normal. Not that she'd know. He was her first proper boyfriend. She hoped Rose wasn't all Incredible Bride today because she was going to need a girly night.

His thumbs stroked her cheeks and his eyes softened. 'Natalie, I was done for the first time I saw you. You're beautiful, smart, funny, and all that makes you sexy as hell. How could I not want you?'

She remembered the first time she saw him. Later he'd been with the redhead. It didn't help make her feel better.

He must have noticed her expression, because he released her face and pulled her closer, gripping her waist with his hands. 'I didn't sleep with the girl at Mode. She was a distraction. I wanted you but you were dancing with someone else.' He frowned. 'And then you kissed him.'

Natalie smiled a little. She was glad she wasn't the only one who got jealous. 'But she looked flushed when she staggered out of the bathroom.'

For the first time, she saw his tanned skin turn pink at his cheeks. 'We didn't have sex. I told her I didn't have protection. I did, but it wasn't her I wanted. I felt shitty for leading her on so—'

'I really don't want to hear it,' she interrupted, trying very hard not to imagine what he did to make it up to the girl.

Dean grinned. 'So, we good?'

She *did* feel a little better now he'd explained things to her, but wasn't comfortable with the vast difference in wealth between them. Still, she didn't want to let him go either. And not because of his bank balance. Nope, if it had just been about that, she wouldn't be half as worried about their future.

Instead of answering she pushed up on her tiptoes and kissed him, wrapping her arms round his neck. He held her closer, so she could feel every inch of his body against her and the heat and lust swirled up like it always did with him, taking her breath away.

He broke the kiss first. His breathing was as laboured as hers. 'I better get you home before we're arrested for indecent exposure in a public car park.'

She chuckled. 'It would be worth it.'

Groaning, he pulled her closer for a second. 'Don't tempt me. I have almost no control when it comes to you.'

'Tomorrow night,' she promised, kissing him chastely on the lips.

Tomorrow couldn't come soon enough.

'Not sure if I'll last that long. Then again if you move into the office tomorrow ...' he trailed off, lifting an eyebrow suggestively.

'Hmm.' She ran a finger down his chest, trying hard not to

157

smile. 'At this rate, I'll never get any work done.'

'Well, if you leave your knickers at home again, it will save time ...'

Natalie laughed, playfully slapping him on the chest. '*Behave*. If you do, I might make it worth your while after work.'

Dean opened the car door for her again. 'Get in, before I take you back to mine, tie you to my bed and keep you there for a month.'

Smiling, she slid into the low seat of his McLaren, feeling a little more comfortable knowing her lunatic behaviour today hadn't made him run for the hills.

***

Rose was in full scale Bridezilla mode. She was getting worse the closer the wedding got. Natalie had only finished with one bouquet by the time Rose had four tiers for the cake in the oven and she was currently whipping up batch number two.

No doubt she'd tried a hundred variations of the cake recipe over the last week.

Natalie rose from the kitchen table and cleared away the excess stems and leaves before she brought through the rest of the flowers. 'Can I ask you something about relationships?'

'Of course.' Rose picked up the huge mixing bowl, held it against her hip, turned to face Natalie and started beating like a maniac. 'Is this about the new guy?'

'Mmm.' Her face heated a little, remembering her overwhelming insecurity at the shop. 'He came with me to the fitting, and you should have seen the attendant at the shop flirting with him. She managed to wangle a date in the guise of getting him to give her and her brother an advanced play of a game his company is releasing. Anyway, he took her number and I totally flipped out.'

Rose frowned in confusion.

158

'I stormed out, telling him he was my ex. I swear Rose, I've never felt so jealous. He was only being polite and I went bananas. Then after I calmed down and we'd had lunch, I was overwhelmingly insecure to the point I asked him why he was with me. It was all lethal attraction.'

Her friend laughed.

'It can feel like that when you're crazy about someone and scared you're going to lose them. Nat, you've lost the two people you loved most in the world. It's only natural you're going to find it hard to trust him, or trust it will last. Tom was the same, in a way. Except he's a lot calmer than you. I can just imagine you giving that poor boy hell in the shop.' She snickered.

Natalie pouted. 'The street, actually. That's probably worse.'

Hmm, she'd never thought her insecurities would stem from the loss of others she loved. It made sense in a way, but she didn't want to be the kind of girl who needed constant reassurance about her relationship from her man. She knew what, if any, kind of future she'd have with Dean – he'd been straight about it with her. There was no way she was going to chase him off just because she was a nervous wreck about how he felt.

'Remember it's all still new. Take it slow. And this isn't exactly the easiest month for you.' Rose stopped frantically whipping to squeeze Natalie's shoulder.

'I know, and now I don't have a job, it's even more insane.'

Rose's chin dropped. 'You quit?'

'No, I was sacked.' She told Rose the story about getting caught last night, admitting ruefully that Tom had been right. 'So I'm going to clear up my desk tomorrow then start working on an event for Dean's company.'

It might have been her imagination, but she thought Rose's face paled for a second, but her friend shook her head, and the colour returned to her cheeks. 'So you're going to work for him?'

She tried to understand why her news would bring out that kind of reaction in her friend, then decided she didn't really need another reason to say no to Dean's offer. It was her only option unless she wanted to live out of a cardboard box. 'Not exactly. I'm the new events coordinator for Tech Solutions and they're loaning me an office until I get on my feet. There's a launch party they want me to work on for the release of the computer game next month, so it will be handy to be close, in case I have questions.'

'Wow, that's really nice of him. Honestly Natalie, I don't think anybody who wasn't into you would offer you a place to start up your business. It sounds like he's crazy about you too. You shouldn't worry so much.' Rose's smile managed to comfort and reassure her almost as much as her words did. 'Where did you say you met him?'

Heat scored her cheeks. She focused on trimming the stems of the white roses so Rose wouldn't see her face. 'We crashed a few of the same parties, and it was like an enemies-to-lovers type of thing.'

Rose grinned. 'Very romantic.'

Natalie wrinkled her nose. 'Not really. I told a girl he was chatting up that he'd slept with half the office and had given them crabs. She screamed at him and slapped him in front of everyone. I'm surprised he gave me the time of day.'

Her best friend burst into laughter, having to put the bowl down on the sideboard before cake mix number two decorated the floor. Natalie joined in.

After a second, Rose said, 'Thanks, Nat. I needed that. Everything's been so stressful lately. I can't wait to meet him on Wednesday. You're bringing him to the wedding, too?'

She wanted to ask him, but wasn't sure how he'd take it. Had he ever been at a wedding before other than his own? She didn't know, and didn't want to cause him pain by bringing it up.

'Come on, ask him. We have room for one more,' Rose urged.

'I will, tomorrow. He's taking me to clear my desk and giving me a lift to his office.'

Rose's eyes softened. 'I really don't think you have anything to be insecure about. He's going out of his way for you, Nat.'

Warmth filled her heart in a rush of emotion. 'I think so too.'

***

Dean pulled up in front of Natalie's flat, then tugged at the knot in his tie. He really hated wearing suits, but he couldn't roll up at her office to lay down the law dressed like a teenager – so Jeffrey had told him.

'Get in the back,' he ordered his brother.

Jeffrey cocked an eyebrow. 'Are you having a laugh? What happened to "bros before hos"?'

Dean gritted his teeth. 'Call Natalie a "ho" again and you'll be walking back to the office.'

His brother rolled his eyes. 'Keep your lacy knickers on. It's just a saying.'

He glared.

'Okay, okay!' Jeffrey got out of the car, then slipped in the back behind the passenger seat. 'Never thought I'd see the day you'd get obsessive over a girl.'

'Can it, Jeff.'

He probably should feel bad for snapping at Jeffrey, after all the guy was doing him a favour. But his stomach was in knots. He hadn't broached the subject of what he was planning to do today with Natalie yet. After she'd freaked at him for taking Louise's number, he didn't want to push her too far. She had enough to deal with, losing her job this close to Christmas. That was enough to upset anyone. And he really shouldn't have taken that girl's number, even if he didn't find her attractive at all.

Natalie came out of her flat with a cardboard box that had the name of a brand of flour on the side. Where would she have gotten that? Before he could ask, she climbed in the car and smiled at them both, though her eyes widened a little when she

161

spotted Jeffrey.

Shit. Confession time.

'Morning,' she said, shooting him a quick, questioning glance.

'Good morning, Natalie. Ready for the big move?' Jeffrey asked.

'Yes. It's a bit scary though.'

'I can imagine. Can't be easy going from having a steady income to starting a business with only one client,' Jeffrey went on.

Dean regretted asking his brother to shift. It would be nice if he was in jabbing distance. He pulled out onto the road and thought now was as good a time as any to come clean. 'So, Jeffrey has a meeting with Mick this morning. It shouldn't take long.'

'Why?' Her voice was a whisper as she looked anxiously at him, then Jeffrey.

Jeffrey answered, ignoring Dean's warning glance at him in the mirror. 'He can't just sack you. It's against the law. You could have him for unfair dismissal. Dean didn't think you'd want the headache of taking your boss to a tribunal though. And since what you did was in breach of your contract, there are no guarantees you'd get a huge pay-off. But if you could manage to get a Settlement Agreement, he'd have to give you some remuneration and wouldn't be able to discuss you with any future employers or clients in a negative way.'

Her eyes widened, but she said nothing.

Dean squeezed her knee, just below the hem of her pinstripe skirt. 'Jeffrey looks after HR at our company too. It's not fair for you to be kicked out after all you've done, Nat. Not without getting something in return.'

'But I broke the rules. He was right to sack me.' She drew in a huge breath. 'You're not going to do anything ... harsh, are you?'

As Dean was all for leaving Mick black and blue, he looked at Jeffrey in the mirror meaningfully, knowing his brother's answer would be more reassuring.

This time Jeffrey took the hint. 'Of course not. Dean's going to help you clear up, and I'm going to be your acting lawyer.'

Her cheeks flushed pink. 'Thank you, that's a lovely offer, but I don't want you to go to any trouble over me.'

'It's not any trouble,' Dean said, squeezing her knee again. She took his hand in both of hers and he could feel her gaze on him. 'Natalie, you told me he was going to bad mouth you so you'd never get a job again. If Jeffrey can convince him that signing a Settlement Agreement would be cheaper than hiring lawyers and dragging this to a tribunal, then you won't have to worry about it. And you can keep looking for work if you want while you're starting out. If he signs, he won't be able to say a bad thing about you, or why you came to this arrangement.'

'Here.' Jeffrey handed her a document and she released his hand.

She was quiet for so long, he worried he'd really offended her. Then she gasped. 'I'm glad I'll not be there to hear what he says when he sees this figure. It's more than I make in a year. Seriously guys, I appreciate the thought, but Mick can be scary.'

Dean frowned, pulling into a space near her building. That figure was at the lower end of the pay scale for her job from what they'd been able to find online.

Jeffrey took the agreement back, then slipped it in his briefcase. 'I'm not scared of anyone, even Dean. Though he'd like to think otherwise.'

She rolled her eyes, then smiled. 'Thank you. And whatever he says, I really appreciate you both doing this.'

***

Her stomach fluttered as she packed the paltry possessions she'd accumulated over the years into one lowly cardboard box she'd borrowed from Rose's bakery. Hankies, lip gloss, a few tangerines, some mascara, her highlighters, coloured pencils, a drawer full of multi-coloured post-its, and she was done. Dean didn't do much, except watch her with a worried expression.

She was not going to cry. After all, she hated working for Mick. He'd underpaid and undervalued her for years. All she got was overworked and ridiculed. So why did she want to burst into tears?

'Are you mad at me, for asking Jeffrey to speak with your boss?' he asked.

She turned to him. He was leaning on her desk, watching her warily.

'No. I'm … it's a lovely gesture. I don't think Jeffrey will get far with him though. But I really, really appreciate you both trying.' She'd been gobsmacked when they'd told her what they were going to do. And it had made her feel closer to him, and his brother. She felt like she'd seen what being part of Dean's family would be like, how they'd both look after her. Like they probably looked after Alana.

They didn't have perfect parents, but they had each other. And she'd wanted to be included. Then she'd remembered Dean wouldn't ever marry her, so she'd never be part of the family. Not really. Was that why there was a lump in her throat?

He took her hands, then pulled her against him. Natalie gasped.

'Ever done it in your office?' he asked with a wicked grin.

Her pulse pounded and her breath caught in her throat. 'We can't! What if Mick walks in? Or your brother. Or anyone else!'

'Dean, please,' she sighed.

He leant down and chuckled at her collarbone, sending shivers through her. 'Is that a *please stop*, or *please more*?'

His tongue invaded her mouth and her wits scrambled immediately to the point she only had instinct and need.

'Holy fuck, will you two give it a rest for an hour.'

Jeffrey's voice sliced through the passion and she pulled away, slamming her head against the cheap hardboard desk.

Dean tilted his head to glare at his brother. 'Never heard of knocking?'

Natalie's face burned so hot she bet it was scarlet..

'I didn't think I'd have to worry about that here! Get into Mick's office. He's agreed to sign, so I need Natalie to sign it too. We'll both witness.' Jeffrey closed the door behind him with too much force.

The shock of his words sunk through the lusty fog in her brain.

'He's agreeing?' she gasped.

Dean's grin made her heart stutter. 'Told you Jeffrey was relentless. Speaking of, we better take a rain check here. He'll be back if we're not there in sixty seconds.'

After some readjusting on both parts, they headed to Mick's office. Her stomach flipped with nerves, and her hormones were screaming for release – probably not the best combination for seeing her ex-boss for the last time.

At the door, Dean lifted her hand and brushed her knuckles with his lips. In a voice she could only hear, he asked, 'Are you ready?'

If he wasn't here today, she'd have been a mess. She'd even ducked the intern manning the reception desk. But now, with her hand in his, she'd happily strut past on the way out with a wave and a smile. She felt like she could face anything with him.

Natalie nodded.

He opened the door and led her in. Mick narrowed his eyes and glared at first Dean then her as they took the spare chairs next to Jeffrey.

'Natalie, you just have to sign here and here on both copies.' Jeffrey pointed to the spaces below Mick's signature on each page. 'Then this renunciation to say you're waiving your right to legal advice.'

He sounded so calm, it relaxed her, and she took the pen he offered.

She froze as Mick leaned forward. 'So, are you sleeping with them both to get them to help you? If it were up to me you'd be out on your arse with nothing.'

The blood drained from her face as she took in his menacing expression. Where was her temper to save her now?

Dean's fist clenched at his side, distracting her and she looked up to see he was glaring at Mick with the most livid expression she'd ever seen. And she thought he'd been teasing when he'd told her he'd wanted to punch her boss. Ex-boss now.

Jeffrey must have seen Dean's expression too, because he jumped in first. 'Mick, Natalie hasn't signed. We can still tear this up and have this argument in court. It's up to you.'

Mick gritted his teeth, but leaned back in his chair and folded his arms in front of his chest. 'Fine. Let's do this.'

Natalie wondered briefly if this could be construed as blackmail. Still, the fact that she could escape today with enough capital to see her through for a while, *with* a written agreement preventing her boss from badmouthing her was too tempting. She signed quickly, then Dean took the pen and acted as her witness.

Jeffrey completed the documents and Dean held her hand again. When he was done, he handed a copy to Mick. 'When will the funds be in Natalie's account?'

'It'll go through with her final salary payment on Friday,' Mick said reluctantly.

She blinked. So soon? Wow.

'Nice doing business with you again, Mick.' Jeffrey stood, then leaned over to shake Mick's hand.

Mick grunted.

They left with a copy of the agreement, and scooted into the lift. Natalie couldn't believe what had happened. She was tongue-tied and couldn't find words to express her gratitude. In the end, all she could do was fling her arms round Jeffrey, then Dean, whispering 'thank you' to them both. It wasn't nearly enough.

***

The morning flew by in a whirlwind of IT people setting up her PC, Dean explaining how their system worked and showing her around the building, but now she was left alone in an office bigger than the whole of Mick's, with a corner sofa complete with coffee table and coffee machine on one side, and empty filing cabinets on the other. And her desk was actual mahogany, not hardboard. Her swivel chair was like a throne compared to the nonadjustable one she'd used for years, with soft black leather so padded she felt like she was sitting on clouds.

She'd promised to call Rose when she was settled, but it was now lunchtime and Rose's little bakery would be swarming with customers. Natalie wasn't hungry enough for lunch, she'd not managed to eat all day, she'd been so nervous about the move.

A knock sounded at her door. It was unexpected, especially since people usually just walked in to her old office. 'Come in.'

Jeffrey did wearing a grin that matched his brother's. He even had the same indents on his cheeks and she felt at ease immediately. 'How are you settling in?'

'Great, thank you. And thanks again for this morning. I didn't think Mick would entertain a Settlement Agreement.'

She could thank him a thousand times and it still wouldn't be enough. She owed them too much. Then inspiration hit her. 'You usually deal with the events, don't you?'

He sat on the chair across from her desk and nodded once.

'Can we go over a few ideas for the launch? I want to make this a party you'll both never forget. And of course, this one's on the house.' It was the least she could do.

Jeffrey's expression was carefully blank. 'Do you want to do a good job because you feel you owe us?'

Despite the central heating that had made her flush when she'd moved in with her paltry belongings, she shivered. The warmth had disappeared from Jeffrey's voice and there was a hint of worry beneath his cool gaze. She realized he was concerned for his brother.

Natalie shook her head. 'I know how much this launch means to Dean. Releasing this game is his dream, isn't it? I mean, the rest of the business was just playing it smart. But this is what he's always wanted to do. I want to make it special for him.'

A whisper of a smile curved the edges of Jeffrey's lips, but then it disappeared. 'He'll probably kick my arse for saying this, but I need to make sure we're clear about something. Dean's been buggered over enough. He's reminded of that every time we're with our parents. I don't want you leading him on if you're not serious about him, because it's clear he's really fucking serious about you.'

His tone and insinuated accusations should have been enough to set off her temper and put her on the defensive, but instead she thrilled with pleasure. Not for Dean's pain, obviously not that. But that he was serious about her.

And she wanted his brother to know there was no going back for her now. That she wanted to be part of their family, and not just because she no longer had one. She wanted to be in this for keeps, even if Dean could never offer her more than what they had.

'I'm really serious about him too,' she admitted, her voice breaking with the depth of her emotion. 'Even if we can't be more than just a couple.'

Jeffrey's eyebrows pulled together. Frick, she shouldn't have said the last bit. It really wasn't any of his business.

'Why not?' he demanded.

Natalie glanced down at her hands, watching her fingers fiddle with the hem of her skirt. 'I shouldn't have said that last bit.'

'Why? Are you just using him to get your business off the ground? Is that it?' His voice was cold, threatening.

Her temper flared. 'Of course not! I didn't ask for anyone's help! I'm grateful for it, but I can get by on my own. I was referring to the fact Dean made it perfectly clear we couldn't have what you and Alana have. We'd never live together, get married, none of it. I know all that and I'm accepting it because I want to be with him however I can. So if you're finished insulting me, I need to work on your brother's launch.'

Jeffrey surprised her by bursting into a fit of laughter. She had to bite her lip and dig her nails into her palms to keep from screaming at him to get out. It was his building after all, and his company's resources she was using. And she probably shouldn't be giving away so much about her relationship to Dean's brother.

When the laughing ebbed, he said, 'Sorry. I'm not laughing *at* you, really. I now know why he's with you.'

'What, because I can't keep my temper in check?' she asked through her teeth.

He chuckled. 'No, because you're a ball buster and he needs that. Give him time, Natalie. You've only known each other a few weeks. The whole relationship thing is new to him. Even with his ex, he just sort of fell into the whole marriage thing. With a few shoves in the right direction by our parents. Or the wrong direction, depending on which way you look at it.'

She blew out a breath, and her ire seemed to escape with it. 'I thought she was his first love.'

Jeffrey's lips twisted to the side, like he was trying hard to remember something. 'So did I at the time. Now though? I think they loved each other as friends and getting involved just ruined everything.'

Natalie didn't know what to say to that. She'd assumed Dean had been heartbroken and scarred for life because of it and that's why he couldn't commit to any kind of future with anyone. Not that she was ready for marriage, or living together or anything more than what they had right now. That stuff came later, or so she thought. Well, at least a year, if she was going by Rose and Tom's relationship.

Anyway, Jeffrey couldn't know for sure how Dean had felt. If they really had been friends first, the split would have been a double betrayal. Getting hurt by your best friend and lover at the time it mattered the most, with your family, friends and whoever else his parents invited scrutinising his pain?

Natalie burned with rage. How could anyone have done that to Dean? He wasn't perfect, but he was the loveliest guy she'd known. She was just glad she'd probably never meet the girl, because right now she was in the mood to scratch her eyes out.

'He has told you about this? Shit, if he hasn't, pretend I said nothing,' Jeffrey said, his expression creasing with mock worry.

Reluctantly, her lips curved. 'You scared he'll kick your backside?'

'Like he could.' Jeffrey grinned a full megawatt Fletcher smile. 'I've never seen him get violent. Though he was close to it today in Mick's office. Can't say I blame him. Your old boss is a piece of work.'

'Thank you again for today. You really didn't have to do that.'

Jeffrey stood, then winked. 'You're under Fletcher protection now, you need to get used to it.'

Despite the fact she'd strived for self-sufficient independence, Natalie couldn't help the flood of joy that filled her chest. But she warily beat it down as far as she could. It was early days, everyone kept saying that. Although it didn't feel like only a few weeks since she'd met the brothers, or even Alana. More like months. And she was beginning to care about them all, not just Dean.

She rose to see Jeffrey out when her phone rang. 'Crap, how do I answer?'

It had a gazillion buttons, no receiver she could see, and was flashing a four-digit extension number.

Jeffrey quickly rounded the desk, and smiled. 'This is the easiest way.'

He hit a button that looked like a megaphone and nodded to her.

'Hello?' she said, feeling a bit stupid.

170

'How's my little thief settling in?' Dean asked, his voice thick with warmth.

She blushed at the quizzical look Jeffrey shot her.

'Er, good, thanks. How was your meeting?' She sat back down, expecting Jeffrey to leave but he just stood over her and raised a finger, pressing it to his lips. She frowned in confusion.

'Couldn't concentrate. Spent the whole two hours wondering if you'd left your knickers at home like I'd asked.'

Her whole face was on fire now. She'd bet she could cook bacon from raw to crispy in sixty seconds using her forehead alone.

Jeffrey covered his mouth to muffle a snicker.

She couldn't let this conversation get any more humiliating. 'Dean—'

'Natalie, get up here. Let's finish what we started this morning.'

Jeffrey had both hands over his mouth now and his shoulders were shaking with restrained laughter. If she'd thought her one-nighter with Stephen had been mortifying when she gave his flatmate a floor show, this was much, *much* worse.

'Dean, listen '

'Come on, Nat. If you knew what I was doing to myself under the desk—'

'You are one dirty bastard, brother.' Jeffrey interrupted, his face screwing up. 'My lunch is about to take a return trip.'

There was silence for a few minutes, then Dean snapped, 'What arc you doing there?'

'Making sure Natalie's settled in. Now I'm going to have to explain to her how we deal with sexual harassment claims in the workplace, you filthy S.O.B.'

She covered her scorching face with her hands, wishing a crack would form beneath her feet. Surely falling from up here on the tenth floor would end this humiliation?

'Funny, Jeff. Natalie, ignore him. Let's go for lunch?'

No, she wanted to die. Felt like the embarrassment would do

171

the job for her soon enough. But since that was only wishful thinking, she whispered, 'Yes.'

'I'll be down in a second.'

A dial tone sounded, indicating he'd hung up.

Jeffrey snickered again, this time louder and switched the phone off. 'Welcome to Tech Solutions, Natalie. I have a feeling you'll fit right in.'

Chapter 14

When she'd gotten over the embarrassment of Dean's sexy call in front of his brother, she'd been really disappointed that his afternoon was filled with conference calls and meetings – all centred around the launch of their new game.

Lunch was a short half hour at a café across the street where, after he'd gotten over his irritation with Jeffrey, he'd told her Zone Craft had been bought by Nintendo for release and though she loved the way his whole face lit up when he talked so excitedly about the game, she felt nervous.

Was she the best person to organise their launch? It sounded epic and important and obviously meant the world to him. Christmas party planning was where she shined. She could plan and organise and cater and go all out for people because she loved the season, and there was no guilt in organising a magical night for others.

She frittered the afternoon away, worrying she'd screw up his special day. It was 5pm before she knew it, which was when Dean entered her borrowed office. Guilt tightened her throat when she saw him, realising she'd wasted her time.

'Hey, can I show you something before I take you home? I wanted to show you on Saturday.'

'Okay,' she answered automatically.

He closed the door and her heart jumped into her throat. She didn't know if she could muster enthusiasm for sex just now. Not feeling as awful as she did.

'Can I borrow your chair?' he asked and she rose automatically. But he pulled her onto his knee, scooted them forward and reached for her mouse. His breath in her hair sent shivers through her and her libido stirred to life. Feeling his thick thigh between her legs made her forget about the guilt, and she twisted her neck to look at him.

Dean was focused on the PC. Clicking and typing away, but she couldn't drag her gaze from the dusting of stubble along his jaw, or the way his sensual lips pursed a little in concentration. She remembered what his lips could do. And his teeth. And his tongue.

He turned to face her suddenly, but there was no heat in his eyes. In fact, his expression was a cool mask. 'Obviously this is only a rough design, and it's not really my forte. But we can work on it together if you want.'

'What?' Couldn't he feel her about to combust with need?

But his eyes melted with heat and he smiled. Slowly, he turned her face away until she was forced to look at the computer screen.

'When I said *something* I wasn't using an innuendo,' he clarified.

Blinking, she cleared her vision then focused on the monitor. The light pink and cream panes on the screen were elegant, the pictures of parties she'd organised for Tech Solutions filled the page she was on with little quotes beneath each, praising her for her innovative work. Her eyes stung as he clicked tabs above, noting services, a booking and contact page.

'Dean …' Her voice trailed off, she didn't know what to say.

'I didn't get a domain name or anything. This is just something I threw together. Like I said, I'm not an expert in web design, but I thought it could get you started. I've tweaked our new booking system so it works on your mobile too. Once you pick a business name and input all the services and anything else you want to add, we can publish your site.'

She choked on a sob.

Dean pulled her round. His profile was blurry. 'Hey, what's wrong? Is this too much?'

Unable to speak, she shook her head, then threw her arms round his neck. She was overwhelmed with an emotion so strong it almost cut off her air supply. How could she have thought he didn't want her? He'd done so much for her. And she'd done nothing for him.

His arms wrapped round her and he kissed her hair. 'Please, Nat. Don't cry. I didn't mean to upset you.'

Oh, her tears had pooled over and soaked his collar. She sucked in a ragged breath. 'You didn't. You've … made me so … happy. Thank you.'

She hoped he could hear how grateful she was through the sobs. Dean crushed her closer.

'I'm glad. You deserve to be happy.'

Pulling back and swiping her eyes, she smiled up at him 'So do you. I want you to be happy too.'

He kissed her softly and far too briefly. 'I am, don't worry about that. Want a lift home?'

'Will you stay the night?' she asked, not ready to let him go until tomorrow, even if that meant she was becoming clingy.

His grin made her heart swell with hope. 'I'd love to.'

***

There was only dessert in the apartment and as much as Natalie didn't mind eating test run wedding baking she doubted a man like Dean would be satisfied with that. 'We'll need to order a takeaway,' she grumbled, poking her head in the empty fridge.

He was behind her in an instant, sliding his hands up the side of her thighs, then clenching his fingers round her hips. She shut the door too quickly as her breathing spiked, rattling the empty shelves.

He leaned down to her ear. 'Dinner can wait. I'm not hungry for food right now.'

Neither was she, but she thought she'd be polite. She twisted in his arms and began sliding loose the Windsor knot on his tie. 'What are you hungry for?'

Not that she didn't know, but it was hot when he said it out loud.

'My little thief,' he answered, leaning down to kiss her.

Natalie put a finger on his lips and teased him, 'That's not the sexiest endearment I've ever heard. I think you can do better.'

His lips curved beneath her digit. 'I'll think of something.'

'Okay,' she acquiesced.

Dean sucked her finger into his mouth, swirling his tongue around. Her lips parted on a gasp and her eyelids drooped. She was lost already, and he hadn't even kissed her yet.

The front door slammed shut and a male voice said, 'Natalie, you home yet?'

Dean released both her finger and her, his eyes narrowing slightly.

Tom appeared in the kitchen doorway, toting a massive cardboard box. 'Oh, sorry. I didn't know you had company.'

She smiled in welcome. It felt like ages since she'd seen Tom. And until a few weeks ago, she would have been thrilled about it. But, she realized now, she'd missed him a little. 'It's cool. Tom, this is Dean. Dean, Tom.'

Dean held out his hand but his expression was guarded again. Tom placed the box on the table and returned the gesture.

'Nice to meet you,' he said, then turned to Natalie. 'We wondered if you'd mind helping with the favours? We've got so much left to do and it's getting overwhelming.'

Eyeing the box with a sense of dread, she nodded reluctantly.

'When do you need them by?'

'I was hoping I could take them to the restaurant before work tomorrow just to cross it off the list. There are only going to be thirty-six guests in total. Well,' Tom looked at Dean, 'Thirty-seven if you come as Nat's plus one.'

Frick, she hadn't had the chance to ask Dean yet. How would he take it? His expression was too smooth and the smile didn't touch his eyes. It was his careful smile. Tom didn't seem to notice.

'I'll have them ready,' she promised quickly, throwing a worried look at Dean. He was too quiet. Shit.

'Thanks Nat.' Though he wasn't a hugger, not that she'd seen, Tom wrapped his arms around her and gave her a squeeze before retreating to the door. 'I'll by round at seven tomorrow.'

'Bye.'

When the front door closed again, Dean strolled over to the box and picked out a small gift bag, no doubt one Rose had made already as an example. It was pearly white and had a pink ribbon woven intricately through little holes in the top, then finished off with a bow. Crap, this was going to take forever.

'Well, this isn't our day, is it?' he said, then smiled a very Dean-like smile, winking his dimples.

All the tension drained away, disappointment taking its place. 'This looks like it will take all night. I'm sorry.'

She walked over to the box and he kissed her hair. Inside was organised in a way only Rose could. All the gifts were neatly banded in individual piles and the ribbons were carefully flattened on the top. There was also sheets of pale pink tissue paper and when she took the bag from Dean and undid the ribbon, she saw that the inside of the bag was lined with it.

'We had better get started if we want done by midnight,' he said, lifting the box. 'How about the living room? More floor space?'

Natalie nodded, then led the way. As they worked, they chatted about nothing and almost everything. He still hadn't mentioned

Tom's invite to the wedding, but then again she'd never asked him to go. After seeing his reaction, she wasn't sure she wanted to put him through that, and had to wonder if Jeffrey had been wrong earlier when he'd said Dean hadn't been in love with his ex.

'When's the wedding?' Dean asked, surprising her.

She studied his face, but couldn't see anything more than casual curiosity. Maybe it was a little too casual. 'Boxing Day.'

He nodded, stuffed some crepe paper into a little bag, then filled it carefully with four miniature gifts – a small bar of Green & Black chocolate, love birds salt & pepper shakers, a small photo frame and a bar of luxury soup. She hadn't noticed earlier but the gift bags had a small R & T in fancy script just below where the ribbon was woven through the holes.

Unfortunately, it took longer for her to weave the ribbon than it did for Dean to fill the bags with gifts, and she needed her focus so much that she couldn't try to read his expression.

'You weren't going to invite me.' His voice was flat, distracting her from her task.

The mask was back.

'I wanted to ask you, but wasn't sure if you'd want to come after …' She focused on tying a bow which was nowhere near as perfect as Rose's had been.

'After my own wedding went tits up?' he finished for her.

Her eyes widened as she met his gaze. Thankfully he was grinning.

'That's not the phrase I'd have chosen.'

Dean rolled his eyes. 'That was ages ago. I'd like to come with you.'

The idea that she'd get to have him as her plus one made her beam. 'Then consider yourself invited.'

'I'll look forward to seeing you in that dress again, and peeling you out of it.' His irises seemed to melt as he stared at her through low lids.

178

Her heart stuttered. 'Me too.'

'I think it's time for a break.' He got off the floor, held his hand out to her and winked.

Natalie eyed him all the way from his polished dress shoes, up his charcoal trousers and to his white shirt. His tie was already hanging loose from earlier and he'd taken off his jacket, opening a few buttons below his chin. He really was delicious in a suit.

She took his hand and he pulled off the floor, then his mouth claimed hers.

***

They didn't get much sleep after finishing up the favours and Natalie spent her Tuesday knocking back coffee. Dean had a breakfast meeting with Nintendo on the other side of London on the Wednesday, so he couldn't spend the night again. By the time she got home on Wednesday, she was dying to see him for longer than five minutes at a time.

At least tonight was his office party and not only was she spending the night with him, but she'd get to introduce him to Rose. And Jeffrey mentioned Alana would be there too.

But as she and Rose caught a taxi, part of her wished they could just have some time alone. Her need for him wasn't ebbing in the slightest. It seemed to be getting more prominent as time ticked on. She really did have it bad.

A slither of fear made her shift in the seat. She tried to quash it, taking Rose's advice to give it time and try not to worry, but it was easier said than done.

'You look nervous, Nat. Are you okay?' Rose asked.

'It should be the other way round. You're the one getting married in a few days,' she teased, trying to distract her friend with the upcoming nuptials.

Rose grinned, then shook her head. 'No wedding talk. This is the only hen night I'll get without turning Tom into a nervous wreck, and I've had enough stress this month already. Tonight is about you and me.'

Guilt pushed away her earlier concerns. She was right, tonight was probably the last night they had together before Rose became Tom's wife. 'Then let's paint the Savoy red.'

Rose's grin was infectious, and Natalie's mood brightened, especially when the taxi pulled up in front of the hotel. Above the silver sign overhanging the entrance, six Christmas trees with blue twinkling lights framed a golden statue.

It was completely gorgeous, though of course, she was more excited to see inside. After all, she'd been left to run wild with the planning of this party and she'd gone all out.

They stepped out into the December chill, then darted across to the entrance where a man took their names, then their jackets in exchange for tickets. Another man dressed in a dark suit escorted them to the banquet room booked for Tech Solutions which was already packed with people. She'd been at Dean's company for three days and had no idea this many people worked there. She tried to catch a glimpse of him, but nobody was seated yet and she couldn't find him in the crowd of glittering dresses and sharp suits.

'Wow, Nat. This is like walking into a Christmas fairy tale,' Rose said, her voice and expression filled with wonder.

Smiling, she paused her search for Dean to admire the work for herself. Everything was modern, glitzy and glamorous. From the fairy lights sweeping down from the high ceiling, to the tables and chairs dressed in snow-white sheets. There were even Christmas themed chocolate and champagne fountains in the shape of angels and though every wall was covered with decorations, it didn't look tacky.

Beneath her awe though, her stomach was churning. She'd never come somewhere this Christmassy, and definitely never as herself. People here knew who she was and she'd be celebrating the season with them, not as her stranger alter-ego. It was too close to what she'd avoided for the last three years.

But before the guilt could overwhelm her, Rose took her hand and pulled her over to the fountains. 'None of that, Missy. Tonight is about *fun*. Here.'

Natalie accepted the crystal flute and leaned over to fill it with the pink champagne that flowed over the see-through Angel fountain. Amazingly, the liquid was still bubbly.

'Where's this boyfriend of yours? I'm dying to meet him,' Rose said with a bit too much enthusiasm.

Her friend knew she was clinging onto a ledge in her mind and if she slipped, she'd be done for, sinking into a depression so crushing, she only permitted herself to feel it one day a year.

'I'm not sure. Let's go look.'

Natalie led Rose through the crowd, pausing to shake hands and chit chat with a few people she'd spoken to over the last few days. Then she spied Alana deep in discussion with Tech Solution's receptionist, so she tugged Rose over to meet her.

'Hi Natalie!' Alana said, then pulled her into a hug. 'This party is absolutely stunning. You're a genius.'

When Alana released her, she returned the greeting and thanked her. The receptionist – Claire? – excused herself to get a drink. 'This is my friend, Rose. Rose, this is Alana.'

'Nice to meet you,' Alana said and Rose voiced her agreement, then asked Natalie, 'Does Dean know you're here?'

'I've not seen him yet. We haven't been here long.' Natalie threw an anxious glance around, hoping this time she'd find him. Was it crazy that she missed him already?

Both Rose and Alana giggled at her as she got up on her tiptoes and tried to see *over* the crowd. Then Alana asked Rose about the wedding and her friend bit her lip, shooting a glance at Natalie.

'I don't mind wedding talk. Alana's getting married soon too.'

Reassured, Rose threw herself into a detailed description of her experience with a hasty wedding, and Alana agreed that it was far too stressful. In fact, she'd been thinking about hiring someone to do it for her.

Natalie was only half-listening, because she'd spotted Dean in the crowd, making his way towards them with Jeffrey. When he saw her, his eyes lit up and he smiled in that way that flashed his perfect white teeth and the indents on his cheeks. She was so full of warm, tingly emotions that she felt winded by them.

'You look stunning,' he said when he was in front of her, then bent down and kissed her.

It wasn't exactly a peck, but nowhere near enough. She suddenly felt starved, but not for food. He had that same, clean crisp smell that made her blood simmer, and the connection that pulsed between them was like both a balm to ease her guilt and an electric current that kickstarted her libido.

'Oh, *fuck*,' Jeffrey announced.

Dean broke the kiss to glare at his brother, and as she had her free hand on his shoulder, she felt him tense beneath the navy suit. Rose was gaping at Dean in horror, but the shock seemed to burn away swiftly with a sudden fury.

Natalie could only stare. She couldn't remember the last time she'd seen Rose angry, never mind enraged.

'Rosaline,' Dean said, eerily slowly.

A horrible, sinking feeling hit her at the same time Rose said, 'What are you playing at?'

Stepping back from them both, the blood drained from her face. *No, it can't be. Something else. Please, anything else.*

Dean's expression was stony as he raised an eyebrow.

'Is this some kind of sick, twisted payback?' Rose demanded to Dean, looking so aggressive it should have frightened her.

But instead her stomach turned with nausea and she had to put down her glass of champagne in case she needed to make a run for it.

'Excuse me?' Dean asked, and she heard a dark, nasty edge to his voice.

She couldn't rip her gaze from either of them, even though

182

she wanted to turn and run, to not let the comprehension of what was so obviously happening click in her consciousness. Then she remembered, the first time she'd used Rose's name with Dean and the way he'd clammed up. And again when she'd told Rose who she was seeing. Right before they both shook it off, because the city was so big, hell, the *country* was so big, there was no way the fiancé Rose left without an explanation was the Dean who'd been humiliated on his wedding day.

But even as her vision filled with tears, she knew. Stunned by a feeling so crushing, she could only watch as Rose tore into Dean.

'She's my best friend! And you knew, didn't you? Is that what this is all about? You want payback for what I did?'

Someone took her hand – Alana she thought, but couldn't turn to check.

Dean's scowl was livid. 'Get over yourself. And get the fuck out of this party.'

'My pleasure.' Rose stormed over, but when she saw Natalie's face, she froze. 'Let's go home. I can explain.'

Natalie tugged her hand free, then shook her head.

'Natalie?' Rose pleaded, reaching her hand out. 'Nat?'

'Leave her alone,' Dean's voice was sharp, but his expression softened as he stared at her. 'Don't listen to her, Nat. She has no fucking idea what she's talking about.'

He stepped towards her and panic clawed its way up her throat. She was past nausea, past upset. And the two most important people in her life were the last people in the world she wanted to be near.

'Stay away from me,' she tried to sound harsh, but all she managed was a choked whisper before turning and fleeing the party.

***

Dean frantically searched the banquet hall, doing his best to ignore Rosaline a few steps behind him. Surprisingly, that wasn't difficult. He'd always worried about seeing her again, wondered if it would break him in two. But the only thing that had achieved that tonight was seeing the look on Natalie's face. She'd been utterly destroyed.

Frustration and anxiety had his feet moving faster until he was out in the street, searching left and right, hoping she hadn't run off on him again. He took his mobile out of his pocket and dialled her number. The message of her voicemail kicked in. After the beep, he said, 'Natalie, I'm sorry. Where are you?'

'So I was right.'

He turned, scowling down at Rosaline and saw Jeffrey and Alana at the doorway to the Savoy. Jeffrey was as livid as he was, and Alana watched him with sympathy in her eyes. All he could focus on was his ex though.

'Why would I do that? I don't *give a fuck* about you. I haven't for a decade. Now if you're done trying to ruin my relationship, I need to go find Natalie.'

'You need to stay away from her,' Rose argued. 'Nat's been through enough. She doesn't need to be played. Just because our parents don't talk anymore, that doesn't mean they've lost touch with the social circle. I've heard how disposable women are to you. I'm not going to let you do that to my friend.'

His anger reached a level that made being around her dangerous. 'You don't know what you're talking about.'

Instead of getting into it with her, he waved down a taxi.

Irritatingly, she got in with him and when he gave the driver their address, Rosaline's glare went thermonuclear.

'Why are you doing this? If you think I haven't suffered at all over the last ten years you're wrong. The guilt is so bad sometimes, it eats me up inside. Leave Natalie alone, Dean. She doesn't deserve this.'

'I'm only going to say this once more, so you'd better pay

attention. I don't give a shit about what happened back then. This isn't about you. This is about Natalie.'

An image of her huge blue eyes and pale, broken expression flashed in his mind and he gritted his teeth. He had to convince her that Rosaline was wrong, prove to her that he had no idea who she'd been talking about. After all, Rosaline had hated it when people shortened her name growing up. How was he meant to know she'd be known by it now?

The taxi pulled up outside their flat and he tossed a note at the driver, then got out. The windows were dark, making him hesitate for a second before vaulting the stairs and knocking the door. Silence.

Until Rosaline said, 'You're not coming in.'

'If she's there, I am.' He shifted to the side, giving her enough room to open the door without risking touching her.

Right now, she made him sick to his stomach. He didn't think he'd ever hated anyone this much, and it had nothing to do with her standing him up all those years ago. It was because she told Natalie he was using her. Which was so far from the truth it should have been funny. But he was too anxious to feel any amusement.

He glared at her until she sighed, fished her keys out of her bag and unlocked the door. Dean went in first, making his way through the hall and opening her bedroom door, but it was dark and there was no sign of her having been there moments ago.

Rosaline overtook him, flipping on light switches and ducked her head around the kitchen doorway. She turned back to him, her fury sliding away as worry creased her forehead. 'She's not here.'

Rosaline tried calling, but must have got Natalie's voicemail too, because she ended the call.

'Where else could she go?' He couldn't remember her talking about other friends, not even Rosaline's new fiancé. And by the awkward way Natalie had returned Tom's hug, he doubted she'd go to him.

Rosaline paced round the living room, her arms folded across her chest. 'I don't know.'

He'd grown up with this woman. They'd known each other better than they'd known themselves at one point. He could hear the slight hesitation, noticed the way she squirmed her chin away so he couldn't see her eyes, just before the lie was delivered.

'That's shit and we both know it. Where is she?' he asked again, harder this time.

'What are you doing with her? You had her all tied up in knots on Sunday. Even if you're not with her to get back at me, I'm not going to let you hurt her.'

Rosaline met his glare head on, not backing down an inch.

'Natalie and I are not your business. I'm not the one who made her feel like a pawn in a twisted revenge plot tonight.' She winced, but he couldn't muster any sympathy for her. 'Tell me where you think she is.'

'Okay, but only if you answer this question and answer it honestly. You know I'll be able to tell if you're lying.' She stopped in front of him, too close that he had to fight the urge to step back.

'What do you want to know?' If she was about to dredge up the past, he wasn't sure he could give her the satisfaction of admitting anything. But if it helped him find Natalie? Helped him make this right?

'Are you in love with Natalie?' Rosaline asked, her voice softer.

Dean staggered back a step, away from her questioning eyes. His heart pounded in his chest and a fine coat of sweat dewed on his forehead. His first reaction was to tell her it was none of her fucking business. But he needed to find Natalie, and if sieRo cared about her at all she wouldn't let him near her until he told the truth.

He took a deep breath, then answered the question honestly.

Chapter 15

Tonight seemed to be a night for slaying her heart, Natalie thought as she inputted the code into the pad at her storage unit, then opened the door. If the revelations at the Savoy were anything to go by, every bone in her body should be crushed by now with the overwhelming grief she felt.

As she flicked on the light and the room before her got blurry, she knew she'd need a course of Prozac after this. But where else could she go?

Natalie closed the door and made her way over to the sofa, slumping down and wrapping herself in the dust sheet. She couldn't go home, not now. She remembered her conversation with Jeffrey on Monday, how she'd been so mad at the woman who'd left Dean she'd wanted to slap her.

Putting her face in her palms, she let the tears spill over freely. Rose had lied to her. She'd claimed she left a fiancé, said absolutely nothing about leaving him on their wedding day. *No wonder* she'd been so upset, so filled with self-disgust. So she bloody well should!

Natalie welcomed the familiar flare of anger. Being angry was much better than being depressed. She stared in front of her, seeing nothing but the scene at the Savoy. Rose's accusations about Dean, that he was using her for payback …

Her ire was snuffed out under a wave of crushing agony. Was she right? Was Dean using her all this time? She'd never thought much about it before, but it was a coincidence that they'd met this year, after all the years of both of them apparently doing the same thing every December. Had he been keeping tabs on Rose all along and, the first year Natalie was left alone to crash, he made his move?

The thought made her stomach twist viciously and if she'd had more than a few sips of champagne in it, she'd have been sick all over the floor.

The familiar beep of buttons being pressed on the entry machine had her sucking in a breath. When the door opened, her heart seemed to rip apart in her chest, the pain was so intense.

Dean let himself in, his face creased with concern. 'Natalie, thank god. I was so worried about you.'

He crossed the room, stepping round boxes she still couldn't bear to look at, but stopped when she squirmed back into the couch. There was no taking her eyes off his though. It was like they'd been locked open with the stunningly acute devastation ripping through her soul.

'What Rosaline said back there was a fucking, lie, Natalie. I—'

'Why do you keep calling her that?' she interrupted.

'What, Rosaline? That's her name.'

She shook her head. 'Rose is her name.'

He looked at her like he was worrying about her sanity and she supposed she should be too. What did it matter what he called Rose? In the face of everything else, it was pathetic.

'She never used to like being called Rose,' he said reluctantly, then sank to his knees in front of the couch but didn't try to touch her. 'You know that, don't you? You know I'm not with you for revenge.'

Tremors racked through her with the effort it took to hold herself together. 'No, I don't know what to think.'

He took her face in his hands and locked his gaze with hers. The splinters that were left of her heart seemed to block her throat.

'I'm crazy about you. I had absolutely no idea who your flat-mate was until tonight. But it doesn't change anything for me. I still want to be with you. More than ever.'

His expression was open, his eyes clear and his tone rang with sincerity. Or was she just believing what she wanted so badly to be true?

'I … I …' She couldn't think right, couldn't trust this hope.

But then she remembered everything he'd done for her, every sweet and caring thing he'd said to her. And Rose, well, she'd not exactly been forthcoming with the truth. She'd lied about the break-up. Could she be lying again? Although why would she do that, why would she want to hurt Natalie that way?

'You don't believe me, do you?' Dean said, rubbing away the torrent of tears that refused to slow.

'I'm not sure it matters anymore,' she whispered.

He released her at once and sat back on his knees, his expression crumpling with agony.

Natalie couldn't stand the guilt of knowing she'd been the one to put it there, so she tried to explain. 'Say I do believe you. You say nothing's changed for you, but for me …'

Now that the shock was wearing off, other things had started to occur to her. Dean and Rose, *together*. The thought brought with it another round of nausea. But worse than any of that, the idea that he'd loved her friend. That he'd been prepared to marry her, spend his life with her …

'Nothing has to change,' he said, interrupting her thoughts. 'I'm still me. I still care about you more than I have about any woman, Nat. Please, don't walk away from what we have.'

More than Rose? She wanted to ask, but wasn't sure she was in a sound enough place emotionally to deal with the answer. Instead she tried hard to focus on how he stared at her, like he was warily eyeing a skittish kitten who might bolt at the tiniest sound.

And she realized then that he really did want her, not just for revenge. Not to hurt her. He was crazy about her, and despite all the mess of insecurities in her head, she wanted to be with him.

'I'm not going to run,' she said, climbing off the couch to kneel on the floor in front of him. 'You said we had to trust each other for this to work, didn't you? And I promised I'd try.' His lips. Natalie snuggled into his chest. 'I just need time to process everything. But I don't want you to leave.'

Dean enveloped her in his arms. 'I'll stay as long as you want me to.'

A while later he lifted her onto the couch where he held her snuggled against his chest, stroking her hair and cheek, but never interrupting her thoughts. She had so many banging around in her head she'd completely forgotten where they were. Until she spied a box containing something she doubted she'd ever be able to open.

'Natalie, please talk to me.'

He must have felt the sudden tension in her body. She lifted her head to look at him, willing everything else to slip back out of her mind. 'I can't stay here. Too many memories.'

His face creased in understanding. 'Come on.'

When they were outside, she pulled her jacket in tighter and welcomed Dean's arms around her. 'Let's find a taxi and I'll take you home.'

'No.' Rose would be there. She couldn't face her right now. She didn't know if she'd ever be able to.

'Do you want to come back to mine?' he asked.

Natalie stared at him, surprised her eyes weren't bugging out of their sockets. She couldn't sleep with him, in his bed. Not tonight. Not after all she'd learned.

'Relax. I have more than one bedroom.'

She ignored the flash of hurt she saw in his eyes. She'd been hurt enough tonight. And his offer was all she had. Hotels would cost a fortune this close to Christmas and Mick hadn't paid her yet. Not that she had her bank card with her, and there was no way she could deal with Rose right now.

'If you don't mind. I can't face going back to the flat.' She couldn't even call it home anymore. It was a stranger's house.

'Of course I don't. You can stay as long as you need to.'

He took her hand and led her down the street.

***

Dean unlocked his front door and held it open for her, trying to keep his expression calm. Inside he was anything but.

It hadn't escaped his notice that she'd snuggled into his chest earlier, effectively making it impossible to kiss her. And he worried that if she had somewhere else to go, her decision to try to make this work after tonight's drama might have gone the other way.

So he tried to focus on the fact that she was here and that he had time to find a way to win her back, as he led her down the hall. He paused outside his bedroom, then opened the door. 'You can stay here.'

Part of him wanted her to be surrounded with his things, especially if he couldn't be with her.

Natalie walked into the room, warily eyeing the king-sized bed he'd thankfully put clean sheets on this morning.

'I'll sleep somewhere else if you want to be alone,' he said.

'I can't kick you out of your bedroom,' she said, having obviously seen the clothes through the open door to his closet.

'You're not. I'm kicking myself out.' She was hugging her waist, then he noticed she didn't even have a handbag, never mind a change of clothes. 'There's tee-shirts and shorts in those drawers. You can help yourself.'

Natalie followed his gaze. 'Thanks.'

Seeing her like this was more painful than anything he'd been through before. 'Do you want something to drink?'

A ghost of a smile curved her lips. 'Definitely.'

He led her through to the open plan living area and kitchen. It was the one part of the flat which had nothing but windows on either side. London was lit up below, but the view didn't make him pause now. He was too wrapped up in Natalie.

So when she froze at the edge of the room and gasped, he noticed. She bit her lip as she looked around, and for a moment he wondered if she was scared of heights. Then he followed her gaze and saw what an idiot he'd been. Fuck, the Christmas tree.

Not just that either, but when Alana had brought round her old lights, she'd stuck them to the windows and switched them on.

'I think I'm going to turn in,' she whispered.

'Sorry, I forgot they were even here. Alana put them up.'

But Natalie was already heading through the house. 'I'm tired, Dean. I'm going to go to sleep.'

Shit.

'Goodnight Natalie.'

The sound of his bedroom door closing softly behind her made him curse under his breath. He glared at the tree, not believing that he'd been so stupid. She'd already told him how she couldn't bear to even let her flatmate put up decorations. Sighing, he went hunting for the boxes. This was going to be a long night.

***

Whoever said, 'things always look better in the morning' was a liar.

Natalie crawled out of bed and stretched. Everything smelled like Dean here – even the tee-shirt she wore. It was green and had a logo she now knew was the brand for the off-shoot company of Tech Solutions they were using to release his game.

Leaning over, she opened the bedside cabinet and pulled out a pair of loose cotton boxers. Yesterday she'd left without underwear having planned for a different kind of evening, so she'd have to borrow Dean's. Once she'd slid them on, she decided it was time to face the music.

How silly was it anyway that she felt guilty for looking at a Christmas tree? It's not like she lived here and had put it up for her own enjoyment. It was Dean's house and he had a right to decorate any way he wanted to. Cloaking herself with a false sense of bravado, she left his room and headed for the living room.

He distracted her from everything, even the panoramic view she'd glimpsed last night. At the kitchen island, looking sexier than anyone in striped pyjama bottoms had any right to, he was pouring himself a coffee. Of course, the fact that he was shirtless helped with the whole distraction thing and so did the sculpted muscles on his smooth back.

He *had* to work out. And going by the lack of a tan line – and his jammies hung low enough for her to see – he must use sunbeds. It didn't matter though, because her libido was back with a vengeance wiping every other thought from her mind.

Just as he was raising the cup to take a sip, he turned and froze. His wary expression was more effective than a bucket of iced water. He'd been with Rose. They'd … she squeezed her eyes shut. No, she couldn't even think about what they'd done.

'Morning,' he said, his voice low and careful like he didn't want to startle her. 'Would you like a coffee? I could heat up some milk and make you a latte.'

Natalie tried to shake off the unwelcome image of him and Rose together, not screaming at each other like they had the day before, but … No! She wasn't going to think about it.

'I can drink it black too.' Forcing her legs to move, she paddled across the wooden floor. The early morning chill seeped into her bare feet.

'Here.' He handed her his cup, then grabbed another out of

the cupboard and poured some for himself out of the coffee pot. 'I like that tee-shirt on you.'

'I borrowed some of your underwear too. I hope that's okay.' Of course, his top was so long they were hidden beneath.

His eyes heated and her pulse sped in response but he broke eye contact, pulled out a stool and sat at the island with his coffee. 'Help yourself to anything you need.'

Anything? Right now, she needed him to kiss her, make love to her, make her forget … Hugging the mug with her hands, she ignored the unwelcome reminder that they'd never made love. It had been amazingly passionate sex at best.

She imagined you had to be in love, to make love, but she wasn't really an expert.

'Are you going to work?' She couldn't tell how early it was. Outside the city was still shrouded in darkness.

'Yes, I have a meeting this morning. Do you want to stay here?'

'I don't think I could face going in after last night. Your staff must have heard everything.' She hadn't even considered the potential gossip until now. It was a horrifying realization.

Besides, she couldn't exactly go anywhere in boxers and an oversized tee-shirt.

He frowned. 'I don't think anyone was close enough to hear.'

'I hope you're right.' Natalie slid onto the nearest barstool, then took a sip of coffee. It was harsh going down and a bit too strong for her. But maybe that's what she needed. She felt like she was in the middle of a nightmare and couldn't wait to wake up.

'Are you going to speak to … Rose … today?' he asked.

She quickly shook her head, hating that he was even saying the name. 'I'm done with her.'

He didn't say anything more, and his face was smooth of all or any reactions. The perfect poker face.

Natalie tried to explain. 'She's been lying to me all along. About what happened with her ex – you. Her name. Your motivations.

I have nothing to say to her and I'm not interested in hearing more of the same.'

'Come here.' Dean rose, then rounded the island and opened his arms.

Depositing her coffee, she took him up on the offer and snuggled into his throat. The tangy scent of him was warmer somehow and it made her think of the two nights she'd fallen asleep in his arms. She couldn't believe that was all, just twice. Being with him felt so comfortable, so natural, it was like they'd been doing this for years.

But she had no idea if she'd ever be able to get past the fact he'd been about to marry her best friend. Well, ex best friend.

'I don't want to lie to you. I know why she ... left.'

Dean stiffened in her hold and the tension radiated out of every knotted sinew of muscle. 'I don't want to know.'

She pulled back to study his face. The mask was back. 'But—'

'I really don't care why she left. She did, I'm over it. I don't need closure.' He released her and stepped back. 'I need to shower.'

He walked past her, his quick movements betraying his calm, reasonable tone. She noticed for the first time that something was different about the space and scanned the room carefully. The whole kitchen and living area was massive. The flat she'd shared with Rose would probably fit in here twice.

There was a fifty-inch flat screen on the wall, which was somehow dwarfed by the vast dimensions, towering speakers in each corner and a desk, two massive sofas, coffee and side tables made of glass and steel. But it looked plain somehow. What was different?

Then it clicked. The decorations were gone. The tree, the lights, the window features ...

Frick. How long had he spent last night packing it all away? And she'd made him sleep alone because she'd been tormented by the idea of him with Rose. She was such a bitch.

He came out of his room a little while later in another expensive looking suit. For someone who hated them, he owned a lot.

'Can I make you breakfast before you go?' she asked, jumping off the stool, eager to do something for him.

Her change in attitude made him pause for a beat. 'No thanks. I need to get going. Can I bring you anything back? Some clothes maybe.'

As much as she really didn't want him spending money on her, there was no other choice. 'Thanks. I'll pay you back when I get … my stuff.'

Not that she knew what she was going to do with it all when she did. And she didn't have her phone, so flat hunting wasn't a possibility either. Unless he'd let her use his laptop.

'Don't worry about that.' Dean came close, like he was going to kiss her, but stopped a foot away like he'd thought better of it.

Her heart twisted. She wanted his kiss, *craved it.* So Natalie closed the distance, getting up on her tiptoes and pressing her mouth to his. Sucking in a breath, he wrapped his arms around her and kissed her back. He tasted like mint and coffee and something even more delicious she couldn't put a name to.

She slid her arms around his neck and he tugged up her borrowed tee-shirt till his palms splayed across the bare skin on her back. Then they slid lower.

A picture fixed itself to the back of her eyelids – one of Dean in a passionate embrace with a familiar woman, a woman she'd loved so much she wished they were sisters. All the heat drained out of her and she pulled away from him with a jerk.

The dazed lust in his eyes cleared until blank understanding had the mask slipping back into place. 'Make yourself at home. I'll see you later.'

He turned and left the flat, not noticing her eyes filling with tears.

The rest of the morning crawled by torturing Natalie with thoughts she tried to push away. She needed to be reasonable and worry about the most important issues first, like where she was going to live now.

Dean and Jeffrey had gotten her a bigger settlement than she could have dreamed of, so as long as her business kicked off, she'd be able to survive for a few more months. As soon as she had clothes, she was going to hit the newsstands and get the letting ads.

But her thoughts kept drifting to Rose's betrayal – of both her and Dean, and she got mad. So mad she wanted to hit something, preferably her callous ex-friend. How could Rose have said he was unambitious? He was successful, driven and completely gorgeous – inside and out.

That led to reflecting on Rose's guilt over the whole thing. Did she want Dean back? Would Dean take her back?

Those were things she couldn't think about because the pain almost crippled her.

Then inspiration came just before noon. She went on the hunt through his apartment, checking cupboards and opening closed doors in the hall until she got to the room he'd slept in last night. In the wardrobe, on the shelf above a gazillion suits, she saw the boxes she was looking for.

Trying very hard not to think about what she was doing, she pulled them down and carried them carefully to the living room. She opened the longest box first, ignoring the black bristles as she methodically retrieved the sections. Focusing on clipping the pieces into place and straightening the branches, she managed to ignore the part of her brain that told her she was a selfish cow for doing this.

Next were the lights. White and sparkling as she recalled. She wound them from the bottom up, being careful to space them out like her mum had shown her a thousand times. Bobbles were next. These weren't personalised. They were part of a set – white and silver and all different sizes. She could do this. She could do this for Dean.

Finally, she placed the simple metal star on top and twined the lights round the base.

It was harder than it should have been to plug in the socket, and her hand shook as she clicked the switch on the cable. But the rush of pleasure that came when the tree lit up brilliantly was what really knocked her for six.

Crossing her legs, she stayed on the cool wooden floor for an age, trying to process the happiness of seeing a tree decorated to perfection, with the conflicting guilt that told her she shouldn't be enjoying it.

Bittersweet. Pain and pleasure. Right and wrong. The thoughts took over her mind completely, blocking everything else out.

Until she heard the front door open and she bounced off the floor guiltily. She had hoped she'd have time to decorate the windows before he got back. But it was not Dean who walked into the room.

'Alana?' she asked, confused.

'Hi. Dean asked me to get a few things for you.'

Alana put a familiar suitcase down on the black leather sofa, then handed her a handbag. Natalie's handbag. Her throat swelled. 'Did he …'

She couldn't even finish the question, didn't want to know if Dean had gone to Rose and asked her for this.

'No, no. He asked me to stop by and gave me his spare set of keys for his place, here.' Alana deposited the keys on the coffee table, then sat next to the suitcase. 'Your friend was glad to hear you were safe, she was so worried.'

Natalie put her clutch on the coffee table, then lowered herself slowly onto the white leather corner suite across from Alana. She felt better knowing it wasn't Dean who'd gone to the flat. But with the relief swiftly came the guilt as what the rest of Alana said sunk in.

'She's *not* my friend, and I don't care if she was worried.'

Unlike Dean, Alana didn't hold her tongue. 'Natalie, I know you must be going through hell just now, and don't get me wrong, Rose is not my favourite person in the world. Still, she *is* your friend. True friends don't come along very often.'

Natalie just shook her head, refusing to give in and feel bad for Rose. 'She lied to me. She hurt Dean.'

'Can you put yourself in her shoes? She must have felt really bad about what she did to keep it from you like that. Last night was a shock for her. I saw her face when she registered Jeffrey. You could call it the perfect expression of guilt and remorse. And then when she saw Dean, she almost fell to bits. But she pulled herself together, put everything she was feeling on the backburner and tried to protect her friend. She was totally wrong, of course and she knows that now. But she said those things to protect you.'

Deep down, Natalie recognised that maybe, just maybe, what Alana was saying fit in with the Rose she thought she knew. 'I can't ... I'm so confused.'

And, embarrassingly, tears started streaming from her eyes like a faulty tap. By all rights she should be severely dehydrated by now.

Alana was beside her in an instant, pulling her into an awkward hug because Natalie couldn't bear to let Alana see her face.

'I get that. And I have an idea of how you must be feeling. That's why Dean called me.'

Natalie tried to blink away the tears so she could see the dark-haired beauty's face. There was no way Alana would ever have a reason to be insecure. She was absolutely gorgeous.

She smiled a little. 'Has Dean ever told you how I met Jeffrey?'

'No,' Natalie answered, curious to where this was going.

'I met him in my kitchen. I was wearing these awful flannel

pyjamas that made me look completely huge, and there was him, all tall and lean and gorgeous, wearing nothing but skin-tight boxers.' Alana laughed at the shock on her face. 'You see, he'd had a one-night stand with my flatmate.'

Natalie didn't mean to gasp, but how could she not be shocked? That was the last thing she'd expected.

'I know, right? That's what you call awkward. Sarah was a total commitment-phobe. She never entertained dates or even second nights. I was pissed off she'd slept with Jeffrey because there was an instant spark between us. And I knew I'd never be able to date him. How could I knowing he'd been with her?'

Alana gave her a meaningful look. Unbelievably, she'd cut right through to the core of Natalie's pain. How to deal with the fact her best friend and boyfriend had been lovers. 'But you're getting married. What changed?'

'We chatted, spoke about work and stuff. But he didn't make a move or anything. I was glad. Then about a month later we bumped into each other outside my office.' Alana rolled her eyes. 'He was all 'what a coincidence, how are you' but I knew it wasn't. He asked me out on a date. I said no. I couldn't, not knowing he'd been with Sarah. And not because she would care. Sarah had been through six more guys by then.'

'I know exactly what you mean. But how did you ... get over that?' Natalie asked. This conversation was starting to give her hope that all was not lost.

'Time, I suppose. And the fact Jeffrey never gave up.' She smiled warmly at the memory. 'He started turning up everywhere I went – the supermarket, nights out with friends, everywhere. Each time I saw him, I wanted him, more and more. In the end, I knew I had to forget about him and Sarah or I could end up regretting it. So, I left it in the past where it belonged.'

Natalie smiled weakly. 'You make it sound so easy.'

Alana frowned, like she was trying to remember. 'No, it wasn't easy. The first night we were together was the hardest. I kept wondering if he was making comparisons or whether anything I did disappointed him.'

That's exactly what she was worrying about. Except of course she had the added fear that he'd never gotten over Rose. 'How did you cope with it?'

She shrugged. 'I told him how I felt. He was so sweet and reassuring. I think by then I was already in love with him, but the way he was with me after that made me realize he was the man I wanted to spend my life with.'

It may not have felt it to Alana, but her situation had been easier. She knew happy ever after was a possibility with Jeffrey. Natalie knew it was never going to happen with Dean. 'I can't let myself look that far ahead.'

'Why?' Alana asked, her tone perplexed. 'I've seen you both together. If that's not love I don't know what is.'

Natalie's chin dropped.

'Oh, come on. It's so obvious a blind person could see it. You're totally smitten and so is Dean.' Alana grinned. 'Whatever happened in the past doesn't matter to him anymore. He's become a different person since he met you.'

Natalie couldn't confirm that last part and didn't want to look too closely at Alana's assumptions either. She was very much in danger of hoping the woman was right. But then that could end in disaster, because if she let herself feel what she'd been trying so hard to suppress, she'd be inviting in the possibility of agony if she ever lost him.

'Do you mind if I get dressed in my clothes?' she said, hoping that would end this discussion.

'Sure. Mind if I stay for a cup of tea?' Natalie shook her head and Alana went on, 'I'll not say another word about this if you don't want me to. I was actually hoping to ask you for a favour.'

'Oh?'

Alana got up, shaking her head. 'Tea first, then we'll talk. Do you want a cup?'

'Please. Milk and sugar.'

Feeling curious as to why Alana would need a favour from her, Natalie picked up her case and wheeled it to Dean's room. Rose, or maybe Alana, had packed everything she needed and it was comforting to have some of her stuff again. She plugged her mobile in to charge, then left it on the bedside table.

Once she was in a pair of jeans and a snowman themed Christmas jumper, she went back to the living room. Alana smiled at her, like a friend might on seeing her penchant for seasonal clothing, but didn't say anything.

'What do you need?' Natalie asked.

'Well, I was hoping you'd let me hire you to do my wedding. The way you did the party last night was incredible and I'd love to get married there. They're booked up for two years though.' Alana pouted.

Wow, another client. Courtesy of Dean? She shook off the suspicion. If anything, she should be grateful for the work. And she owed Alana after today. 'I'd love to. Don't worry about the Savoy. I know the events manager. They always say they're full but usually have a few openings. You might have to settle for a Sunday though.'

'Really?' Alana beamed. 'I don't care if it's a Monday as long as it's this year.'

'I'll see what I can do. So, what are your thoughts on music ...' And as they spent the rest of the afternoon discussing plans, Natalie was glad to fall back into some semblance of normal.

***

Before he went home, there was something Dean had to do. The last twenty-four hours had been fifty shades of fucked up. He'd never vault these stairs again and knock on the door if it was for anyone other than Natalie.

The door flew open and Rose glanced around hopefully, before her face fell. 'Is she ever coming back?'

He didn't know the answer to that. Natalie had told him no, but he wasn't about to stick the knife in. He knew right now she was just hurt and confused. Probably even mad about what Rose did to him. 'She's upset. Can I come in?'

'Of course. Er, I mean, Tom's here.' Rose blushed.

It didn't evoke any emotions in him at all, not even discomfort at being in the same vicinity as his ex-fiancée's hubby-to-be. 'We can do this here. It won't take long.'

'Okay. How bad is it? She must hate me.' Rose seemed to forget about Tom for a second. 'Tell me Dean. Please.'

And because he felt nothing, absolutely nothing for her anymore, he could relax as he told her the truth. 'Confused. She feels betrayed that you didn't tell her.'

'I know you hate me but please, please don't make it worse. I can't lose her. She's my best friend. I love her.' Rose's eyes widened as she pleaded with her hands clasped in front of her chest.

The reminder of the end of their conversation last night distracted him for a second, but he shook it off and focused. 'I don't hate you. Really. I thought, seeing you again, maybe I would, but I don't.'

Though if it had gone the other way and he'd lost Natalie for good? Yeah, he'd hate her.

'But I was awful to you. I just left you hanging without a word. And your mother ...' Rose shuddered. 'She came straight to our house and called me out for being a horrible person. She told me that you deserved better than a would-be baker like me. That she was glad you left because it stopped you from making the biggest mistake of your life.'

If his mouth was hanging open, he wouldn't have noticed. His mother said all that? She'd defended him.

'I didn't leave because of you. I was selfish. I thought I wanted more than a life in the country attending one boring social func-tion after another. I wanted to move to the city, start a business and live like a normal person. I knew your parents would never give you the trust fund if you came with me, and I didn't think you wanted to work.'

Dean was still too in shock from her revelation about the Wicked Witch to stop her from going on. He just couldn't comprehend his mother sticking up for him for any reason, especially something she'd openly said was *his* failure.

'Will you ever forgive me, Dean?' she whispered.

Shit, he had to focus. 'We weren't in love, Rose. We were friends more than anything. You were right to leave. It would have been a mistake for both of us.'

As he said the words, he realized how true they were. The way he'd felt about her came nowhere near the feelings he had for Natalie. They weren't even on the same chart.

'You're right,' she whispered.

'That's not why I'm here though. I came to ask you not to give up on Natalie. She's strong-willed and stubborn, but from what she's said about you before, you were her whole life.'

The tears in Rose's eyes spilled over. 'Of course I won't. I never will.'

Her fiancé must have heard her choked sob because he was in the hall, glaring at Dean in an instant. 'Good, that's all I needed to know.'

He turned and went back to his car. As he drove away he caught a glimpse of them both in his rear view mirror. Rose was wrapped in Tom's arms. It was weird to feel sort of happy for her, even though seeing her again was a little strange. He doubted they'd ever be friends again, but he could keep things amicable for Natalie. He was beginning to realize he'd do anything for her.

And today, finally, he knew he'd really moved on from the past. Now if only the future was as easy to deal with.

Chapter 16

'Frick, frick, frick.'

The smell of burnt garlic butter wafted through the air and Natalie fiddled with every knob she could see, not remembering which one turned the gas off. She found it in time to save a disaster.

She was fairly sure he'd kick her out if she set fire to his kitchen.

Now the heat was reasonable, she picked up the chopping board that was topped with chopped mushrooms and onions, then slid them into the wok. Using a silicone spatula, she spread the veg round the pan, soaking them in the garlic butter.

This was the only thing she knew how to cook and, well, she'd cheated for the most part. The prawns were already cooked and the pilau rice was microwaveable. She couldn't even take credit for the chilli poppadoms sitting in the packet on the kitchen island.

Still, this was a thank you dinner. Dean always knew what she needed, even from the first time she met him – blackmail notwithstanding – and he'd asked Alana to come over, knowing she needed both a friend and reassurance.

She was working on putting the past behind her. It was still so fresh she was struggling, but trying. When the mushrooms softened, she added more garlic butter, then the prawns. A glance at the kitchen clock told her he was later than usual. It had just gone 7.15pm and he usually got home around 6.30pm. In a way she'd been glad, because it meant she had time to finish redecorating after Alana left and change into a shimmery purple knit dress.

There wasn't much she could do about the puffy eyes though. She heard the front door open. 'Dean, is that you?'

'Yeah. Something smells good.' He appeared in the room, undoing his tie and the top two buttons. He then took off his suit jacket and slung it over one of the barstools.

She almost forgot to breathe, especially when he rolled up his shirt sleeves giving the beautiful contrast of tanned skin against his sharp white shirt. He was a complete contradiction. Nerdy games programmer, company CEO, country manor aristocrat …

But more than that, he was smart, funny, kind, charming and so sweet to her.

And his smile. It made her forget her name sometimes.

'You didn't have to do all this,' he said, gesturing to the kitchen island.

She'd lit candles, set down placemats and poured them a glass of white wine from the bottle that the man in the off-licence had assured her went perfectly with shellfish. Frick, the food! She shut the door on the microwave and the two packets of rice started spinning inside. Next she turned the gas off – she hoped – to avoid the whole burnt food, setting the flat on fire thing.

'I wanted to. How was work?' she asked, smiling at how normal a topic of conversation it was.

The microwave dinged and she used a dishtowel to retrieve their plates from the oven.

He took a seat at the island. 'Busy. Jeffrey scored a new client – an international hotel chain. We've started upgrading their systems. How was your day? Did Alana get some things for you?'

'She did. Thanks for sending her over. It was nice to talk to her and she hired me to do her wedding.'

Natalie emptied the pouches of rice onto the plates, topped it with the garlicy prawn, mushroom and onion mix and took them over to the island, handing him one.

'That's great, Nat. Another client,' he said, picking up his fork. He scooped up some rice and a prawn and popped it in his mouth. 'This is really good.'

Just like it had before, his praise made her light up inside. Which reminded her. 'I hope you don't mind, but I put those back up.'

She pointed behind him and he glanced over his shoulder, freezing for a second. 'Are you okay with this? I never bother with decorations but Alana brings over her cast-offs every year and insists on glitzing me up.'

Natalie laughed. She had gotten to know Alana relatively well, and she knew the girl didn't shy away from speaking her mind. She could just imagine her taking over his space and imposing festivity on him. 'It's fine. I love them. Really,' she added, when his brows pulled together. 'It's still hard, I feel guilty for enjoying it, but I wanted to do it for you.'

His eyes melted. 'Just when I thought you couldn't get any more amazing you go and do something like this.'

Natalie didn't know what to say to that, so instead filled him in on her plans for Alana's wedding, ignoring the nagging thought that Rose's wedding came first and she should be dealing with that. But she quickly pushed the guilt away, not wanting to admit to Dean that she was having second thoughts about her friend. It felt like she was betraying him.

The rest of the night went by in a flash. Dean was really easy to be around and much to her relief (and also disappointment), he never sat too close or even tried to touch her. They just lounged on one of his sofas after changing into their pyjamas and watched rubbish on the television.

But it had been an exhausting couple of days and before long she yawned. 'I think I need to turn in.'

'Me too. I had an early start.' He leaned closer, maybe to kiss her, but hesitated. 'Can I grab some things out of my chest of drawers before you go to sleep? I went commando today because I didn't want to disturb you.'

Natalie giggled at the thought, but then realized he wasn't going to be sharing the bed with her, and disappointment surged. 'You don't have to leave your room, Dean.'

He shrugged, a little too casually. 'I wouldn't put you in a guest room. The mattresses are new and hard.'

'I meant, share with me.' He raised an eyebrow. 'I like sleeping in your arms,' she quickly added, not knowing if she was ready for more than that.

'You sure?'

Natalie nodded.

He took her hand and led her through to the bedroom.

On Friday, she woke earlier than usual, feeling antsy and uncomfortable. It didn't help that he never wore a shirt, and for a second she was tempted to wake him so they could release this tension that had been between them since Wednesday.

It wasn't just her either, Dean was being very careful around her but he was always tense. She still had too many fears about the whole Dean and Rose thing, and didn't want to get him all hot and bothered then put the brakes on. That wouldn't be fair.

She couldn't stop thinking about her friend. Her text messages and whatsapp were full of pleading messages from Rose. Each one had softened her ire a little and now she was starting to feel awful for not replying. This was the longest she'd gone without speaking to her friend since she'd met her, but forgiving Rose would feel like betraying Dean. And she couldn't do that after all he'd done for her.

Dean stirred and his arms around her tightened. 'You're up early.'

'I couldn't sleep,' she admitted.

He leaned up on one of his shoulders and stroked her hair back from her face. 'I know Christmas is hard for you. Christmas Eve can't be fun either. I'm here if you need to talk.'

Natalie frowned. 'Christmas isn't until ...'

But she didn't finish, realising it was tomorrow. She waited for the grief to choke her, but all she felt was a pang of sadness mixed with longing. It was nothing like she'd felt for the last few years. She wondered why that was? Maybe all these new dramas were forcing the old ones to the lower level of her emotional grid.

And if that was true then she might be able to do something she'd never been able to do. If the Rose and Dean drawer couldn't be closed yet, maybe another could.

'Do you have to work today?' she asked.

'Nope. We're closed until the second week of January. Why?'

'Will you come somewhere with me?'

His thumb caressed her cheek. 'Ok. Where are we going?'

Natalie took a deep breath, then said, 'The storage unit. I'd like to sort it out.'

Understanding softened his expression.

***

They arrived shortly after 8 o'clock, with a couple of rolls of bin liners and some fresh boxes for the stuff she wanted to keep. Though she would need to hang onto the unit a little longer if she was also flat hunting.

Dean typed in the key code and a thought hit her.

'Why did Rose give you the combination?' She'd been careful not to mention Rose around him until now.

His reaction surprised her. He smiled, without any hint of caution, and said, 'She realized I really do care about you and wanted me to find you.'

'Oh.' There was no malice, no anger, not even bitterness when he spoke about her and all Natalie's insecurities came back to the forefront of her mind. She almost asked if he still loved Rose, but was too afraid of the answer.

Which was probably a good thing. As they flicked on the light and started sorting through the boxes, she was too distracted to really think about the severity of what she was doing. They started with clothing, shoes and handbags. Natalie told him stories behind some of the stuff, but all she kept was a handkerchief which had belonged to her grandmother, and some of her mum's dressy neck scarves. The rest would go to charity.

Old vinyls were next, and Dean suggested she keep those as he had a player somewhere, in case she ever wanted to listen to them. They made their way through the drawers of the display cabinet similarly, with Natalie hanging on to things she might regret throwing away.

It wasn't until she was faced with just the boxes at the back, bursting at the seams, that she got emotional. 'All these are full of Christmas decorations, and something I've never been able to open.'

She dug through the box with her mum's favourite Christmas tree decorations until she found it. The parcel was wrapped in silvery paper which was now dirty and worn, and the purple ribbon securing it wasn't in better shape. Sinking down onto the concrete floor, Natalie stroked her finger over the top, following the line of the ribbon.

Dean shifted so he was beside her. How did he know she needed him without her having to say the words?

'The year she got sick, Mum said all she wanted was to see another Christmas with me. By November she was … failing and I was terrified she'd never get her last wish, so I decorated the house and the garden and the windows until we were surrounded by tinsel, lights and angels.'

He wrapped an arm around her waist and she leaned against his shoulder, drawing strength from his silent support. 'December came and I couldn't believe it. She was hanging on, despite what her doctors or the home help thought. I started to hope we'd get one last day, our favourite day, together.

'Every Christmas Eve we used to put the presents under the tree. I couldn't think what to get her so went with framing a photo of me, her and my dad from the Christmas we visited London. It had been our last year together. On her last Christmas Eve, she gave me this.'

Natalie stopped, a lump rising in her throat and her eyes stung.

Dean pulled her into his lap so she was straddling him, but there was nothing sexual about it. He took her face in his hands and kissed her, again lending her the blessed support she sorely needed. After a moment, he pulled back to look at her and she could see sympathy etched into his expression, and concern shining from his eyes. He'd guessed, but she had to tell him the rest. Today she was finally strong enough to try and move on.

'She died at 11.57pm. Three more minutes and ...' Natalie just shook her head. 'She was cremated with the gift I got her. The people at the crematorium didn't like it much, but I threw a fit until they agreed.'

Dean's lips curved a little, but the concern was still prominent on his face.

'You should bring this with you tonight,' he said, mirroring her earlier move and running his finger along the faded paper. 'Your mum wanted you to have it.'

She thought about that for a while wondering if she could open it. If she could accept this when her mum didn't get the chance to do the same. She wasn't sure.

'Natalie, you are so strong. You can do it, I know you can. And think, afterwards you'll have something from her that you know meant everything. I don't think she fought to make it to Christmas just because she loved the day. I think she knew you did too, and didn't want to ruin Christmas for you.'

Her eyes watered but she blinked the tears away. 'You really think so?'

'I do. I'm almost positive that's why. I'd do the same.' His fingers swiped away the tears on her cheeks.

She must have looked as torn as she felt because he took her free hand and said, 'I'll be there. You don't have to do it alone.'

Right then she didn't worry about whether she was beginning to rely on him. She was too overwhelmed with an emotion she didn't want to acknowledge.

'Thank you.' Her voice was thick with gratitude and she was thanking him for so much more than today.

***

In the end she didn't keep much else, just some of her favourite decorations and the tree decorations she and her mum had bought together, including the angel that had had pride of place on their tree when she was little.

Dean even switched it out for his star when they got back, and she didn't think she'd ever find a way to make all this up to him. Later, Dean grilled them steaks for diner and afterward, she excused herself to get something from his bedroom.

When she came back into the living room, her stomach fluttered with nerves. They hadn't been dating long, and maybe it was too soon for the present thing, but she'd seen it yesterday in the shop when she'd nipped out for a few things, and thought of him.

And she had to put her mum's last gift to her under the tree.

Dean cocked a brow. 'Another present?'

She slid them onto the floor at the base of the tree, then shifted her weight from foot to foot. 'Actually, the other one's for you.'

His grin melted her anxiety and he crossed the room, lifted her up and kissed her with a passion that sent her blood rushing through her veins. After a week like this one, her emotions had been put through the blender so she welcomed the lusty haze that settled into her brain. Tugging at his tee-shirt she managed

212

to slip her hands beneath.

His hands squeezed her bum, pulling her closer and she almost purred with satisfaction. But he released her, taking a step back and left her panting. Wanting.

'Shit, I'm sorry,' he said, running a shaky hand through his dark hair. 'I know this is hard for you.'

The reminder cooled off the burn. 'It's not. I mean, it is but not because I'm … jealous or anything.'

'Will you tell me why you've been so hesitant with me?' he asked.

Natalie sat on the sofa and he followed suit. She realized they were in exactly the same places as she and Alana had been a few days before. Well, Alana had said talking to Jeffrey helped her. Maybe coming clean with him would put her insecurities to rest, too.

'I hate the idea you were with my best friend but I know that was ages ago and realize it's my problem, so I've been trying to put it behind me. But …' God, this question wasn't as easy to ask.

'But?' he urged.

Natalie drew in a breath like it was her lifeline. 'I'm worried that seeing her again – Rose – brought back feelings for you. I'm scared that you still love her.'

He pressed his lips together and she was irritated when she realized it was to stop from laughing.

'It's not funny, Dean.' Alana was wrong. Coming clean was not the way to go.

'Sorry, it's just that I can't believe you're worried about that. I've told you I loved her as a friend back then, but lately I've realized that it wasn't love, just affection.'

She pursed her lips. 'You don't have to pretend to make me feel better. I need to know the truth.'

'Okay, I'll tell you the whole truth.'

She eyed him warily as he made his way over to her, but he

just sat on the edge of the coffee table. His face was close enough to touch, but she didn't dare. Instead she steeled herself for bad news.

'I *know* I didn't love Rose, because I now know what love feels like. I love you, Nat, and what I felt for Rose didn't even come close.'

She gaped, then scrambled around her stunned stupid brain, trying to find a way to talk, or even a hint of what to say.

'I know it's early and you're probably stunned but you don't have to say anything. I just wanted to tell you so you could stop fretting about Rose.'

A rush of warmth, joy and even a touch of tentative elation washed through her. All she could think to say was, 'Alana was right.'

He raised a questioning eyebrow, but he was smiling. She shook her head, not wanting to get into it. 'I don't know what to say.'

'You don't have to say anything. I just wanted you to know.'

'Make love to me?' she whispered, too dazed to filter the request.

'Are you sure?' his forehead creased with concern.

She nodded not trusting herself to say more.

He took her hand and led her to the bedroom. 'I'm going to show you how much I love you with my body and soul,' he said gently.

***

When Natalie woke she was sprawled across Dean's chest and her legs were twisted through his. They were both still naked beneath the duvet, but with skin on skin like this, she didn't even feel the chill of the early morning air.

Dean was still asleep and it was impossible to resist staring at him. He looked so young like this, even with the dark stubble dusting his jaw. And she remembered what he had said last night. He loved her.

214

Right now, her joy wasn't tentative. She marvelled in the glow. The love she'd been trying very hard not to acknowledge burst through the careful guards she'd put in place to keep it hidden.

He stirred, then smiled sleepily up at her. 'Good morning.'

Her answering grin almost split her face in two. 'Morning.'

'I love seeing you so happy.'

'It's because of you,' she told him, then leaned down to kiss him softly. 'Merry Christmas, Dean.'

He wrapped his arms around her. 'Merry Christmas, Natalie.'

She waited for the usual grief to crush her, but the love inside was stronger. And she was eager to give him his present. 'Time to get up.'

'I am up, see.' He nudged his hips against her.

Her belly quivered. 'We have all day to be naughty. Come on, I want to give you your present.'

She wriggled out of his hold and slid on her Christmas pudding jammies, trying to ignore the way he watched her with a carnal expression. When she was done, she tossed his pyjama bottoms at him.

Dean faux sighed. 'Fine, I'll be good.'

Grinning like an overexcited child, she darted through to the living room and flicked on all the switches so that the Christmas decorations that illuminated the dark morning. It had always been tradition in her house, and the thought that she was continuing that didn't bring the same horrid guilt it used to. All she could find was a dull ache in her heart.

She sat down on the floor by the tree, pulling his present out from beneath. When Dean came into the room, he had his hands behind his back.

'Here.' Natalie lifted the box and held it out to him. 'Open it.'

He laughed, then came over to sit across from her. As he took the present, he handed her a small gift bag. 'You first.'

'You got me a present?' she asked, a little stunned.

He nodded, watching her warily.

Beaming, Natalie opened the bag. A long jewellery box was inside and she pulled it out. Slowly, she lifted the lid and gasped. It was a thin platinum bracelet woven round little pink and white diamonds. Actual diamonds, if the Cartier inscription inside of the box was any indication.

'Dean, this is ... beautiful.' A lump formed in her throat.

'You like it?' he checked.

'Love it.' She carefully removed the bracelet, draped it over her right wrist and clasped it together. The diamonds glittered in the white Christmas lights. 'Thank you.'

She tapped the top of the box she'd given him. 'Your turn.'

His mouth pulled up in a lopsided grin and he tore through the paper. He lifted the lid and laughed. 'A Christmas jumper?'

Natalie joined in. 'You can't trust a man who doesn't wear a Christmas jumper.'

'I will, on one condition.'

His tone was teasing but his eyes grew wary. Bracing herself, she waited.

'Can we go to Alana and Jeffrey's for lunch? We've been invited.'

She didn't say anything, waiting for the familiar misery to creep in. But nothing had changed, all she had was a longing ache, overruled by the way she felt in his presence. Could this hold long enough to survive Christmas lunch? Natalie wasn't sure.

Then again, the idea of spending the day with a family she'd hoped she could be a part of was tempting. 'I'll wear mine so we can match.'

'Are you sure?' he asked.

Natalie nodded. 'You know, I didn't just get you a Christmas jumper. Keep digging.'

He lifted the thick knitted jumper out and picked up the envelope from the bottom of the box. Smiling, he opened it and his eyes lit up. 'You got me a racing day!'

'Yup. I thought if you liked fast cars, you might like this.'

'Thanks, Nat. I love it. There are two tickets. Are you coming too?'

'I can't drive, but I thought you might want to take Jeffrey.'

He shifted the empty box and wrapping paper out of the way so he could reach over to her. Natalie climbed onto his lap, her heart bursting with love at his joy.

'I can't wait to beat him.'

She giggled. 'What if he beats you?'

Dean rolled his eyes. 'Not likely. He drives an old man Jag and won't edge past fifty on the motorway.'

She clasped her hands behind his neck, briefly eyeing the stunning bracelet. Maybe she should show him how grateful she was. 'Back to bed?'

This time he shook his head. 'You still have one more.'

'Oh.' Her muscles tensed.

Dean picked up the faded silver box and held it between them. With shaking hands, she pulled the ribbon so the bow unravelled. Holding her breath, she carefully removed the rest and peeled back the two strips of sellotape beneath. It came away easily. Then she peeled off the paper, exposing a plain, rectangular black box.

Curiosity drove her to open the lid. She could barely see the delicate silver chain through the moisture in her eyes. But she saw the oval locket edged with pink gemstones. Picking it up, she pressed the button on the side until it popped open.

On the right was the exact same picture of the three of them she had framed and was going to give to her mother, only minia-ture. On the left, were four words that made her heart swell.

We'll always be together.

'You look like her,' he said softly.

Natalie nodded, gazing at her mum's beaming smile. Natalie was only ten with bright blonde hair the exact same shade as her dad. He had his hands wrapped around them both. 'It was freezing that winter, that's why we're all huddled up in knitwear.'

Stroking her thumb over the promise, she realized what her

mum was saying. She had them in her memories, her heart and soul. 'I'm glad I opened this.'

She put the locket back in the box and placed it on the coffee table. 'Now, how about that naughty I was promised.'

He pulled her face to hers, kissing her fiercely and they misbehaved late into the morning.

Chapter 17

Warm ribbing, mostly from Jeffrey at Dean's Rudolph jumper, filled the afternoon. Alana put on a mean spread with all the trimmings, and as crackers were pulled, stringers popped and champagne poured, Natalie's smile got wider and wider.

Since they'd met Alana, this had been the tradition on Christmas day and now her annoying flatmate Sarah had buggered off to live in France, Dean could really start to enjoy it. He didn't expect to feel like the happiest man alive with Natalie there.

She seemed to struggle to keep her eyes off him, even when Alana monopolised her with conversation about the wedding. He'd been worried that telling her he loved her might have freaked her out. He'd also been pissing his pants at the idea she didn't love him back, but his confession seemed to help her open up more with him.

And she might not love him yet, but the emotions glowing from her eyes and smile when she looked at him was close enough.

Later, after he and Jeffrey had washed the dishes, he found a quiet moment to speak with her alone. 'How was today?'

'Amazing. Thank you for bringing me.'

Because he couldn't resist, he kissed her. It was only supposed to be a peck, but Natalie twinned her fingers in his hair and upped the intensity. He was beside her on their sofa, but she climbed onto his lap and he pulled her closer.

'Jesus, I'm glad we don't have kids,' Jeffrey complained. 'You two would scar them for life.'

They broke apart, Natalie's face turning bright pink. Dean turned to glare at his brother, but it was hard to stick to when he was so happy and he gave in to a grin.

Alana, who'd been packing away the table, swatted Jeffrey with a placemat. 'Leave them be.'

He grinned at his fiancé. 'Maybe we should kick them out so we can practice baby making.'

Natalie gasped quietly. 'Are you trying for a baby?'

This was news to Dean, too.

Alana shook her head. 'Not 'til after the wedding. I don't want to be a fat bride.'

'You won't be fat, you'll be pregnant.' Jeffrey sounded exasperated, like he'd had this discussion a million times.

'Well, I don't want to be a pregnant bride. I want to be a sexy bride.'

Natalie bit her lip, like she was trying not to laugh. Dean couldn't quite manage to hold in a chuckle.

'See, Dean agrees,' Alana said. 'Listen to your brother.'

Jeffrey frowned at him, then turned back to Alana. 'Dean's a knob. Nobody cares what he thinks.'

Dean rolled his eyes and Natalie caressed his face.

'He'll be your baby's uncle. You'd better start being nicer to him.' Alana wasn't great at pretending to be mad at Jeffrey. Her smile gave her away.

Jeffrey helped her pack away the rest of the place settings, theatrically shuddering. 'God, I forgot about that. Our kid will have him as a role model.'

'I'm sitting right here,' he teased. The idea of becoming an uncle was … amazing, actually.

'At least aunty Nat will be there to balance out the crazy,' Jeffrey added.

Natalie's immediately looked wary. Dean stared at her, trying to understand her reaction. Didn't she want to be around that long? He'd thought after everything that happened the last week that she did, more than anything.

'That's true. But Natalie, please tell my husband-to-be that brides don't want to be anything but perfect on their big day.'

He could see the strain in Natalie's smile. 'Sorry, Jeffrey but brides like to look their absolute best.'

Jeffrey sighed in defeat. 'Fine. Seven months. But I'm knocking you up on the honeymoon.'

Alana laughed.

Dean was too busy wondering what Natalie was thinking to come up with a suitable ribbing remark for Jeffrey. He squeezed her hips in question, while Jeffrey and Alana continued to clear away the fold-up table.

Natalie turned to him, and though some of the strain had left her jaw, her eyes still looked haunted.

'What is it?' he whispered, so only she could hear.

'I'm fine,' she replied. 'Are you ready to go?'

No, he wasn't. But it was getting late, and he'd put off this conversation long enough. 'Let's say goodbye.'

He punched Jeffrey lightly on the shoulder and hugged Alana, while Natalie hugged and kissed them both goodbye. They'd only known each other weeks but it was like she was supposed to be with them. She'd slipped into their family seamlessly, and even had enough backbone to stand up to his mother.

The reminder of the Wicked Witch had him dreading Boxing Day dinner at their mansion. He wondered what she'd say if he turned up in his new Christmas jumper, but then remembered what Rose told him she'd done. The urge to wind up his mum disappeared.

When they got to the elevator, he forced himself to focus. Natalie was gazing at his gift to her, circling the diamonds with her fingertips.

'I thought the bracelet would go with your bridesmaid dress,' he admitted.

Her head whipped up to look at him.

'Are you ignoring Rose because you're still mad at her, or is it because you think you'll be hurting me by forgiving her?' he asked. Natalie didn't seem the kind of person who held grudges. She had forgivven his awful behaviour more than once.

'I can forgive her for lying to me, but what she did to you ...' She shrugged. Her eyes betrayed her. They were full of sadness.

'I forgave her.'

Natalie blinked at him.

'Last Thursday. I went to your flat after work and asked Rose not to give up on you. I know how much you care about her and I didn't want you to lose a friend because of me. She told me why she left, even told me that my mum hauled her over the coals for it. I'd already let the past go, but I realized I didn't hate her. I'm even sort of happy that she's found someone she loves.'

Her chin dropped and her lips parted.

'Meeting you changed me, and loving you wiped away any bitterness I had.' The elevator stopped and the doors opened. He took her hand, leading her out.

She pulled him to a stop in front of the building. 'You don't mind if I go to her wedding, be her maid of honour?'

He shook his head. 'I'm guessing she's a mess right now worrying about you. I thought you might want to spend the night with her.'

Natalie's expression looked torn. 'I've had the best Christmas I've had in years. I don't want it to be over, but ...'

'You don't want to leave Rose on the night before her wedding either?'

She nodded.

Tugging her closer, he leaned down so his forehead was pressed against hers. God, he craved her touch. 'We have next year, and the next, and the next.'

He sensed apprehension in her silence, and was reminded of her reaction when Alana had said she'd be an aunt. Pulling back to read her expression, he saw the same guarded edge tightening her eyes.

'Natalie, I'm in love with you. I could never leave you now. You can be around for as many Christmases as you want. It's up to you.' He ignored the shiver of fear that ran through him. He was done letting it rule his life.

She reached up and cupped his face in her hands. 'I want them all.'

The tension drained from his body. 'Then they're yours.'

***

Despite the fact Natalie and Rose had been up all night talking and bawling onto each other's shoulders, Rose was the most beautiful bride she'd ever seen. The simple but elegant white dress sheathed her slender frame, her joy her most extravagant accessory as she recited her vows in the registry office.

Dean hadn't come. She'd wanted him to, and missed him like crazy, but they all decided it would be a bit weird especially with Tom's insecurities. Though he certainly didn't look insecure now. His elation and pride were almost palpable, especially when the minister declared them man and wife.

The reception, as promised, was a quiet event. Just close friends and family. Natalie chatted away to Tom's family and Rose's colleagues, eyeing the clock in the restaurant more than she should. Dean was spending the night at her flat and Rose would be at Tom's. With the theme of the day being love, it was hard not to miss him.

Rose took the seat next to her. 'I wish he could be here for you.'

She smiled a little. It still felt strange talking about Dean with his ex, even if it was her best friend. But there was something she wanted to know. 'Why do Jeffrey and Dean know you as Rosaline?'

Rose's smile was sad. 'That's my name. It was also my grand-mother's. When she died, I didn't want anyone shortening it to keep her memory alive.'

When Natalie's brows furrowed in confusion, she sighed.

'It felt like an appropriate punishment, letting people call me Rose when I moved to London. It eased the guilt a bit. Not much, though.'

'Oh.' She felt a pang of sorrow for her friend. She really was lovely, and caring. Just because someone makes a shitty decision, it didn't make them a bad person. Rose had suffered enough. 'I don't mind calling you Rosaline.'

Rose smiled. 'I don't mind anymore. It was actually weird on Wednesday being called by my old name.'

That really wasn't the weirdest part of the night for Natalie, but she didn't bring it up.

Rose changed the subject. 'I couldn't believe it when you came over yesterday. Not because I never thought you'd forgive me, but because I saw the change in you. Nat, you were so happy. I've never seen you anything other than in agony on Christmas day. And wearing this ...' She touched the locket Natalie had round her neck. 'He is so good for you. I wish I'd never known him growing up, because then he could have come.'

The honesty and conviction in Rose's words melted away the last shreds of Natalie's resistance. 'I'm in love with him.'

Suddenly she was wrapped in white, trying very hard not to choke on the veil as Rose hugged her hard enough to cut off her air supply. 'I know you do, and I'm so happy for you.'

When she was released and could breathe properly again she said, 'He told me he loved me. I didn't say it back. I didn't want to let myself feel that way.'

'In case you lost him?' Rose asked, immediately understanding it was more than just a minor insecurity.

Natalie nodded. 'But I can't not live my life because I'm scared to lose someone. The inscription in the locket is true. You never really lose the ones you love, they're always with you.'

Rose's eyes welled up. 'Definitely.'

'So I'm going to tell him. Tonight.' Natalie was sure.

Rose took her hand and squeezed. 'What time is he back from his parents?'

Natalie glanced at the clock again. It was getting late. 'He should have been back a while ago.'

'Then why are you dallying round here? Go get your man.' Rose engulfed her in another bone-crushing hug. 'Married or not, we'll see each other all the time. I love you too, you know.'

Tears pricked her eyes. 'I feel the same way.'

***

Dean picked her up from the restaurant and his eyes were appreciative as he took in her dress. He drove to her flat quicker than usual, but the streets were empty. She didn't know whether to talk about the wedding or not, so instead asked how his day was.

He grinned. 'Mum assumed you'd dumped me. You should have seen her face when I told her you were at Rosaline's wedding.'

Natalie giggled, but then got serious. 'Did you tell her you knew what she did?'

'Yes. We talked for ages and for once, she wasn't patronising. In fact, we came to a sort of compromise.'

'Oh?'

'Hmm,' he said, staring at the road. 'She wanted us to go over every Sunday for lunch.'

'You agreed?' she asked.

'I agreed to two Sundays a month, and only if you wanted to,' he said, his eyes still focused ahead.

The idea of being showered with pretentious and unlimited meals every other Sunday with a couple she barely knew shouldn't have made her giddy with joy, but it did. Probably because it felt like he was going out of his way to bring her into his family. Giving her what she wanted again, without her having to ask.

'I suppose I could, for you,' she said lightly as he pulled up against the curb at the side of her flat. 'That's what people do for those they love, isn't it?'

He looked at her this time, his eyebrows raised in surprise. 'Did you say—'

'Love, yes I did. I love you Dean Fletcher. I just thought you might like to know.' She couldn't keep the cheek-splitting smile off her face.

'You thought right.'

Even though the inside of his sports car didn't have much room for manoeuvre, somehow she managed to climb into his lap, honking the horn in her haste. He was staring at her like he still couldn't believe what she'd said.

'I really, really love you. In fact, I'd say I was head over heels.'

His hands cupped her face gently, almost reverently, and his eyes glowed with the love he felt for her. 'You've made me happier than I ever thought I could be.'

'Back at you. But do you know what would make me happier?' she asked.

'Go on,' he said, smiling.

'Something a little bit nice, but very, very naughty.'

'I think I can rise to the challenge,' he said, face perfectly smooth.

Natalie couldn't help it, she laughed at the bad joke and he joined in. She was glad she'd let go of her fear, of the past, because she wanted nothing more than whatever future she could have with Dean.

Epilogue

Natalie poured another glass of wine for her and Rose, ignoring Alana's pout.

'Here, I forgot. I made raspberry brownies,' Rose said, taking a tin out of her handbag and handing it to Alana, whose eyes lit up like it was Christmas.

'Thanks Rose! Junior and I love your baking.' She stroked her still flat stomach and beamed. 'I miss the wine though.'

Natalie chuckled. As promised, Jeffrey brought Alan back from honeymoon very much pregnant, and she was now thirteen weeks along. It didn't stop their Friday nights in at Natalie's flat, even though both her friends were happily married. She tried to push away the first tingling of depression, being the only unmarried one in the room.

'Are you going to find out the sex?' Rose asked.

'I want it to be a surprise, but Jeff's desperate to know. He'll wear me down before the next scan. He always does.' Alana rolled her eyes.

It was difficult not to feel insanely happy for her friends, but the day of Alana's wedding wasn't as happy an event as Rose's. For Natalie, anyway. Back at Christmas, there was so much going on she didn't have time to yearn for anything more than just Dean.

By July, things had changed. They spent half the week at his flat, half at hers. They'd never spent a night apart since Christmas. But every hint she dropped about taking the next step and just moving in together went unnoticed.

So at his brother's wedding, she'd been sad knowing Dean wouldn't even commit to living with her, never mind marrying her. Still, he'd told her right from the start how it would be and she was trying to accept it.

'What's wrong, Nat?' Rose asked.

'Nothing.' She couldn't tell Rose that Dean wouldn't marry her, the why would make her friend feel awful. So she tried distraction. 'I got this really weird email today.'

Pulling out her mobile, she flicked through her business account. *Every Occasion* was thriving. She'd had enough bookings for weddings, baby showers and Dean's company to keep her ticking over. She hadn't made much of a dent in the settlement she got from Mick, except to set up a home office in Rose's old room.

When she found the email, she read it out to them.

'I've heard good things about your company. I want you to do my fiancée a surprise wedding.'

'That's not too strange. It's actually kind of romantic,' Alana said.

'I thought so too, until I replied asking what kind of thing he was going for,' Natalie said, while she scrolled to the next email.

'What did he say?' Rose asked.

Natalie read his reply. 'I'm not sure. Doesn't every woman have an idea of dream wedding? I'm sure she'll love whatever you choose.'

She looked at her friends. 'He wouldn't give me his name either, said he couldn't because he didn't want to risk ruining the surprise. And when I pointed out that different women have different dreams, he told me he'd already asked previous clients about my skills as a wedding planner and was satisfied I'd make it a day his fiancée would never forget.'

Rose and Alana shared a look that made her suspicious. 'What?'

'Nothing,' Alana said, too quickly. 'Maybe he's a celebrity and doesn't want it getting out to the press.'

Rose nodded her agreement.

Natalie didn't want to take it on though. She wasn't sure if she could do her dream wedding for someone else, knowing she'd never get the chance to walk down the aisle to Dean.

'Obviously you have to do it. Imagine if he is a movie star or something, your business would blow up,' Alana said.

'You can't pass up that kind of potential opportunity, Nat. Go for it,' Rose agreed.

She sighed, then polished off the wine, resigned to her fate.

***

Dean arrived later with Jeffrey, who had come to pick Alana up but they stayed a while. Natalie fired off a quick email to the mysterious client while Jeffrey and Dean's playful ribbing filled the room with laughter.

She asked for the date, a budget and if he'd thought about a dress, then re-joined the conversation, not as into it as before. A little while later, Jeffrey and Alana took Rose home and she went to the fridge to fill up her glass.

When she returned to the sofa, Dean frowned. 'You okay?'

'Yes. What are you watching?' she asked, turning to the television rather than let him see she wasn't being completely honest.

'Nothing yet, but A Christmas Carol is on soon.'

Oh, she loved that film and couldn't believe it was screening already. It was still a week until December. She took her phone and snuggled in beside him. There was a new email from her mystery client so she opened it. Her earlier suspicion flared as she read the words, but she could never dare to hope, could she?

Natalie shifted so she could study his expression. The poker face was back.

'I was contacted by a potential new client today,' she said, trying to sound nonchalant.

'Oh,' he commented, not looking at her.

'Mmm. Seems he wants to throw his fiancée a surprise wedding. He asked me to do it how I would want my dream wedding to be. Strange, don't you think?'

Dean just shrugged, seemingly more interested in the Rimmel lipstick advert on TV.

'Do you know what day they want to get married? 1st December. That's the night we met. Crazy coincidence, isn't it?' She couldn't keep the sarcasm out of her voice, since she was almost positive her suspicion was correct.

He pressed his lips together, like he was trying very hard not to laugh at her tone.

'And when he suggested I should pick a dress, because I was about the right size, well that got me thinking ...'

'Are you going to take the job?' he asked, turning to face her but his expression was too careful.

'That depends,' she hedged, wondering if her mind was playing tricks on her. After all, he'd made it very clear he was not into marriage.

'This might help you make up your mind.' Dean stood up, then pulled a little black box out of his pocket.

Her eyes froze wide with shock. He couldn't be about to propose, could he?

When he looked at her now, his expression was glowing with love.

'Natalie Taylor, you are one hard woman to surprise. Which is why I kept this with me.'

Dean got down on one knee and opened the box. Inside, there was a platinum ring with a white square cut diamond, on either side of which was a small pink one. With a shaking hand, she covered her mouth as her eyes filled with tears.

'I love you more than I could ever explain with words. I want you to be my family, officially, as my wife. Will you marry me?'

Tears were streaming freely down her cheeks as she was filled to bursting with joy. 'Of course I will.'

His triumphant smile knocked the air out of her lungs. She couldn't take another breath until he'd slid the beautiful ring onto the fourth finger of her left hand. It matched the bracelet round her wrist, and she loved them both. Unable to stop herself, she threw her hands round his neck and kissed him with all the joy she felt.

When they stopped to catch their breath, she laughed. 'I can't believe you were trying to surprise me with a wedding. Just FYI, you should have gone to another company if you wanted to keep it a secret.'

'I want our wedding to be perfect and exactly how you want it to be, so my hands were tied.'

'As long as it's with you, I don't think I'd care if we got married at a strip club.'

'Was that an option?' he teased.

'Not if you feel particularly attached to your privates.'

Dean sobered. 'I can live without those, but not you. You're my *everything*.'

'That's a much sweeter endearment than little thief.' Natalie's vision got blurry again. 'You want to get married on the 1st?'

'Is that enough time?' he asked hopefully.

Natalie laughed. 'No. But I'm sure I could throw something together.'

'We can do it next year,' he said, but sounded reluctant.

She shook her head. 'The 1st of December is perfect.'

After all, her dream wedding had nothing to do with centre pieces, the venue or even the dress. She just wanted to finally be part of his life, officially, and start living it. She marvelled again at how he knew what she wanted, needed even, without her having to say a word.

Natalie couldn't have asked for a better happy ever after.